Bowman met M

trusting me to c

activity?"

She paused, letting herself get a little lost in his brown-green eyes. Was she going to trust him? He'd been fantastic this week, but he was still a daredevil at heart. He shifted, his gaze probing hers, wanting her trust.

"Y-yes? Yes."

"Okay. I've got an idea. But you've got to promise not to lose it on me."

Maisy bit her bottom lip. "Can I promise to try?"

His full smile broke out under the rim of his Stetson. For the sake of his smile, she was going to try very, very hard.

"Hey, gather up, everybody." Bowman indicated that the kids should circle around. "We're gonna go to one of my favorite places. But when we get there, we have to talk about safety."

Maisy was unable to hold back a snort. Bowman glared at her. *Sorry*, she mouthed.

Dear Reader,

Welcome back to Outcrop, Oregon, for *The Firefighter's Rescue*! Bowman may be the quiet one in the boisterous Wallace clan, but he's got a few surprises up his sleeve.

Maisy Martin is a pragmatic young doctor just out of residency. Bowman is a daredevil firefighter, famous for his willingness to take risks. She's good with details, he's good with disaster. Together they find strength in compromise as they run a kids' Cowboy Camp at Wallace Ranch.

The Firefighter's Rescue draws on personal experience. My husband never met a cliff face he wouldn't climb and takes calculated risks with confidence. Me? Not so much. Fortunately, humor and patience kept us moving toward a middle ground. Now you can find us rock climbing (safely!) together and up for all kinds of adventures.

I hope you enjoy this story. Love, Oregon is my first series with Harlequin Heartwarming, and I'd love to hear what you think. You can find me on social media and at my website, anna-grace-author.com.

Happy reading!

Anna

HEARTWARMING

The Firefighter's Rescue

Anna Grace

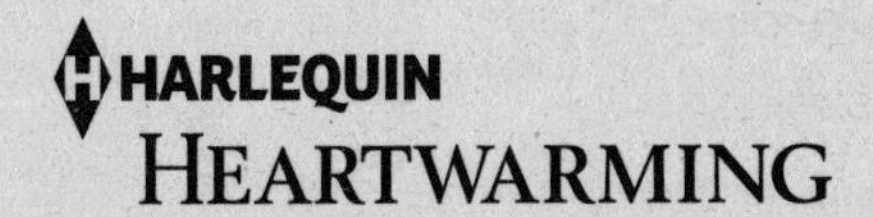

Recycling programs for this product may not exist in your area.

ISBN-13: 978-1-335-58497-7

The Firefighter's Rescue

For questions and comments about the quality of this book, please contact us at CustomerService@Harlequin.com.

Harlequin Enterprises ULC
22 Adelaide St. West, 41st Floor
Toronto, Ontario M5H 4E3, Canada
www.Harlequin.com

Printed in U.S.A.

Anna Grace justifies her espresso addiction by writing fun, modern romance novels in the early morning hours. Once the sun comes up, you can find her teaching high school history, or outside with her adventure-loving husband. Anna is a mediocre rock climber, award-winning author, mom of two fun kids and snack enthusiast. She lives rurally in Oregon, and travels to big cities whenever she gets the chance. Anna loves connecting with readers, and you can find her on social media and at her website, anna-grace-author.com.

Twitter: @AnnaEmilyGrace
IG: @annagraceauthor
Facebook: Anna Grace Author

Books by Anna Grace

Harlequin Heartwarming

Love, Oregon

A Rancher Worth Remembering

Visit the Author Profile page
at Harlequin.com for more titles.

CHAPTER ONE

TRIPPING OVER A chair in the middle of a crowded restaurant wasn't the first impression Maisy Martin had envisioned for herself in Outcrop. She righted the chair with feigned confidence. *All cool. Nothing to see here.* She risked a second glance at the man sitting in the last booth by the front windows in Eighty Local.

Was that the firefighter guy from the poster?

Stetson pulled low over his brow, muscular forearms resting on the table, sullen gaze directed outside. She checked her phone again to confirm she was meeting a representative from Wallace Ranch at the last booth by the front windows. Then her eyes swung once more to the poster by the door.

Same guy.

A copy of that poster was the heart-stopping introduction she'd received when she rolled into town two days ago. It was plastered on the side of an old brick building next to a Wanted flier alerting locals to an escaped emu. When she saw the emu, she figured she'd like the locals. When she took a look at the poster, she fell in love.

Firefighter of the Year! was scrawled across the top. The original poster had one exclamation point, but several more had been graffitied on to copies around town. The poster gracing the door of *this* establishment included a handwritten note on the bottom that read, *Literally one of the three best brothers in the world, ever!*

And while the information was all very interesting, it was the picture that threatened to blow valves in her heart. It was a candid shot of a firefighter emerging from a wall of rubble and flame. The firefighter walked with confidence, clutching an intricate piece of beadwork in one hand. His turnout gear was unzipped, and peeking out from the safety of the suit was a glossy blond puppy. The firefighter of the year was grinning at the camera, like there was nothing he enjoyed more than narrowly surviving with his life. Humor lit his hazel eyes, and a small, slightly off-center gap between his front teeth gave his smile a wild, dangerous quality.

The guy slumped in the booth, however, was not grinning. She checked her messages again. The text was from Ash Wallace—polite, straightforward, businesslike. Those adjectives didn't seem at all appropriate for the man in the booth.

"Can I help you?" A woman with sparkly brown eyes and blond hair, wearing an Eighty Local tank top, smiled at her from behind the espresso machine. Maisy blinked. *Help?* Well, she was standing in the middle of a crowded restaurant, eyes running from her phone to a gorgeous man, and back to the poster of that man, on repeat, for who knew how long. She needed help alright.

"Um, yes. I'm here to meet Ash Wallace?" Ugh. Why did she end the sentence like a question? She was here to meet Ash Wallace; it wasn't a question, it was a fact. Maisy could feel herself start to flush, and took deep breaths before she would turn bright red.

The woman's eyes lit up. Apparently, she wasn't nearly as disturbed by the choice of punctuation as Maisy was. "Are you Dr. Martin?"

"Yes," she said decisively. She *was* Dr. Martin. Twelve years of primary school, three years of an accelerated undergrad, four years of medical school, four years of residency. Two full weeks of being Dr. Maisy Martin.

Maisy clamped down on the very strong urge to groove in celebration.

"I'm so super-thrilled to meet you!" The

woman turned and called over her shoulder, "Hunter? The new doctor is here!"

"Hey, welcome to Outcrop!" a voice called from the kitchen.

Maisy warmed. *These were nice people. This was going to be fine.*

She'd debated the offer from the Healthy Lives Institute, listing the pros and cons of the decision on endless legal pads. But from the start the pro column held one weight far too heavy to ever really be tipped. Two hundred and fifty thousand dollars in education debt. HLI was willing to pay back those loans if she committed to seven years as a general practitioner in a rural area and agreed to roll out a series of community health initiatives. It was good, important work and she believed in it. The only real concern was this kids' camp she was supposed to help with. She'd had her choice of communities and picked Outcrop because of the town's reputation as a hub for the outdoor activities she enjoyed. But with Outcrop came three weeks helping out with something called Cowboy Camp. It would be a lot easier if she could have settled in with her medical practice first, rather than start her tenure here working with children.

She shivered, closing her eyes against the trepidation. She could do this. In her life she'd climbed mountains, bicycled across entire states, run marathons…

Okay, fine—run-walked marathons. Point was, she could take on a challenge. Kids were a challenge.

Let's do it.

The woman grinned at her. "I'm Clara Wallace, Ash's sister and, like, basically everyone's sister around here." She waved her hand to indicate an undisclosed number of siblings. "I don't technically work here, but right now I'm here all the time because my brother's expanding the restaurant and it's insane." She leaned across the counter and lowered her voice. "My brothers can get a little cranky. Lovable, but certifiable grumps when they get in over their heads."

"I heard that!" the voice called from the kitchen.

"They also eavesdrop," Clara yelled back.

Maisy laughed, relief filling her chest. "Thanks. The kids' camp will be a new challenge for me."

"You'll be amazing," Clara said, despite the complete lack of evidence to back up her statement. "Now, I'm going to make you the best coffee you've ever had, on the house, to celebrate. What looks good?"

Maisy instinctively glanced over her shoulder at the firefighter of the year.

Wow. Could you be more obvious?

Heat threatened at her neck. When she'd gotten a cute, short haircut that exposed the back of her neck, with long bangs sweeping across her forehead, she'd thought about the carefree, confident woman she aspired to be. She *hadn't* thought about how, when she blushed from her neck to the roots of her cute, chic hair, it was now visible from all angles. Maisy focused on the coffee menu to distract her from the thought of lighting up like a fire truck. Caramel chocolate mocha, honey cardamom latte, iced cinnamon sugar cold brew. *Oh, yummers!*

But, no, she was a representative of the Healthy Lives Institute now. She was a doctor, in a public place. This was an opportunity to set a good example.

"A regular cup of coffee is fine."

"Really?" Clara eyed her.

"Yes," she said, nodding to help herself believe she'd prefer a straight-up cup of coffee. "Thanks."

"Okay, I'll make you a pour-over." Clara grinned. Maisy smiled back, relief washing through her. If Clara was any indicator, the people of Outcrop were going to be great. "Go ahead and join Bowman over there. I'm sure Ash'll be here any minute."

The relief washed right on out. Maisy swallowed hard and asked the question she was pretty sure she already knew the answer to. "Who's Bowman?"

Clara gestured to the sulking poster-come-to-life in the last booth along the front window. "Bowman Wallace, also my brother. Your partner in crime for the kids' camp."

"That...guy?"

"Yep. You know he's the central Oregon Fireman of the Year?"

"Um, yeah." Inasmuch as every vertical surface in Outcrop held a poster advertising that fact. "So I should go sit with him?"

Clara was kind enough *not* to acknowledge how stupid the question was. She just smiled and headed over to a coffee grinder. "He's nice...when you get to know him."

Maisy took a deep breath and approached the table. This was no big deal. So she'd be working with a good-looking, puppy-saving guy. So he had an off-kilter smile with the power to knock things out of orbit. Whatever.

In fact, with a smile like his, and the reputation as a firefighter, he was probably great with kids. In the poster, he looked like the kind of guy to give piggyback rides and steal noses in a nonthreatening manner. The type of nose stealer a child could be confident would put their nose back. He could be the fun camp counselor, and she'd run things quietly in the background.

"Um, hi?"

She startled Bowman from his meditation on the parking lot.

Ugh. Why did she have to put everything in the form of a question? What was this, *Jeopardy*? She blinked, then pushed back her blond hair and tried again.

"Hi, I'm Maisy."

Bowman's gaze flickered briefly over her face, then returned to the front window. He nodded. "Okay."

Okay? That's all she got in greeting from the person she was supposed to be running a camp with? The flush she'd been successful at keeping at bay earlier flooded her face. She knew she was lobster-red, and probably looked a lot like the fires he put out for a living.

Fortunately, she was also mad.

He might be gorgeous, and she might have a truly reprehensible habit of ending statements with a question mark, but that was no basis for rudeness. She was a doctor, here to help this community. Even if her face did look like a four-square ball at the moment.

She crossed her arms over her chest and

lifted her chin. It was a pose that always worked when another resident tried to intrude on her time with an attending doctor. "Clara said you're Bowman Wallace. I'm Dr. Maisy Martin, with the Healthy Lives initiative."

His eyes, a compelling mix of brown and green, flickered up to meet hers. A spark of attraction raced between them. Or, more likely, raced from her to him, but whatever. There was one flickering moment of…something before he rolled his eyes. "You gonna check my cholesterol?"

She blew out a breath. Maisy had met some rude people in her day: patients, doctors, doctors who'd had to submit to being patients. But this? *This* was impressive.

She brought up the text from Ash on her phone and held it out for Bowman to see. "Ash Wallace, who I'm assuming is some type of relation to you, texted and asked me to meet him here at two o'clock." She looked pointedly at the clock hanging over the cash register. "In the last booth by the window." She gestured to the booths. "So I'm sorry if you're not looking for friends, but I have to be here. I don't have a choice."

His jaw twitched at the mention of Ash. He opened his mouth to speak, but nothing came out.

Scratch her original thought. This was the

type of guy who stole noses from children, pocketed them and left the room.

"Dr. Martin?"

Maisy looked up at the deep voice. A serious man, several years older than her, came jogging up to the table, hand held out in greeting.

"Ash Wallace. Please excuse my lateness."

The minute hand ticked past the two, making him a little over 120 seconds late.

"It's fine—"

"I see you've already met my brother Bowman. Did you tell him why you're here?"

She glared at Bowman, not because she was much for glaring, but because if ever there was a time, this was it. "I was just about to confirm I won't be checking his cholesterol, but other than that we haven't gotten very far."

Ash gave her a brief, conspiratorial smile, then gestured for her to sit down across from Bowman. Maisy slid into the booth as Ash pulled the Stetson from Bowman's head and placed it on a hook at the end of the booth.

"Bowman, you're not going to like what I'm about to say."

Bowman ran both hands through his hair. There were twenty-four different muscles in the human arm, and Bowman managed to flex all of them in the simple action of getting his brown hair temporarily off his forehead. "This week can't get much worse, man."

Ash sighed, looking sympathetically at his brother. "You're running Cowboy Camp this year. With Dr. Martin."

"WHAT?!" BOWMAN BOLTED UPRIGHT. Ash was joking. This had to be some elaborate joke his siblings put him up to.

He glanced over to the counter, fully expecting to see Hunter and Clara laughing.

No one was laughing. And Ash looked gravely serious. "I intended to do it myself, but we've got two out-of-state deliveries and the ranchers' federation is having an emergency summit over this county-commissioner debacle. Over the next three weeks I'm gone more days than I'm here."

"Ash, I can't work at Cowboy Camp. I'm the last person in our family who's suited for it."

"Exactly. You're the last person in the family."

This wasn't happening.

When was he going to bolt upright, out of this nightmare of a week? The suspension from the fire department had sent him into a free fall. But every possible landing place was filled with women who thought he did nothing all day but carry around puppies and save important cultural artifacts. He could kill his sister Piper for sending in that picture from the Heritage Museum fire. The posters made him into a hero he'd never wanted to be, and forced him into a spotlight that had the fire chief evaluating his every move. It didn't take long for Chief Hanson's scrutiny to translate into a suspension for breach of protocol. Not that he wouldn't break the same rules all over again.

And now he'd been rude to this woman who was apparently volunteering to help with camp. He glanced up at Maisy. The angry flush had subsided, giving way to pale skin, intelligent blue eyes and a wash of freckles across her nose.

The freckles were really pretty.

"Camp starts Monday—"

"What about Hunter?" Bowman interrupted, gesturing to the counter. "He's great with kids."

Ash shifted and glowered at him. "Hunter? In all his spare time?"

Bowman glanced back into the kitchen, where their brother was working frantically: arguing with someone on the phone, sautéing something on the stove and communicating with one of his employees about something else entirely.

"Yeah, I know. It's all gotta get finished by December."

Hunter, his twin and best friend in the world, was incredibly successful with this restaurant. He worked hard, overcame every problem imaginable and was doing so well he'd broken ground on an addition. It was fantastic.

But also, not fantastic.

He and Hunter were a team; they'd gotten into every kind of trouble as kids, played sports together in high school, built this restaurant from the ground up. But now Hunter was always busy, and building a new kind of life for himself. Bowman would never begrudge his brother his success—Eighty Local was fantastic.

He just really missed Hunter.

Bowman swallowed against the pressure in his jaw. The pretty doctor was watching him.

"What about Jet and Clara? Or—" Bowman bit back the urge to crack a joke about having a few of Jet's emus run camp. His habit of laughing when things got serious annoyed his whole family, but no one more than Ash. "Jet's great with the football team, and Clara's used to dealing with big groups of people."

Ash scoffed. "They got engaged two weeks ago."

"So kids' camp'll be a trial run for them. They can decide if they want kids."

Ash placed a hand on his shoulder. Never a

good sign. "I'm not going to ask Clara to add one more thing to her schedule. Moving forward with Jet was a big step for her, and I don't want anything to hinder their relationship."

Bowman nodded. Clara managed her anxiety disorder well, but major changes were hard for her. "Piper is in Portland, and I have to run the ranch. Our parents spent over thirty years teaching, so I think they've earned the break. My son Jackson can help out, but he's got daily doubles through the end of the month. It's time to family up, man. Camp's on you this year."

Bowman sat back in the booth. This was unfair. First the posters, then the suspension, now camp. All he wanted to do was work for the fire department, help out his brother around Eighty Local, go rock climbing when he had a little time off and enjoy hanging out with his family.

But now he was looking down the barrel of a minimum three-week suspension, and he'd be spending it with strange kids and this woman he'd already offended.

Bowman's sisters, both overly enthusiastic psychology students in college, had pegged him as a classic introvert. He got his energy by being alone and felt drained when forced to be around others he didn't know well. He was used to his buddies in the fire department and had always felt comfortable with his family. But the newfound fame that came with Firefighter of the Year, exacerbated by the ridiculous posters, suddenly put him at the center of everyone's attention.

"I'm no good with kids."

Ash looked at him sympathetically, shook his head, then said the most annoying thing possible. "You're not good with kids *yet*."

Bowman groaned. "Did you take an online class on turning into Dad, or does it come naturally?"

Ash chuckled, then gave Maisy a wink. "He'll warm up, and he knows the ranch inside and out. I'm sure you'll both do great."

He turned, like he was going to leave, but Maisy's hand shot out and grabbed his arm. A pink flush appeared at her neck. "Wait." She pointed at Bowman, concern deep and wild in her eyes. "He's *not* good with kids?"

"He's fine," Ash said. Bowman could tell his brother was getting frustrated. Ash liked to stomp in, drop orders and have those orders followed without complaint. The fact that his siblings had yet to hold up their end of this scenario never seemed to factor in to his plans.

"He doesn't think he's fine. He doesn't want to be here at all."

Ash glowered at him. "What did you say to her?"

"Nothing," Bowman replied.

Ash sighed.

"I can confirm," Maisy said. "I got about five words."

"I didn't know who you were." Bowman sat up and finally gave in to the pun that had been building in his chest since she'd introduced herself. "Doc Martin."

"Ha ha." She glared at him.

Bowman twisted his lips, working to hold back the smile. "It's kinda funny."

"Um? If it were funny I'd be laughing."

Bowman tried to keep a straight face, but he'd never been good at being serious in a serious situation. The more tense things got, the more likely he was to start laughing. Yet another reason he wasn't very good with people. But there was something about her blue eyes and freckles, the insanity of the situation. How could he be expected to suppress a laugh when her professional title was the name of a clunky hipster shoe?

No, the joke was gonna slip out at some point. What surprised him was her reaction. Most people would be good and mad by now. But when he smiled, she seemed to relax. She sat back in the booth and shook her head, the blond hair falling across her forehead. She smiled back, and it felt like the first good thing that had happened in a month.

Which Ash completely ruined by smacking the back of his head. "What's wrong with you?"

"It's okay," Maisy said. "It's like the billionth time I've heard the Doc Martin joke, so whatever. The problem is, it doesn't sound like Cowboy Camp is very well organized. That concerns me."

It was almost funny to watch Ash react. He was diametrically opposed to being rude to strangers, but this stranger was accusing him of being disorganized. For the former lieutenant in the Oregon National Guard, it was about as low as she could strike.

"Summer-vacation Cowboy Camp is a twenty-year tradition at Wallace Ranch, founded by my parents to help local kids get outside and active in their free time," Ash said, with what Bowman knew was strained patience.

"So I was told," Maisy responded calmly, as though Ash was an irrational patient in the ER. "But here we are. I have almost no experience with children." She gestured across the table. "He doesn't seem to like kids at all, and we're the ones running this camp?"

"We have lists of activities and past schedules you can look over. We're partnering with the Healthy Lives Institute this year, and that comes with a specific curriculum."

"That's great." She kept calm, and Bowman had to admit he was impressed with the way she handled Ash. "Activities and past schedules will help. But again, I've never worked with kids. I didn't even babysit as a teen. I'm smart and capable, but I'm not good with children. I expected to be working with someone who knows kids and can help me implement the Healthy Lives curriculum."

Ash shifted, looking over his shoulder to where Hunter and Clara were laughing together, then out at the parking lot. Bowman almost thought Maisy was going to win this argument, and he'd be free from Cowboy Camp. Then Ash rested his hands on his hips, looked down at Maisy sympathetically and said, "You're not good with children *yet*."

Maisy blinked, and a flush rose up her neck. Of all of the stupid, unconscionable things that had happened in the last week, his big brother dropping a *yet* on an unsuspecting newcomer had to be about the worst.

"Did you just *yet* her?"

"Growth mindset," Ash said, defending himself.

"She's a *doctor*. I think she probably has a

growth mindset already." Bowman shook his head. "I can't believe you laid a *yet* on her. You don't even know her."

Bowman looked at Maisy and shook his head in disbelief.

"Two hundred and fifty thousand," she muttered to herself.

"Two hundred and fifty thousand what?" he asked.

"Dollars." She gave him a weak smile. "The Healthy Lives Institute will pay back my loans from med school if I work out of Outcrop and help implement their initiatives, starting with this camp."

Bowman glanced up at his brother and pointed at Maisy. "See? Serious growth mindset right there, along with good financial planning."

She laughed. "Ash is right, though. I can learn to get more comfortable with kids." She cleared her throat, then said quietly, "It'll be good for me."

"You two will be fine," Ash asserted. Bowman slowly shook his head, getting another smile out of Maisy. "Look, how bad could it be? You both have considerable outdoor skills. You're a doctor and he's a firefighter. If nothing else, parents will be assured their kids are safe and will make it through three weeks alive."

The blood drained from Maisy's face. Ash had meant to be funny, but it clearly wasn't funny to her. As much as Bowman wanted out of this whole situation, she was upset and that didn't sit well with him.

Ash was right. It was time to family up.

"Look, if I have to do this, I'm gonna do it," Bowman said. "I'm the only Wallace with time right now. I'm *not* good with kids, you should know that. I'm not good with people in general. But when I make a commitment, I honor it. I'll do my best with this camp."

She looked up, her blue gaze connecting with his. She was stuck, too. They were just gonna have to do this thing.

The bells on the front door jangled, signifying the entrance of another patron. Or rather, six other patrons, all wearing a lot of makeup and noisy shoes, and looking in his direction. One of the young women waved, then they all exploded into giggles. Bowman closed his eyes. Piper was seriously going to pay for sending in that picture.

Ash laid a protective hand on Bowman's shoulder. "Maybe you and Maisy should take a walk. You could show her around town and pick up supplies for the camp." He pulled a list out of the pocket of his jacket. “I’ll email you Mom’s activity lists tonight, and you two can confirm your schedule when you meet at the ranch tomorrow, how’s that sound?”

Getting out of the crowded, groupie-infested restaurant? *Good idea.*

Spending time with this doctor he’d known for fifteen minutes and already managed to insult? It would be easier to summit Mt. Hood barefoot.

Bowman nodded to Ash and grabbed his hat. Maisy stood uncertainly, unaware of the dark cloud of aggressive flirtation heading their way.

Behind the counter, Clara caught his eye and held up two to-go cups of coffee. If it had been her choice, they wouldn’t serve the groups of women who came in to gawk at him, but Hunter had an annoying habit of wanting to stay in business.

Maisy had caught the whole exchange. She tilted her head and asked Bowman, “Who are those women?”

“Nobody.”

She held his gaze. He focused on looking as disinterested as possible. “We’ll get the supplies in town.”

She checked her phone. “Okay. There’s someone from the Oregon Medical Federation stopping by my house to drop off some welcome materials in about an hour—"

"It won't take long."

"Coffee!" Clara approached their table, shielding Bowman from the fan club. She handed Maisy the cup, overly proud of her ability to run hot water through ground-up beans, as always.

Maisy took the cup and breathed in, then smiled. "Thank you."

"Just doing my part. You two want to exit through the back?"

Exit was the only part of the sentence Bowman understood—yes, it was time to go.

Problem was, these days it didn't seem to matter where he went in this town, everyone had an opinion on his business. And the family he would have once gone to for shelter had scattered in a hundred directions, leaving him on his own.

CHAPTER TWO

"HEY, BOWMAN!"

"Hey." He kept his head down and didn't pause to greet the woman who stopped on the sidewalk in front of him. Maisy gave her a brief wave, then scrambled to keep up with Bowman's long strides.

"Bowman! Great to see you," a guy about their age called from across the street.

Bowman gave him an obligatory bro nod. "Yup."

"Oh, hey." A young woman stepped out of a store as they passed. "You're Bowman Wallace, aren't you?"

Sullen nod.

Sunlight bathed the sidewalk leading down Main Street, but Bowman didn't appear to be feeling the warmth. Watching him interact with others made *her* introduction to him seem downright welcoming.

He hadn't spoken to her since leaving the table in Eighty Local. Communication came in the form of a nod as she thanked him for holding the door for her, and something that might have been agreement when she commented on how great the coffee was. Other than that, he kept his eyes forward and his thoughts to himself. Everyone who spoke to him seemed to push him further back into his shell.

She glanced up at him. "Are you always this lively and social?"

He stopped abruptly and glowered at her, brown-green eyes washed in annoyance. She held his gaze and took another sip of what really was an extraordinary cup of coffee. He glanced up, and she nearly choked on her beverage when she realized he was trying to repress a smile again.

"Yep."

Maisy laughed. His expression softened at her laughter, then he took off walking again.

"Where are we headed?"

Bowman gestured with the list Ash had given him. "Supplies."

She tried to look at the list, but got distracted by the strong, work-calloused fingers holding it. She shook her head. "And we get these supplies where?"

"At OHTAF." He pointed ahead to a deep red, wooden building with a wide, wraparound porch. Outcrop Hardware, Tack and Feed was painted in large letters over the entrance, but given the purchases she observed people leaving with—garden starts, climbing gear, children's books—it was hard to determine exactly what was being sold in the establishment. They seemed to have everything.

"Do they sell capable adults there? Because that's what we need—two grown-ups to run this camp."

Bowman glanced at her from under his Stetson, his lips set in what she now understood to be a pre-grin. "Nope. But they've got Advil."

Maisy slowed her pace, then stopped walking even as Bowman trotted impatiently up the steps to OHTAF. Main Street in Outcrop was beautiful. Old brick buildings had been updated, and a collection of thriving shops had their doors propped open to the summer day. She'd researched the town and knew it had experienced a resurgence over the last decade. Outdoor sports, like hiking, rafting and skiing, were a major industry. Smith Rock, the world-famous climbing destination, was fifteen minutes from her front door.

No, Outcrop was a great town. She liked what she saw, but she did *not* like what she was feeling. This camp was her introduction to the community, and if she failed, it would taint her standing here. The treatment of a community's children mattered, and she was on a fast track to failure within her first month.

"I'm serious."

Bowman turned around at her words.

She held her arms out, hopeless. "What are we going to do?"

He rolled his shoulders and looked up at the cloudless sky. He didn't speak. There were probably a hundred trivial words he could have scattered to make her feel better about the situation, but that didn't seem to be his style.

His concerned gaze met hers. "I don't know."

"Bowman Wallace!" The words boomed across the front porch of OHTAF, and for once, her terse companion didn't flinch at a friendly voice—it was the opposite actually. Bowman bounded up the last two steps toward a man in his midfifties and yelled, "Coach!"

He gave the man a high five and began an animated conversation about offense, defense and a team emu named Larry. Maisy drifted up the steps behind him, taking her time to get the full measure of OHTAF. The porch was home to scattered rocking chairs and benches, and a few tables set up with chess games. Fireman of the Year! Posters hung at regular intervals. She peeked in the window but kept her focus on Bowman's conversation. He'd been so sullen, with only occasional rays of humor. Now *this* guy got a jovial reaction?

"Who's this?" the man asked, gesturing to Maisy.

"Doc Martin. She's the new—"

"*Doctor* Martin," she corrected, holding out a hand. "Or Maisy."

"Doctor Maisy Martin, it's great to have you in town. We've been looking forward to your arrival."

"Thank you." Maisy nodded. "I'm glad to be here."

"I'm Coach Kessler—" he raised one hand, like a Boy Scout pledge "—and I promise to eat better, exercise and not make unnecessary work for you."

Bowman shook his head, the pre-smile morphing into the real deal. "I don't know about that."

Coach's chuckle gave way to a confused frown. He pulled back his head and looked at Maisy, then at Bowman, and back again. "I gotta ask…how long have you known Bowman?"

"Um…" Maisy glanced up at Bowman. "Are we going on thirty minutes?"

"And he's speaking to you?" Coach clarified. He mugged an impressed face at Bowman.

"I wouldn't go that far. We're only up to about twenty words?"

"Nicely done." The coach offered her a high five. "That's probably a record. What brings you to OHTAF?"

Maisy looked at Bowman, waiting for the terse "supplies" she'd gotten earlier. Instead, he sat heavily on a bench, pulled off his hat and ran his hands through his hair. "Ash wants me to run Cowboy Camp."

Coach burst out laughing. "You?"

"Yeah." He gave Maisy an apologetic nod. "Doc's stuck with me."

"Hey," the coach said sternly, "I don't like that attitude."

"No, it's bad."

"Nothing's ever that bad."

"Seriously, Coach. It's like the 2010 district semifinals."

Coach Kessler shuddered, but quickly recovered from what looked to be a bad memory. "You haven't even started. What if you'd had this same attitude with the Heritage Museum fire?" He gestured to the poster behind them. Bowman looked defeated and exhausted—the complete opposite of the confident, energized man in the photograph.

"He tell you about the fire?" Coach asked Maisy. She shook her head. "Right, you're only at twenty words." He clapped Bowman on the shoulder. "The old barn on the Amondson place caught fire, and the crew arrived and got busy putting it out. But this guy—" he indicated Bowman "—notices sparks from the flames are drifting. The Heritage Museum building is made of stone, but has timber framing and a shingled roof. The second level holds Amondson's personal collection of Paiute artifacts." Coach tapped the poster behind them, drawing her attention to the beadwork. "So Bowman scales the stone wall, while the roof is on fire—"

Maisy held out a hand to pause the story. "You climbed a burning building?" Her heart lurched against her lungs, like it was trying to hide there.

Bowman shrugged.

"By the time he breaks in the second-story window, the roof is in flames, but he keeps yelling at the guys to hold the water until he can clear out the important pieces. Then he's about to leave—"

"I think she gets it, Coach—"

Kessler continued, "He's about to leave, and he hears Mr. Amondson's new puppy whimpering in the background."

Maisy glanced up at the little blond puppy,

peeking his head out of Bowman's turnout gear in the poster.

"I wasn't going to leave the dog," Bowman said, as though everyone rushed burning buildings to save artifacts and family pets.

"Bowman might not be much of a talker, but he's a hero. He's brave, has physical abilities you can't even imagine and he's always here for his community."

"And he's suspended for three weeks," Bowman muttered.

Suspended? Okay, she needed to know a lot more about that.

Coach, on the other hand, chose to ignore the comment. "He's gonna do great with camp. You both are." Coach checked his watch, a smile growing across his face. "Sorry, kids, but I gotta go. It's chocolate time!"

"Chocolate time?" Maisy asked.

The coach tapped his watch. "Every day I buy my beautiful girlfriend, who owns that store over there," he said, pointing at a clothing shop, "a piece of chocolate from *that* store over *there*." He gestured to a storefront with Three Sisters Chocolatier etched in the glass. "Chocolate's good for you, right?"

Maisy blinked. "Um, in moderation. One ounce of dark chocolate a day has some health benefits."

"And multiple dating benefits." Coach winked at Bowman, then jogged down the steps as he waved over his shoulder. "Nice to meet you, Maisy. Good luck with the camp! And with Bowman."

Bowman leaned back on the bench, once again engaging all forty-eight muscles in his two arms to push his hair back. Then he put on his Stetson and stood abruptly. He gestured to her empty coffee cup and held out his hand in what she understood as a silent offer to dispose of it for her.

Did he think she was going to hear this fascinating story about his heroism and not talk about it?

"That's incredible," she said. "About the fire."

He shrugged, turning his back to her as he found a recycle bin.

"What was in the museum?"

"Cool stuff. Artifacts, some documents and old photographs. Amondson used to let school kids come through and taught us about Paiute history. It's just his personal collection, but I learned a lot from it as a kid. I thought we should save it if we could, you know?"

She glanced back at the picture, seeing the burning building behind him in a new light as a result of this information. "Still. It's impressive."

He scoffed. "Don't get your hopes up. I'm good with disaster, not kids."

"Well," she said as she headed for the door, "that's what camp is setting up to be—an unmitigated disaster."

BOWMAN STARED AT the list, trying to make sense of it.

> Glue sticks. String. Cornstarch. Birdseed. One hundred feet of eight-gauge wire. Paint stir sticks. Ask Mr. Fareas for empty feed sacks.

"What are we supposed to do with the string?" Maisy asked.

Bowman shrugged.

She leaned closer, reading over his shoulder. Her hair smelled a little like the flowers that used to bloom along his grandma's front porch in early spring.

"What are we supposed to do with birdseed, and eight-gauge wire?"

"And twelve kids," he added.

Maisy shook her head, then looked around. OHTAF was one of his favorite places, and despite the trouble they were in, Bowman still enjoyed showing it to Maisy. The wide-plank floors softened the clunking of footsteps. Newborn chicks peeped in a galvanized steel water tank, while locals and out-of-towners buzzed through the warrens of merchandise, each finding exactly what they needed.

Mr. Fareas, the keeper of OHTAF, was as astute as any big-city businessman, even if he did wear overalls to work. He ran the tack and feed sections with an eye to quality and economy. As Outcrop became a popular destination for outdoor adventurers, he expanded his offerings, taking care to note what people were likely to forget, or not know they needed until they got here. He carried a small selection of books, featuring local authors and gardening books alongside climbing guides and *The Farmers' Almanac*. If a customer couldn't find an item when combing through the store, he'd be sure to have it in stock the next time they showed up.

Bowman and his siblings had loved any trip to OHTAF as children. They'd played endless games of I spy, hide-and-seek and tag as their parents bought supplies for the ranch. Once Bowman thought it would be funny to hide from his parents, resulting in forty minutes of thrilling fun for him, extreme panic for his mom and the longest lecture on record from Dad.

"What are you smiling at?" Maisy asked.

Bowman shook his head and refocused. He wasn't a kid anymore, and his family all had better things to do than wonder what he was up to. He studied the list again, trying to make sense of the items. What even *was* cornstarch?

It didn't matter. They'd spend at least half the day in the barn, anyway.

"We've got the horses," he said. "So that's most of the camp right there."

Maisy pulled a face, rearranging the freckles across her nose.

"It's Cowboy Camp," he reminded her. "We run a horse-breeding operation. Horseback riding is the whole point of sending your kid to Wallace Ranch."

She hid her expression, turning to look at a rack of brightly colored socks as they walked past. "There are helmets for the kids when they ride?"

Bowman tried to conjure up an image of Piper or Clara teaching one of their riding lessons. Were the kids wearing helmets? He couldn't remember.

"Probably."

Her blue eyes met his. "I'm sure there are helmets. There have to be."

He nodded. If helmets were a thing, his parents would have helmets.

"Okay." She inclined her head, like she was convincing herself of this fact. "Horses will take up part of the time. And I've got the Healthy Lives curriculum."

Bowman imitated the face she'd made when he brought up the horses. The family's decision to partner with Healthy Lives for Cowboy Camp was based in necessity, rather than a desire to switch up camp with more nutrition information. The cost of insuring camp had risen dramatically, and HLI offered to cover that cost and supply a second camp leader.

When Bowman had cast his vote, it never occurred to him that he'd be the first camp leader.

"I think the curriculum is supposed to be pretty good," she said. "I honestly have no idea. I wouldn't know good curriculum if it walked up and tried to educate me."

"You haven't looked at it yet?"

"Oh, I looked at it." She shook her head, her blond hair falling back into her eyes. "I just couldn't figure out how to implement it. I'm a doctor, not a teacher. Plus, I—I thought I'd be working with someone who was experienced with kids, who could help me make sense of it."

Bowman groaned. "I'm so sorry for you. And me."

"And those kids."

Bowman chuckled. Maisy was cool, and the first hour of working with her hadn't been horrible. She was no-nonsense, from her simple jeans and tank top, to her unwillingness to sugar-coat the situation they were in.

He glanced around. The store was getting busier, like it did in the late afternoon. He was about ready to get back to the ranch. There was a climbing crag on the property he co-owned with Hunter, adjacent to the family place. Maybe he'd hike up to Fort Rock and do some bouldering after they finished up. The promise of fresh air and the stillness of being outside alone relaxed him. He smiled at Maisy, and something seemed to shift in her eyes, like she relaxed, too.

It felt good.

She pushed her blond hair out of her eyes, and Bowman noticed her smoothly muscled arms. She might like rock climbing, too.

"So, string?" she asked.

String? He glanced around. There were bales, balls and skeins of string in every weight and size imaginable on the shelves. "Right." He shook his head. "I don't know much about string."

"I probably know more about string theory than I do about literal string."

Bowman laughed. Maisy's arm brushed his as she reached for the nearest skein, warming him.

"Wallace." The statement was like a bucket of water on warmth of any kind. The fire chief, Josh Hanson, was clunking down the aisle.

Bowman took half a step in front of Maisy. Like he had to protect her from getting suspended by Hanson, too?

"What are you up to?" Hanson asked.

Bowman shrugged. He *really* didn't feel like talking to the fire chief right now.

Hanson glanced at Maisy, as though he expected an introduction. When he didn't get one, he sighed, as if Bowman was the one being unreasonable. "Look, I'm not any happier about this than you are."

Bowman felt the walls moving in on him, the merchandise in OHTAF crowding closer. This was one of those times he was supposed to say something, and he really didn't have anything to say.

He knew he didn't fit in this world and didn't need Hanson pounding it into his head. He was an introvert at a time that not only celebrated, but also demanded constant, gregarious human interaction. He was an intuitive man in a world that valued logic, where every action was judged and evaluated against a rubric. In a different place and time, his skill set could have grounded a community. Here, he just seemed to rub against everyone the wrong way.

Bowman did his best to get along, but the battle was exhausting. At best, he was misunderstood. At worst, he was hassled to become someone wholly different from who he was at his core.

"We have protocol for a reason," Hanson continued.

"I know," Bowman snapped. "You explained the whole thing at the meeting."

"It doesn't look good for our department to have the Firefighter of the Year suspended two weeks after the posters go up."

"Then take the posters down."

Hanson put a hand on his shoulder. Bowman tried not to flinch it off. "I understand why you broke protocol."

"Mrs. Stamm would have lost everything."

"I know. But you can't go with your gut every time. In this case, you were right. But if you'd been wrong, you'd be dead."

Bowman felt Maisy shudder. Her face went gray, blue eyes shining out in contrast.

"I don't know what you want me to say." Bowman crouched down and grabbed a ball of string. If Ash hadn't cared enough to specify what kind of string, he wasn't going to spend time trying to figure it out. "I'm not sorry, Mrs. Stamm's not sorry and neither of us is dead."

Hanson didn't walk away. Bowman managed to spit out another few words in an attempt to get him to do so. "I can't chat right now. I got Cowboy Camp at the ranch to get ready for."

Hanson shifted. "You're working Cowboy Camp?"

Bowman nodded. *Where did Mr. Fareas keep glue sticks?* Probably in the office-supply section Clara had coerced the man to set up.

"Sami's really looking forward to it."

Bowman stilled. Keeping his back to Chief Hanson, he asked, "Your daughter's coming to camp?"

Hanson replied, but Bowman was no longer listening. Up until now, the kids attending this camp had been a vague notion. An annoying and potentially frightening notion, but vague all the same. Sami was real. The only upside to the suspension was not having to be around Josh Hanson for three weeks. He needed the time to cool off and remember that the chief was actually a good guy.

But Sami would be at camp, having a miserable time, reporting back every inadequacy of Bowman's to the fire chief. This was too much. Bowman was just a guy trying to do his best in the world. But recently it seemed like every instinct he had got him further and further into trouble.

He glanced up to see Maisy talking with Josh. She smiled with a forced confidence, and seemed to be reassuring this smug rule monger that everything was going to be okay for his precious daughter.

"We need to grab the rest of the supplies," Bowman interrupted.

She gave him the calm, controlled doctor look, which was probably something she was taught in med school and practiced in her bathroom mirror. Then she turned back to the chief and offered her hand. "Nice to meet you. I look forward to seeing Sami when camp starts on Monday."

Bowman stalked off in the direction of the office supplies. He knew it was rude, but something about Maisy taking the chief's side bothered him.

"Well, that just got real," she said, catching up with him.

Why did Mr. Fareas carry so many sticky notes?

"Yeah." He grabbed a handful of glue sticks. "I'll get started on the schedule tonight. I've got some ideas, and if we can get the first few days planned—"

"Do we even need a schedule?" he interrupted, keeping his eyes on the list. Birdseed. What were they supposed to do with birdseed?

She took the list from his hand and gave him a look again. "Yes. We have to have a schedule. We can't let them run wild."

"I spent my summer breaks running wild."

"That's pretty clear," she joked. It didn't feel funny to Bowman. "Look, I'll get the schedule started if you—"

"We're not going to know what the kids want to do until they get there. Let's just show up and see how it goes."

The angry red flush began to creep up her neck. "They're not going to know what they want to do at all. We have to tell them."

"That's how kids have fun? Adults tell them what to do?"

"We cannot do this without a solid plan."

"Let's get there first. It will be better if we shoot from the hip, rather than plan everything in advance."

"Shoot from the hip?" She glanced over her shoulder to where Chief Hanson was in conversation with Mr. Fareas. "That's how you got suspended, right?"

Bowman stalked down the aisle, heading for

the feed section. She followed, confused and obviously annoyed with him, and said, "This camp isn't only about having fun. It's about teaching kids to engage in healthy habits."

"So we're going to hijack their summer and ruin it?"

"We're setting them up for a lifetime of freedom in healthy bodies. And from what I understand, your family is willingly partnering with HLI on this."

"Because we can't afford the rising insurance costs of the camp. Look, I'm not against healthy living. I'm just reminding you that kids go to camp to have fun."

"Maybe insurance costs would be a lot lower if you didn't include horses."

"It's Cowboy Camp. Wallace Ranch is a horse-breeding operation—"

He stopped, closed his eyes and tried to get a hold of himself. This mattered to her, and as misguided as she might be, he didn't need to be a jerk. She put a hand on his arm, her light touch tethering him in the moment. Bowman breathed in, then gazed down at Maisy. He needed to be a better man and help her get through this.

She blinked, then pulled back her hand. "I'm sorry if your family's disorganized, but I have a job to—"

"What did you say about my family?" Cold anger flooded through him, snapping any momentary connection. She didn't know anything about his family.

She wrinkled her nose again. It wasn't nearly as cute this time.

"What? Your family *is* disorganized."

He clenched his jaw and tried not to snap at her. "My family is the best group of people you'll meet in this town. Or anywhere."

"Um, okay? And I'd know that because your brother forced you into this last-minute? Or because of the clear and detailed plan they gave us for camp?"

Bowman shifted, fighting to contain the emotion reverberating through his chest. "You don't know anything about us."

She opened her mouth but Bowman cut her off. "My parents are two of the most respected people in this town. If anyone knows anything about science or geography, it's because my folks taught them. This camp? It's free. Any eight-year-old who wants to come is welcome so long as we have room. None of the families will pay a thing for their kids to spend three weeks outside, with the horses, instead of staring at a screen all day. Eighty Local, where you'll have the best food in central Oregon, my brother built from the ground up. And I won't hear you say one word about Ash. He served eighteen years in the National Guard, which is more than either of us can say."

Maisy blinked and took a step back. Then she let out a sharp breath.

"Why are you helping with camp if you don't want to? Aren't there a million small towns that need a doctor? I'm sure some other place would love to learn about healthy habits, rather than letting their kids run around outside and actually get healthy." Bowman shook his head. "I don't have a choice. I'm doing this for my family. What's your excuse?"

CHAPTER THREE

MAISY TURNED AWAY before the flush made it to her face. Unfortunately, she still had short hair, so her flaming red neck was glowing for him and all of OHTAF to see. She crossed her arms over her chest and walked quickly toward the door, the foolishness of her actions looming as she neared the exit. Had she been assuming he'd follow her and apologize? Well, that wasn't happening. Bowman's boots remained solidly on the other side of the store, as she, a full-grown woman with a medical degree, ran for cover.

She rested her hand on the door handle, giving him another beat to catch up.

And now she was a full-grown woman blocking the exit.

Maisy wrenched open the door and marched out into the sunny afternoon.

How had things gone so wrong, so quickly?

One minute they were joking about how unprepared they were for camp, and the next he was furious with her for stating the obvious.

The obvious was clearly a sore point with Bowman.

She shook her head. This was ridiculous. She was a doctor. She'd worked for years, doing hard, grueling work, and yeah, she'd expected a little respect when she came out the other side.

But here she was, in a town run by the Wallace family, forced to work at a camp on their ranch that was going to fail so hard they'd feel the tremors in Idaho.

I'm doing this for my family. What's your excuse?

What were the rules here? Did she have to have an excuse for volunteering in this community? And if so, wasn't the repayment of a massive educational debt enough? Also, why did he have to have that adorable gap between his front teeth? Couldn't they get an orthodontist out here so her pulse didn't have to surge every time he smiled?

Maisy's feet pounded the pavement as she made her way past OHTAF and into the town square. The little house she'd rented was two blocks off Main Street, past the park, and right now she wanted to get home, slam the door and not see another member of this community ever again.

She broke into a run. It felt like the pavement

was pounding back as her feet hit the ground. Her heart rate rose and blood rushed in her ears as she moved faster. Confusion initiated the familiar roar of panic reverberating through her skull, sending her back to the bleak, endless days in the wake of the accident. She could still see Elliot, rolling down the drive on his beloved bicycle, still hear the screech of tires as the car swerved to avoid him, still remember the silence in the days, weeks and months after he passed.

"When will we be happy again?" she'd asked her mom, the day after her ninth birthday.

Mom, situationally and clinically depressed, had shaken her head and said, "We won't be, sweetie."

Maisy slowed her pace and shook off the memory as she exited the town square. She was a doctor now. This job was the goal, the endgame. She'd arrived.

A medical degree was supposed to end her sadness, to bring the tragedy of her brother's shortened life full circle by helping others live longer, happier lives. The kids' camp was a great place to start, even if kids did make her nervous. Maisy had spent her life confronting her fears; she could do it again.

She'd intentionally become a bike commuter in medical school, to overcome the dizzying waves of fear that pounded her when she saw people cycling. It had taken time—and a cycling wardrobe of all the bright orange and yellow known to humanity—but she did it. Starting with making the trek from her little apartment to Oregon Health & Science University, and culminating in bicycling across the entire state.

A paralyzing shock had immobilized her the first time she'd seen someone rock climbing. That was her signal to get comfortable with the sport. In the course of a year, she'd learned to climb safely, and now was perfectly at ease when roped into a route, eighty feet off the ground.

Starting this week, she'd learn to get comfortable around children. There would be some rough patches—there always were when she tried to conquer a fear. Tonight, she'd come up with a fantastic schedule. When she and Bowman met tomorrow, she'd hand him the list of activities, and he could take it or leave it.

Scratch that—he could take it or take it. She was not going to let some displaced firefighter with an attractive smile run roughshod over her.

She glanced up and stuttered to a stop before nearly running into a telephone pole. And, of course, right at eye level, plastered to the wood was the Fireman of the Year. Exclamation point, exclamation point, exclamation point, lipstick kiss, heart, heart, heart.

Maisy grabbed the poster with both hands and pulled it off the pole, crumpling it into a big, satisfying ball. She looked around for a garbage can. Nothing.

Her head swung wildly, searching for a trash receptacle. The whole, adorably cute town had no waste disposal? She took a few steps back toward the town square.

Then she froze.

Had anyone seen her pull down the poster? That would be humiliating. Everyone knew and loved Bowman. She'd be the crazy new doctor ripping down posters of the town hero. She slowly moved her eyes from left to right. Nobody there. Maisy smoothed out the poster and approached the pole. But what? Was she going to reattach it? With what?

She could drop it, as if it had fallen naturally…and just happened to get all crumpled in the four feet from the pole to the ground.

Maisy took a step in the direction of her house. Ugh. She had to do something with this poster. If anybody saw her, it might look like she was stealing it and taking it home for her own nefarious purposes.

She uncrumpled the poster and glanced

down at the image of Bowman, now marred with crisscrossing lines.

Okay, darts might be fun.

But, no, she needed to get rid of the poster immediately. She carefully folded the poster in half and glanced around. There was no one nearby. She folded the poster again, and again. It was thick, but still folding.

Cheerful voices floated up Lemon Street. Maisy folded faster. She now had a very thick stack of paper, but she was less than two blocks from home. All she had to do was walk down the street, take a left and she'd be in the safety of her cottage. Desperately, she shoved the image of Bowman into the back pocket of her jeans. A few threads gave way. Maisy kept her hand over her pocket, her eyes cast down and continued her march homeward. She passed the neighboring homes, all similar little houses built in the 1920s. Leafy green trees lined the street and a neighbor was barbecuing. Maisy was less than seventy-five feet from slamming her front door behind her.

"Hello!" a man called out cheerfully.

Maisy's head snapped up. On the front steps of her cottage was a man in his midthirties with thick glasses and a broad smile. He was sitting with a woman, also smiling, and gazing at her with soulful, violet eyes. In front of them was a basket big enough to house all her humiliation from the last two hours.

"Hi?" Maisy smiled at the couple, readjusting her hand over the pocket.

Nothing to see here, no poster desecration going on in these parts.

"Welcome to Outcrop!" the woman cried.

"Um?" Maisy swallowed and resisted the urge to make her statement a question. "Thank you. I just moved to town."

The man and woman looked at one another. "We know. We're your welcoming committee."

"From the OMF," the woman clarified. "I'm not a doctor, but Michael works at the hospital."

That one word, *hospital*, felt like wrapping her arms around a big, cushy life preserver.

"Y-you work at the hospital?" she asked, and really tried not to hug the man.

He pushed his glasses up on his nose. "I'm in pediatrics. And I know you're the new GP in Outcrop. Welcome to town."

"You're the welcoming committee!" Maisy said excitedly. She'd totally forgotten they were coming in the insanity of the afternoon.

His face lit up as he nodded and Maisy knew, right then and there, that these people were friends at first sight. She allowed her shoulders one quick groove of celebration.

"I'm so happy to meet you! It's been kind of a weird start here in Outcrop."

"Oh, it's hard moving to a rural area." He shook his head sympathetically as he stood. "When I came here, I had one friend." Then he grinned at the woman, offering her his hand. "But now I have a number of friends, and a brilliant wife."

"You have an army of friends." She rolled her eyes. "My husband can make friends during an internet outage at the DMV."

He shook his head. "She's exaggerating."

"Dan?"

"Oh, well, *Dan*..."

"Do you have room for one more?" Maisy asked.

The woman grinned at her. "Absolutely. I'm Joanna Williams, this is Michael."

"I'm Maisy Martin." She held out her hand and the couple laughed as they bumped into each other, both trying to shake her hand first.

"I'd love to get together and swap stories about practicing medicine," Michael said. "You wouldn't believe the ways kids manage to get hurt in Deschutes County."

Maisy shuddered at the idea of kids getting hurt. The camp will be fine. The kids will be okay. It's only three weeks. She was a doctor now—she could heal the kids who got hurt.

Maisy pulled in a deep breath. “I’d love that. I’m really excited to start. I’m working with the Healthy Lives Institute.”

“That’s fantastic! Did you get the loan-repayment gig?”

“I did.” It felt great to say it. She applied for, and got, the loan-repayment grant because HLI thought she was worth the investment.

“Nice! I applied but was rejected.”

“They rejected you?” Joanna asked.

Michael shrugged. “To summarize the email I received, my lifestyle did not adequately reflect the HLI mission.” Joanna laughed. Neither of them looked particularly fit, but if the research on strong relationships leading to longer lives was correct, Maisy suspected these two might live forever.

“When do you start practice?” Michael asked.

“In a few weeks. I committed to helping with a kids’ camp, then I’ll get set up at the clinic and the rotating docs will taper off until I’m the only show left in town.”

“Sounds like a smart beginning,” Michael said.

“We’ll have to get together.” Joanna smiled at Michael. “We live in Redmond right now, but we’re in Outcrop all the time.”

"Eighty Local is the best restaurant in central Oregon."

"Yeah, I've heard that..." Maisy's heart dipped at the mention of Bowman's brother's place. She'd been planning to avoid the establishment from here on out.

"And we're good friends with the Wallace family."

Maisy's heart took a full-on plummet. "Really?"

"It's kind of hard not to be friends with the Wallace family around here."

"Oh, I'm doing a pretty good job of it."

Michael and Joanna exchanged a glance, probably rethinking their offer of friendship. "What happened?"

"Um, have you met Bowman Wallace?"

"Oh, yeah. Bowman." Michael shook his head.

"Have I technically met him?" Joanna asked, turning to her husband. "I mean, we've spent lots of time with him at their family gatherings, but I'm not a hundred-percent sure we've ever spoken."

"I talked to him once," Michael said. "We had a ten-minute conversation about fly-fishing."

"Wow."

"Yeah. It was fascinating." Michael shook

his head. "Remember the time they brought out a karaoke machine for Bob's birthday?"

Joanna burst out laughing. "I was *not* expecting Bowman to sing!"

"I wasn't expecting him to dance!"

Bowman was singing? And dancing? That didn't seem like it could happen in this universe! Then again, his expression on the poster that was busting a seam in her back pocket spoke of a man entirely different from the one she'd stormed out on.

"How'd you meet Bowman?" Michael asked.

"Ugh. We're supposed to be running this Cowboy Camp together."

"Bowman's working kids' camp?" Michael's enlarged pupils reminded her of the classic sign of shock. Which *was* a possibility, given the situation.

"Yeah. Bowman and…me." Maisy hung her head as the reality of the situation set in, once again.

"I'm so sorry," Michael said. "I mean, Bowman's a great guy. He's just not very good with kids. Or people he hasn't known for at least fifteen years."

"And especially new-to-town doctors," Maisy added, covering her face with her hands. "This camp is going to be a disaster."

"It could be okay," Joanna said authoritatively. "If the activities are engaging enough, good curriculum can almost run itself. Is the camp carefully planned out, with a range of activities scheduled in rotation throughout the day?"

Maisy shook her head. "Not even close."

Joanna exhaled, seeming to come to a decision. "Okay, then. I'm going to help you. I teach third grade, and I make it look good. Give me your email address." Joanna pulled a phone out of her purse and typed as Maisy recited her email. "I'm sending you my planning guide. You can get creative and have fun, but stick to a schedule. Kids aren't wired like we are. They can let loose and have a good time when they know the parameters."

Tears pushed at the backs of Maisy's eyes as Joanna's fingers played across the screen, sending her a much-needed lifeline. "Thank you," she choked out.

"We've been where you are, at the beginning of your career in a small town," Michael said. "It's a bumpy start, but if you made it through med school, you can survive a few weeks with Bowman at a kids' camp."

"That's what I keep telling myself."

Joanna tucked her phone away. "You are not to hesitate to call me. Am I clear?" Maisy nodded. “Good.” Joanna grinned and looked at her husband. “Now, check out this basket. It’s everything you need to survive your first few weeks in Outcrop.”

The basket was filled with all sorts of treats and information: fliers for local businesses, coupons, a calendar of town events, baked goods, an Outcrop Eagles sweatshirt. Maisy was particularly happy to see a little box marked Three Sisters Chocolatier.

“Wow, thank you,” Maisy said. “This is so nice.” The basket, like the poster of the runaway emu welcoming her to town, was a reminder: this was a good place. She’d gotten off on the wrong foot with Bowman, but that didn’t mean her future here was ruined. She pulled out a pale pink envelope with gold lettering across the front that read Love, Oregon.

“What’s this?” she asked.

Michael and Joanna smiled at each other, a world of information racing between them. After a long moment, Joanna turned to her. “That’s from Clara Wallace, and honestly it’s the only thing you really need in the whole basket.”

“I met her at the restaurant. What’s she do?”

“She’s a matchmaker,” Michael said. “Our matchmaker, actually.”

"For real?" A funny mix of concern and intrigue mingled in Maisy's belly.

"Best money I ever spent," Michael said, gazing at his wife.

"Mmm." Maisy nodded. A matchmaker sounded so old-fashioned, but also kind of awesome. And Clara had clearly done a great job with these two. "I didn't know matchmakers still existed."

"Clara's a miracle worker. I don't know what your relationship status is—" Joanna began.

"Oh, there's no status," Maisy interrupted. "I haven't even begun to climb the ladder."

Michael and Joanna laughed. He nodded at the card and said, "When you're ready to date, it's the only way to go. Trust me. I tried all the other ways."

Maisy conjured up a picture of her ideal partner. A conglomeration of several of the men she'd dated, along with a strong dose of Patrick Dempsey, began to take shape in her mind. Until an image of Bowman, his errant smile flashing, crashed the party. She shook her head. "When I'm ready."

Joanna reached out and touched her arm. "It's so great to meet you. I included our numbers along with the email."

"We'll take you out to lunch as soon as you finish up camp and get settled," Michael added.

"Thank you." Maisy grinned at her new friends. "I'm so glad to have met you."

"Take care!" The couple waved and headed to their car.

Maisy bounced up the steps to the front porch, basket in hand. The cottage looked a little more adorable, and the sky bluer than it had. She could handle the camp and three weeks with Bowman Wallace.

"Oops! I think you dropped something," Joanna called out.

Maisy turned back, ready to wave away the concern. She hadn't been carrying anything.

Joanna gestured to a rapidly unfolding wad of paper on the path intersecting the front lawn.

She hadn't been carrying anything except a wrinkly, folded-up poster of Bowman Wallace.

Joanna took a few steps toward the poster. Maisy launched herself off the front porch and swooped in to grab it.

"I got it. Thanks!"

The couple looked confused. Maisy spun around, waving over her shoulder as she headed to the house, willing the soft breeze to keep her flush at bay.

She could do this. Ash was sending her activities, she had the Healthy Lives curriculum and now Joanna's framework. So long as she didn't let Bowman Wallace under her skin, everything was going to be just fine.

CHAPTER FOUR

Bowman's chest tightened as he exited the bunkhouse. On a normal day, taking his coffee on the front stoop helped him focus and prepare for the challenges ahead. But today's challenge was Maisy, and she'd be here in ten minutes. No amount of caffeine, or fresh morning air and solitude, could prepare him for her. She was probably still mad, legitimately still skeptical. And no matter what her mood, they had to run Cowboy Camp together, starting tomorrow.

He glanced around the property, her words riling him up again. *I'm sorry if your family's disorganized.*

Hopefully, she'd be more generous when she saw what the Wallaces had built here. It was hard to find anything more beautiful than summertime at the ranch, when grass stretched across the fields and flowers bloomed in a constant rotation throughout the season. The driveway of crushed river rock looped through the property, then gave way to a network of horse trails that reached into the hills. The buildings were all well-kept, and a lot of people got excited about the farmhouse his parents had rebuilt thirty years ago. But Bowman had always loved the simplicity of the bunkhouse. The old building was snug and simple, with four small suites that shared a common kitchen. Clara and Piper kept threatening to fix it up, but so far it had escaped their decorative whims.

But right now, he needed to leave his home and get up to the main house to meet Maisy. He swallowed the last of his coffee and set the tin cup on the stoop. Then he grabbed the scrap of paper he'd been working on and started up the road at a jog. He had to get this right. His family was counting on him to carry on this tradition, and knowing the fire chief's daughter was going to be at camp, there was even more pressure. To get it right, he was going to have to work with Maisy.

Bowman jogged up the back steps of the family home and entered the kitchen, letting the screen door slam behind him. Mom always heard that slamming door for what it was—his greeting. She'd call back "Hello, Bowman," and he'd follow her voice, then give his mom a hug when he found her.

But today there was no one to alert his presence to. Ash was delivering one of the Canadian horses to a buyer. Jackson was off with his friends. Mom and Dad were traveling in the southern part of Mexico, presently at the ancient Mayan city of Calakmul. Dad had texted him and Hunter a video of two monkeys playing in the trees around the ancient stones with the message Looks like you followed us here!

Bowman moved through the silent kitchen, across the dining room and into the big, open living room to the front windows. No sign of Maisy…*yet*.

She'd be here in less than five minutes, and he'd have to be with her for at least three hours, then three weeks.

As a rule, Bowman wasn't one to stew on the past. But he couldn't help replaying the events leading up to her walking out of OHTAF yesterday. Everything was going fine, then Hanson got him all fired up. He could own that. It didn't excuse her comment about his family, but he at least had an idea of what had set her off. Bowman looked down at the scrap of paper in his hand, then shoved it in his back pocket. He'd written up a schedule as his peace offering. His price was exacting an understanding from her that his family was an incredible group of people. When she got here, she'd see what they'd created.

Once they'd established an understanding,

they could get to work. He'd committed to this camp, and he was going to see it through.

Bowman glanced out the front window. No sign of her car along the creamy, crushed-gravel drive. He paced, feeling like one of the monkeys in the video, only deprived of his freedom and a canopy of trees. He pushed open the front door and strode onto the porch.

He jumped up, grabbed an exposed beam and did a chin-up, then another, and another. As a kid he used to challenge his family to chin-up competitions. He pretty quickly outstripped everyone but Dad and Hunter. Then Dad hurt his shoulder. Hunter had all his issues in school and had to spend most of his time with all the academic specialists and tutors they thought could help. Clara had a series of panic attacks, and the family put all their energy into helping her master a crippling anxiety disorder. No one had the energy for a friendly chin-up competition anymore.

Bowman pulled himself up again, enjoying the engagement of muscle. He tightened his core, making it easier to pull his chin over the beam. The flow of movement felt good, releasing the tension of the last few weeks. The work got hard, but he turned his concentration inward, focusing solely on one more chin-up, and one more after that.

"Hello?"

Bowman startled, uncurling his arms and hanging for a moment. Maisy stood next to a dusty Jeep in front of the house. She was dressed in a pair of jeans and a simple T-shirt, her slender, athletic frame on alert, like she was ready to fight or run at any moment. She held on to a thick stack of paper.

Everything Bowman had intended to say—*Hello. Welcome to Wallace Ranch. Thank you for coming this morning*—all evaporated in his mind.

He dropped onto the porch and nodded at her, dusting his hands on his jeans. She pulled the stack of papers to her chest and raised her chin. He needed to say *something.*

"You been to Lost Creek Boulders?" he asked, gesturing at her truck.

She spun and looked at her Jeep, then back at him.

"Um? I was. How'd you know?"

"There's the..." He gestured again. "The mud. On your Jeep. It's got that golden color."

She examined the sprays of dust and mud on the underside of her truck.

"You're a mud reader?" she asked.

"I guess so." He glanced back up at the exposed rafters and clamped down on the urge to challenge her to a chin-up contest. "You're a climber?"

"When I get the chance."

He felt the smallest beat of hope. She couldn't be all bad if she was a climber.

"You?"

He shrugged, then headed for the door. "Come on in."

Bowman held the door for Maisy, observing her as she observed the house. Ash had updated the place when their parents moved out to the apartment over the garage, replacing old furniture and repainting the interior a warm beige. Pictures from their childhood still hung on the walls, accompanied by photos of Jackson and a group shot of Ash and his buddies taken when he served overseas. The house was what Piper called "*magically clean*," as though dust was afraid to settle for fear of getting barked at by their older brother.

No one could accuse Ash of being disorganized here.

"Is this where you grew up?" she asked.

"Yeah."

"It's nice." She drifted over to a bookshelf and scanned the titles. Something caught her eye and she stepped in closer. "Whose copy of *The Insect Societies* is this?" she asked, tapping the spine of a book.

"My dad's."

She studied the shelves. "He's a big E. O. Wilson fan?"

"I guess so." Dad was probably Wilson's biggest fan, judging by the number of times he'd read each of these books. Bowman glanced at the ceiling, then made his decision. He joined her at the bookshelf and pulled out the one about the ants. "This one's signed."

Maisy's eyes ran from the book to Bowman's face and back again. He gestured with the book, indicating she should take it. She set aside her stack of papers and grabbed it.

"Wow!" She blew her bangs out of her face, excitedly flipping a few pages. "This is so cool! Look at this!" She spun the book around so he could see the signature. "I'm sorry, I'm geeking out here. But, hello! E. O. Wilson!"

Bowman wasn't sure how to respond. It was a little weird that she was getting so excited about a signature in a book, but also kind of adorable. "It's okay. My dad had the same reaction when I gave it to him."

She glanced at him from under her bangs, then looked back at the book and pulled in a deep breath. "I was rude yesterday, saying your family was disorganized."

Bowman nodded.

She handed him the book. "I'm sorry."

He nodded again and placed the book back on the shelf. "Me, too."

"This…wasn't what I expected. I really thought I was just helping out with a camp. I didn't know I'd be organizing it."

"Fair enough. We were both blindsided. Difference is, I owe my family, and you don't."

She gave him a glimmer of a smile. "I do, however, owe the Healthy Lives Institute."

He smiled back, feeling better. Too bad they couldn't end the conversation right now and go about with their lives. Instead, they were going to spend several hours together planning a camp neither of them wanted to run.

It was time for his peace offering.

"You don't have to worry about the activities." Bowman pulled the scrap of paper from his back pocket. "I talked to Ash about the previous schedule—"

"He emailed me last night," Maisy interrupted.

He smiled, and she seemed to settle. "I came up with a plan this morning."

"Oh. Um." She picked up the sheaf of papers and held them out. "I came up with a plan, too?" She cringed, like that wasn't what she meant to say.

"Well, let's see what we got."

He headed to the dining table and took the

spot he always sat in. Which happened to be right next to where he'd set a plate of cookies. He popped one in his mouth and held the plate out to her, raising his brow in invitation. Not that anyone should require an invitation to dive into a plate of cranberry jumbles.

She started to reach for one, then paused. "Should we be eating cookies while planning for a healthy-living-themed camp?"

"It's a cowboy camp," he corrected. "Besides, these are healthy. Look." He grabbed a second cookie. "Oatmeal."

She reached for a cookie, smiling. "You can't argue with oatmeal."

"Nope." He winked at her before he could think better of it. "But I bet you'd be willing to try."

She blinked, then her laugh rang out, filling the familiar room with a new sound. He hid his pleasure in her laughter with another cookie.

Maisy settled across from him and set the huge pile of paper in front of her, then took a deep breath.

"So...horses in the morning?"

"First thing," he agreed.

"Or, first thing could be a check-in circle?" She pushed the stack of papers two inches in his direction. "We could start the day by playing a game and talk about the healthy choices people made the night before."

Playing a game sounded good, but he'd yet to meet a kid who wanted to check in about healthy choices at 8:00 a.m. Still, he didn't want to offend her. She could run that portion. "Sure."

She pressed her lips together and Bowman got the sense she was trying not to offend him, too. "Are all the horses safe?"

"Yeah. Canadians are a gentle breed. So long as the kids stay away from Bella, we're fine."

"Who's Bella?"

"A horse the kids need to stay away from." Bowman leaned back in his seat.

She held his gaze, like it was somehow his responsibility to get rid of his mom's devil horse for the duration of camp. He'd have done that years ago if it had been an option.

"Bella won't be a problem," he reassured her. "And the horses will take us up to lunch."

"Okay. That only leaves afternoons, then." She pushed the stack of papers an inch closer to him. Bowman set the slip of paper with his proposed schedule on the table to ward off the encroaching parchment.

"The weather's going to be great this week. Cool mornings, then highs in the eighties."

She smiled, the real kind of smile that sent her freckles shifting across her nose. "Weather can make such a difference."

Bowman rested his elbows on the table and leaned toward her. "Yeah. I was thinking a couple of afternoons we could take them up to the swimming hole. Cougar Den rock is a fun ledge to jump off."

She blinked, confused. "You want them to jump off a rock?"

"It's fun."

"And swim?"

"It wouldn't be much fun to jump off Cougar Den rock if you didn't hit the water." He grinned at her. She didn't smile back this time.

"No."

"No?" He hadn't realized she got to be the final say in these things.

"Absolutely not."

Apparently, she did.

Bowman ran his fingers through his hair, and her eyes followed his arms. "Okay." He'd assumed the swimming hole would get them through several afternoons. "We have an old trampoline we can set up. Hunter and I used to put it at the base of the big cedar by the barn and climb up the tree and launch ourselves onto the—"

She held out both hands, as though shielding herself from his ideas. Maybe he hadn't explained it right. "I mean, you can't jump from too high, or the trampoline sends you back up into the dense branches near the top. I learned that the hard way."

She gave the stack of papers a good shove, moving it past the center of the table. "No trampolines."

Bowman crossed his arms and leaned back in his chair. "I thought we were planning this together."

"Trampolines are responsible for an average of thirty thousand fractures a year in people under the age of sixteen."

"You make it sound like the trampolines are coming after the kids."

"They may as well be."

Bowman worked his jaw and glanced down at his notes. Was it even worth mentioning Mud Battle? She plucked the piece of paper from his hand and scanned his schedule, reacting physically to each of his ideas like an actor in a silent film.

"Why don't we just let them run around with sharp objects all afternoon?"

"Why would we do that?"

She dropped his schedule on the table and sighed. At him. Like he didn't know the first thing about kids.

Which, technically, was true.

But these ideas were a blast. He'd taken a lot of time to compile his favorite childhood activities and figure out how the kids could do them at camp.

"What have you got?" he asked, not loving the defensive tone in his voice.

She pushed the pile of papers the last few inches across the table to him. He lifted the first one. A detailed, minute-by-minute schedule of warm-ups, cooldowns, circles and—

He dropped the paper like a hunk of low-fat cheese.

"We are *not* making these kids do worksheets."

"It's so they can practice the information."

"No."

"Well, what do you want to do?"

"Take them up to Cougar Den rock!"

Maisy stood abruptly and paced to the end of the dining room. She crossed her arms over her chest as she was confronted by more family photos. "These parents are sending their kids here to learn about healthy habits with the power to shape the rest of their lives."

"Parents are sending their kids here to get them out of the house, and away from their screens. As a child, I was lucky to grow up here—"

"You were lucky to survive," she muttered.

A swarm of muddy emotions swirled through him. "You don't say one word about my parents."

"I'm not talking about your parents, I'm talking about *you*. How many broken bones have you had in your life?"

Forearm, elbow, collarbone...whatever. She was just asking to prove some stupid point. "All kids are going to get hurt once in a while. Accidents are part of growing up."

She turned to face him, her eyes steely as she spoke. "Not all kids survive the accidents."

He paused. Something about her tone was different. "I know that."

"You..." She waved a hand at him, struggling for the words. "You like putting yourself in danger. You want to run into burning buildings. That's your choice."

"It's not a choice, it's a calling." Bowman stood, moving around the table to face her. "Public safety depends upon men and women who are willing to take risks. Firefighters, police officers, everyone in the armed forces. It's not about seeking danger, it's about serving the community."

"Does everyone serving the community get suspended for taking unnecessary risks?"

Bowman froze, a complicated mix of feelings immobilizing him. "That's a low blow, Doc."

A flush raced up her neck, through her face, to the roots of her blond hair. Her eyes traveled the room, like she was looking for an escape. She blinked, then looked him straight in the eyes, speaking clearly even as she trembled. "You are a risk taker, and I won't take risks where children are involved. I'm not going to participate in a camp where there's significant chance of injury to children."

"I'm not going to participate in a camp where we're making kids do worksheets on summer break."

They stared at each other. Bowman could feel Maisy's desire to turn and walk away as much as his own, but there was too much holding both of them here. He couldn't let down his family, and she had a lot of money on the line.

"Hello?" A voice echoed in through the kitchen. Maisy dropped her gaze, her chest rising and filling with air.

"I have exactly seventy minutes to help." His sister Piper stalked into the room, dropped her bag on the table and grabbed a cookie. "Having you run Cowboy Camp is literally the worst idea ever, and that includes low-rise jeans and barbecue sauce as a pizza topping. But I'm in town, anyway, to take Clara wedding-dress shopping, so I left early and sped on Highway ninety-seven to mitigate the disaster that is you running this camp. Because I love you." She checked her watch. "I'm leaving here at ten thirty. Are you the doctor?" She turned to Maisy and ran an appraising eye over her.

"Yes?"

"I'm Piper. I love your hair," she said, as though everyone had been waiting for her verdict on the matter. "Shall we go meet the horses?"

MAISY KEPT HER eyes on Piper as they moved across the property. She was Clara's twin, but where Clara was sunny and bright, Piper was sharp and purposeful. Dressed in a black linen shirt, perfectly cut jeans and riding boots, she may have been the most stylishly dressed farm girl in the known universe.

Looking at her made Maisy feel uncomfortable about her own outfit, but she had to keep her eyes somewhere, and she wasn't going to take one more look at Bowman unless she absolutely had to.

This morning was *not* going as hoped. She'd arrived with the intention of apologizing for insulting his family, then laying out a plan for camp. She and Bowman weren't a dream team by any standards. But she'd had plenty of group projects throughout her education where she did the majority of the work, and did it well. All she had to do was meet the rubric. And Joanna had provided her with the rubric the night before.

Maisy's goals were simple: Do the camp. Don't feel anything for Bowman Wallace. Succeed as a doctor.

It really shouldn't be so hard.

But then she'd pulled up to this incredible ranch. She knew from her reading that Bowman's parents had built the place over the years, while both teaching full-time. From the moment she'd crested the little hill of the property, she'd been swept away. There were deep green pastures fed by irrigation ditches, lush grass occasionally giving way to outcrops of golden rock. Two ponds reflected the morning sunshine, and glossy brown horses dotted the pastures. This well-ordered ranch in the midst of the rugged terrain relaxed her, making her feel like this was the only place anyone ever really needed to be.

And as gorgeous as it all was, it was the image of Bowman, doing chin-ups on the front porch, that she couldn't quite shake.

But shake it she must. He didn't trust her, he didn't respect her ideas and he seemed intent on putting her medical degree to swift and constant use at this camp.

"How's the bunkhouse?" Piper asked Bowman.

"Good. Kinda empty these days with Hunter working so hard on the addition to Eighty Local."

Piper turned to Maisy. "I'm planning on stealing the bunkhouse from my brothers. He and Hunter own twenty acres, past that outcrop of rock—" she gestured to the west "—with the most fabulous old house on it, but they insist on living here."

Bowman shook his head, his pre-grin barely noticeable under the Stetson.

"When you and Hunter bought the old place, you made plans to build a home near your climbing crag on Fort Rock," Piper said, sparking another unhelpful image of Bowman in Maisy's imagination, this one of him wielding a hammer as the frame of his home materialized around him. "When's that going to happen?"

Bowman shrugged. "Bunkhouse is fine for now."

They neared the stables, a long building that had little paddocks outside for each horse on one side, and a covered riding arena on the other. Piper pulled open a bypass door and ushered Maisy inside. Light danced down the aisle, illuminating specks of dust in the air. The space was alive with the warmth and energy of the horses.

"You won't find a better breed of horse for a kids' camp." Piper spun and faced Maisy, walking backward as she spoke. "They're gentle and sweet as anything, but full of personality."

Maisy nodded. She knew nothing about horses. She couldn't feel more out of place than she did in this barn.

Bowman, on the other hand, was right at home. He tossed a flake of hay to a horse, then rubbed the animal's graying ears, commenting on the horse's fortitude. A newborn colt tottered to the front of a stall at the sound of Bowman's voice and was rewarded with a slice of apple. The little horse swallowed the treat, then tried to give Bowman a loving nip, sending him playfully ducking away from the colt. All the way down the corridor, horses moved to the front of their stalls to see Bowman, like fans lining a celebrity's red carpet.

Up until now, Bowman had generally seemed on edge, ready to bolt at any minute. But here in the barn, he was in his element. That any one of these animals could unexpectedly kick him and break a leg didn't seem to register. Or trample him or…what? Roll aggressively over him, crushing his body with their massive weight?

Maisy shook her head. "The horses the kids are riding will all be broken in, won't they?"

Piper stilled, and Bowman looked up sharply. Had she said something wrong?

Bowman refocused the young horse. "We don't break horses here."

"*Train* is the correct word," Piper said gently, then she turned to Bowman. "I'm sure that's what she meant."

Maisy felt flustered, like when competitive med students would try to trip her up with semantics. She crossed her arms over her chest. "Bowman mentioned a dangerous horse named Bella. Is there any way she could be stabled elsewhere for the duration of camp?"

Piper laughed. A beautiful horse with a white crescent in her forehead moved to the front of a stall. "Is Bella a dangerous horse?" Piper asked the magnificent animal. "Is she a mean old monster?"

"She's the worst," Bowman said, stepping well behind Piper as he passed the stall.

"She just hates Bowman," Piper said, lifting a tiny piece of straw from the sleeve of her blouse.

"And Hunter. And Ash."

"Yes, because you guys get all up in her business. If you'd just let her run Wallace Ranch, she'd be fine."

Maisy took a few steps toward the horse. The animal eyed her calmly, as though she was assessing her worth. Maisy had an inexplicable urge to blurt out her GPA.

"Ash will turn Bella out onto the western pasture most days. She'll hardly be around at all during camp. That said, she's fine with kids. She doesn't like or care about them, but she understands that kids are to humans what colts are to horses." She gave Bowman a wicked smile. "It's only full-grown men who never learned to properly use a currycomb she has a problem with."

"Nobody else around here seems to have a problem with my grooming technique," Bowman said, gesturing to the rows of horses. "If I had my way, I'd never have to go near Bella again."

"Wait." Maisy turned to Bowman. "Are you afraid of this horse?"

Bowman didn't hesitate. "Yeah."

"You scale burning buildings, jump out of helicopters and who knows what else, and you're afraid of Bella?"

Bowman wrinkled his brow, like this shouldn't even be a question. "Yes." He stepped into the stall of a chubby-looking mare who immediately started sniffing his pockets. Bowman fed her an apple slice.

"Bowman is the most amazing firefighter, and, like, really good with horses. It's people he struggles with," Piper said. "Plus, he literally has zero fashion sense, but you've probably picked up on that."

"What's wrong with the way I dress?" Bowman asked, glancing down at what Maisy thought of as a fairly standard jeans-and-T-shirt situation.

"Everything." Piper turned to Maisy. "My brother dresses like he fell into a laundry pile and had to battle his way out."

Maisy laughed and held out her arms. "I don't think I'm much better."

"You have an effortless, elegant vibe. Bowman looks like he's been lost in the mountains for three weeks straight."

Maisy made the mistake of catching Bowman's eye. He raised his eyebrows in Piper's direction, his lips twisting in a conspiratorial smile.

"Just try not to look at him. It will make this whole process much easier for you."

Piper had *no idea* how right she was.

"I still can't understand why you have six billion groupies, dressed like that."

Maisy's head snapped up. That's what those women at Eighty Local had been? Groupies? Women like her who'd been entranced by his poster?

"Because *someone* sent in a stupid picture of me," he accused.

"It's the best picture of you, and they *had* to have a picture."

"The committee didn't have to have that picture. Do you have any idea how disruptive it's been?"

"You could use a disruption."

"You *are* a disruption."

Piper crossed her arms and glared at Bowman. Bowman shifted and glared right back. Maisy had the feeling this standoff was not the first of its kind, and could possibly last all day. She cleared her throat. "So we'll start each day in the barn?"

"The arena," Bowman corrected her, pointing to the covered riding area connected to the stables. "We can circle up there."

"Arena. And the kids will…saddle up the horses?"

Bowman ran his hand under the mane of the pudgy horse, keeping his eyes on the animal as he said, "I'll have them saddled before the kids get here. We can do a saddle lesson the second week, but there's a lot involved in getting it right. Anytime we ride, I'll make sure the saddles are on correctly."

"Oh. Okay. Good." She turned to Piper. "Helmets?"

"In the tack room, although some kids will bring their own. When I used to teach lessons, I'd have the kids write their name on a piece of tape and stick it to the back of the helmet, so they always knew which helmet to wear. Added bonus, their name was on the back of their head in case I forgot."

Instinctively, Maisy glanced at Bowman again. He was still mad at his sister, but clearly thinking the same thing she was. "You sure you don't want to run this camp for us?" he asked.

Piper kept her eyes on Bella, drawing in a deep breath before she spoke. "I'd do it in a heartbeat, but I've got some stuff going on in Portland right now."

The change in Bowman was immediate. He dropped his focus on the horse and walked back to Piper. "You doing okay?"

For the first time since she'd blown into the house like a whirlwind, Piper's energy dropped. She seemed defeated. "I'm fine. It's just work."

"You sure?"

"Yeah, well, work and life. It's happening."

She glanced up from Bella, mischief in her eye again as she said, "Just like Cowboy Camp."

THE MORNING PASSED in a haze of new information and what felt like a serious cardio workout. Maisy was getting her bearings as she tried to keep up with Bowman and Piper on the ranch. But, somehow, it was now noon, and as difficult as it'd been to craft, they had a plan.

"So we're…finished?" Maisy asked.

Bowman glanced up as they passed a massive cedar tree. "Seems like it."

"We've got an itinerary, activities, supplies, snacks," she said, listing off everything Joanna had suggested they prepare in advance.

"Backup itinerary, backup activities, backup snacks," Bowman muttered. Like it was some kind of crime to be prepared.

Maisy let out a breath. The morning had gotten off to a good start, then she and Bowman came up on a rough patch, a pothole, and finally hit the skids entirely. But in the end, they *did* have a plan for the next day. She stole another glance at Bowman. His eyes were fixed on the house, his boots crunching against the gravel drive.

This was as much her fault as his. He didn't know about her brother's death, or the years spent reliving the accident that took his life.

She knew she was reacting out of fear, but also out of experience. And since she was in no way willing to share her experience with Bowman, she couldn't fault him for not understanding. He was just some guy, trying to live his life and help out his family.

"Look," Maisy said, breaking the silence, "I'm sorry we're such a bad fit for this."

He shrugged, his long legs covering ground as they headed back to her Jeep. "I'm sorry you're stuck with me. Any one of my siblings would be better at this than I am."

A warm breeze lifted the last of the morning chill, carrying the scent of sage and juniper. This must have been an incredible place to grow up, and so much fun with a rowdy pack of brothers and sisters.

Maisy swallowed, and tried again. "So there's four of you?"

"Five. One planned son, then two unexpected sets of twins. I'm smack in the middle."

"Ash is the oldest?"

He nodded. "Hunter's my twin. He beat me out by a couple of minutes. Then Piper and Clara. None of them is perfect, but all of them are better with people than I am."

Was this one of those times she was supposed to say something kind and false about his people skills? She didn't imagine that would go over well with Bowman.

"How about you?"

Maisy looked up, tracking a cloud as it drifted across the sky. "I'm not terrible with people?" She shook her head. "Ugh. I do, however, turn statements into questions. It's the worst habit."

"You do?" he said, with exaggerated emphasis on making the phrase into a question.

Maisy directed her wry smile at the ground. "I've got to break it before I set up practice."

"I can see where that might get you into trouble." He seemed deeply serious, until a spark lit his eyes as he imitated her speech pattern. "'I'm sorry, Mr. Fareas, but you have high blood pressure?'"

Maisy sputtered out a laugh. Bowman's gaze connected with hers, and now it was more than just the breeze warming things up.

"My worst habit is making jokes at inappropriate times," he admitted. "The more tense things get, the more likely I am to say something stupid." He shook his head, then stopped laughing. "You're going to be a great doc."

The words felt powerful, like he was transferring his confidence to her. She soaked it up for what may have been an inappropriately long time before she finally said, "I hope so."

"No, you will." He focused on the road before them. "You're good with details, you ask hard questions, you don't drop something when you think it's important. I'd want you for my doctor." He looked up briefly, then frowned. "I guess you *will* be my doctor, since you're taking over the practice in Outcrop."

A shiver ran through her. "You're probably a repeat customer at the clinic, aren't you?"

He shrugged again. Yeah. This guy definitely came ambling in with a laceration once a month. An image of Bowman limping into a waiting room after another one of his daring saves in a fire had her heart stuttering.

"But, what about your siblings?"

Maisy looked up sharply, heart giving up the beat entirely. Exposed fear wrapped around her lungs, constricting her breath. "My siblings?"

"That's what I was asking, earlier." He gave her one of his pre-grins. "When I used a question mark to end a sentence, it was actually a question."

Maisy blew out a breath. Her regular response to this innocent question was a quick "no brothers, no sisters, next topic." Yet something about Bowman made her want to open up and blurt out the whole, heartbreaking story. He wouldn't try to make her feel better with a rush of words. The shock and sorrow would process across his face and sift into his complex, quiet personality. Of all people, this frustrating, danger-seeking *Firefighter of the Year* might actually get it.

Or he might not. Maisy had learned early on that opening up only made things harder for her. The depth of sorrow and loss crushing her family was met by well-meaning sympathy in others. People would gasp, acknowledge how horrible it was, then move on to a new conversation. They'd forget. Her family's tragedy was a minor blip in the tapestry of their experience. And that, Maisy couldn't stomach. She couldn't tell people, only to have them forget her brother along with the other minutiae of life. Bowman seemed different from other people, but then again, she'd just met him.

She gave Bowman a weak smile. "Only child."

He gazed at her like he could tell there was more to the story. But he was the last person to pressure anyone else to talk. Finally, he shifted his gaze from hers and said, "Bummer."

"Yeah. It was a bummer." Maisy pulled in a deep breath as they arrived back at her Jeep. "I'll make up for all the lost fun at camp over the next three weeks."

Bowman raised his brow in skepticism as he kicked a spray of gravel. "We'll get through."

Maisy gazed out at the beautiful ranch. In twenty-four hours, this place would be buzzing with kids. She and Bowman would show up and try to run this thing.

Earlier, he'd said, "When I make a commitment, I honor it. I'll do my best with this camp."

The question was would their best be enough?

CHAPTER FIVE

"WHAT DO YOU mean they can't keep their phones?" a woman asked, wrapping her arms around an eight-year-old girl engrossed in a game on her device.

Wow. Camp hadn't even started and Maisy was already on her third disagreement of the morning.

She pushed her hair back off her forehead. "I mean they should leave the phones with you." Maisy managed to make it a statement, rather than a question. A small win, but still worth celebrating. "Our goals this week include lots of exercise and team building, and we don't need phones for that."

"Sounds good to me." Josh Hanson, the fire chief, smiled at her, then addressed his daughter, "Hand it over, Sami."

"I didn't bring it. I read the instructions and it said no phones," Sami replied, delivering a superior glance to the other, less-prepared children.

"But what if something goes wrong?" the

woman challenged, as though the computer her child was currently glued to was the only communication device for miles around.

"Then Bowman or I will give you a call. Right, Bowman?" Maisy glanced over her shoulder to where Bowman had been standing, only to find herself staring at his back as he retreated to the barn.

Thanks, partner.

Maisy rubbed her temples. Despite a great breakfast and large doses of positive affirmation, the day was not off to a good start. Marc and his parents arrived forty minutes early, expecting her full attention as she and Bowman tried to prepare for camp. Which was somehow better than Kai's dad, who'd dropped him off a half hour early, leaving Kai to case out all the trouble he then proceeded to get into. Most families arrived on time, and full of questions about Wallace Ranch. But Bowman, the natural choice for answering such questions, kept his Stetson pulled low over his eyes, avoiding as much human contact as possible. When she'd started off camp with a few words to the parents, Bowman said nothing. *Nothing.* He ran no interference, didn't greet the children and when the fire chief arrived with his daughter, Bowman checked out completely.

And now she was fighting with a parent about cell phones?

"You know, that's not going to work for me," the mom said. "Liya needs to keep her phone."

"Okay." Maisy nodded. She didn't make the rules at Wallace Ranch, but she was happy to enforce them. "So I guess camp's not an option for Liya this year?"

Maisy cringed at the question mark, but no one else seemed to notice. The other parents glanced at one another around the circle. Josh hid a smile.

What? Was that the wrong thing to say?

Liya looked up at her mom, who was clearly shocked. "I—I didn't realize it was a major camp rule."

"It's in the instructions," Maisy said. Liya's mom looked flustered. "It's not a big deal."

The fire chief cleared his throat. "You know, Danica, Maisy's the new doctor in town. I'm sure she'll keep Liya safe."

"But what if Liya wants to talk to me?"

"She waits until four o'clock?" Maisy suggested. This really was the weirdest conversation.

Sami sighed, plucked the phone out of Liya's hands and offered it to Maisy. "How about you keep the phone, and if Liya gets scared you can give it to her to call her mom."

"I'm not scared," Liya said. Sami rolled her eyes.

Liya might not be scared, but personally, Maisy was petrified.

And it turned out to be with good reason. Once Danica and the rest of the parents had been briefed and then left, wrangling the children into order proved to be a lot more complicated than the average teacher let on. Somehow, they made it to the riding arena. The plan was they'd play a name game, check in about a healthy choice they'd all made recently, then ride horses. It was Maisy's complete intention to make the check-in last as long as possible, decreasing the time they had to spend on the horses.

"Okay, everyone, let's make a big circle."

No response.

"Circle up, everyone!"

A complete lack of any shape materialized.

She gestured to Bowman. He looked behind him, as though the real adult was hiding in the wings somewhere. Then he sighed and trotted over to her.

"Hey!" he yelled. "Be a circle."

"Be a circle?" she muttered.

Bowman shrugged, then pointed out the circle of children forming in front of them.

Sami fanned her hands in an arc. “It’s supposed to be a circle. This isn’t a circle. Marc, you have to step back. Juliet!” She motioned a girl forward. “Stand here—”

“Welcome, everyone,” Maisy interrupted Sami before the child was able to pull out a compass and make sure every kid was in the exact right spot. “We’re excited to have you here. This is Bowman Wallace—”

“We *know*,” Liya said.

Maisy kept going. “And I’m Maisy.”

“Are you really a doctor?” Juliet asked.

“I am. And we’re going to start by playing a name game and checking in about healthy choices we’ve made recently.”

“What kind of a doctor?”

Maisy pulled in a deep breath. “I’m a general physician. Let’s all get to know one another’s names.”

“Do you cut people open?”

“Um, I can. I have, but surgery isn’t my specialty. Okay. Who can tell me what makes something a healthy choice?”

One innocent question on Maisy’s part went on to light a dumpster fire of a discussion about what constitutes a healthy choice. By the time Sami accused Marc of lying about his vegetable consumption, Bowman cut out entirely, leaving a gaping hole in the circle. As annoying as that had been, it turned out to be a good thing. Bowman put a stop to what would have been a literal fire since he caught Kai playing with a lighter in the hayloft.

By the time Bowman coaxed Kai back into the riding arena, they'd already had one major fight and one child in tears.

Bowman strode over to Maisy. He had the same easy gait she'd come to associate with him, but she could tell he was tense, too. "Should we start with the horses?" he asked.

"Okay." They had to have used up nearly an hour by now. She glanced down at her watch, then flicked the side of it with her finger because the display was wrong.

She met Bowman's gaze. He looked as horrified as she felt. Only fifteen minutes had passed.

"You remember that one time," she whispered, "when we were planning this camp, and you said we'd get through?"

Bowman's pre-grin snuck out, warming her much more deeply than she was comfortable with. "We're still standing. I'll bring the horses in."

Bowman jogged through the bypass door into the stables. "Okay, I want everyone to head into the tack room and grab a helmet," Maisy said.

She managed to get the kids into helmets, and put tape on the back with everyone's name, with little resistance. Bowman had been right. The kids were here to ride and learn about horses. She would sneak in as much of the HLI curriculum as possible, but it felt a little like offering up broccoli florets at a make-your-own-sundae bar.

They returned to the arena to find the magnificent animals saddled and waiting. The kids quieted instantly.

"Sami, you're gonna be on Cricket here." Bowman parked Cricket next to a set of steps. Sami, silent for the first time that day, reverently made her way up the steps, put a practiced foot in the stirrup, then saddled up with a huge grin on her face.

Bowman got the other children situated, directing each kid to the horse he'd chosen for them.

"Can I ride this one?" Kai asked, gazing at a stately black horse.

"I've got Liya on Midnight. Hopper's for you."

Kai glanced at the roan waiting for him, then returned his focus to Midnight.

"I want to ride Midnight."

"I'm sorry, man." Bowman was confused, and clearly not interested in dealing with the situation. He doubled back to check the length of stirrups and adjust saddles.

Maisy didn't like the scowl growing across Kai's face. "Kai, why don't you—"

"I want to ride Midnight," he yelled, startling the horses and further upsetting the group.

"Midnight's my horse. Bowman said so," Liya proclaimed.

Bowman glanced over from where he was checking Marc's stirrups. He'd told Maisy earlier that Midnight was the gentlest horse they had, and while he was jet-black and had a cooler name than the other horses, Bowman had specifically assigned the most docile horse to Liya.

"Then how come you're not even getting on it?"

"Because I don't want to ride horses right now."

Maisy's pulse pounded at her throat as she approached the child and spoke calmly, like she'd learned to in her ER rotation. "Right now, it's riding time. We're all going to ride horses now."

The girl glanced at the horse and shivered, then looked defiantly at Maisy. "I don't have to do anything that makes me uncomfortable. Mom said. Can I have my phone?"

"Nope," Bowman answered. "Let's hop on Midnight here, then we can get riding."

"My mom said I could call if I got scared."

"Are you scared?" Kai sneered.

"No!" Liya snapped, giving Midnight a look easily interpreted as terror-stricken. "I just don't feel like riding horses right now."

"We're going to stick to the schedule," Maisy said.

"I *hate* the schedule."

Out of the corner of her eye, Maisy saw Bowman raise his brow.

Not helpful, Wallace.

That's when Sami burst into tears. "I've been looking forward to this camp all summer! Now everyone's ruining it."

Bowman caught Maisy's gaze. She widened her eyes. He twitched his shoulders. Somehow, they managed to silently agree that as weird as it seemed, they were the adults in this situation, and they needed to fix this. *Now.*

Maisy stared at the children, applying every solution to every problem she'd ever encountered. Nothing was helping. She opened her mouth to suggest they dig into the Healthy Lives curriculum and worksheets early, but was cut off as Bowman crouched before Liya. "You ever ridden a horse before?"

Liya turned her head away, dark curls springing and flowing with the action. "I want to call my mom."

He nodded. "When I learned to ride, I had my brother with me. Over there, that's my horse, Jorge." He pointed over his shoulder to where a massive creature stood nobly to the side. Liya blinked back tears. "What would you think about riding him with me?"

Liya considered this. Bowman smiled at her, and the girl nodded. "Okay."

"You want to wear my hat?" he asked.

Her smile brightened as she dropped her helmet and reached for the hat, settling the too-large Stetson over her curls. Maisy opened her mouth to insist the girl wear a helmet. Bowman caught her eye and gave the slightest shake of his head. He'd keep her safe on the horse. Bowman straightened, then startled when Liya slipped her hand into his. He paused, staring at the little hand in his palm, but he didn't let go.

"Okay, Kai, you need help gettin' up on Midnight?"

Kai was completely caught off guard, having received what he wanted and now having no battle to fight.

"No," he said sullenly.

"Suit yourself." Bowman set Liya onto the saddle and then swung up behind her. The other children had already mounted their horses, and Kai flailed on his belly as he tried to get onto Midnight. Everyone was on a horse, or mostly on a horse, except Maisy.

She gazed up at the animal, then around the arena. The unhelpful wish of getting to ride with Bowman slipped into her imagination.

"You need help, Doc?"

Maisy squared her shoulders and grabbed on to the horn of the saddle. She placed a foot in the stirrup and swung her other leg over the horse, surprised at how high up she was. A wave of trepid excitement rose through her.

"I've never ridden a horse before," she admitted.

Liya glanced at her, adorable under Bowman's Stetson. "Me, neither."

"I have," Sami proclaimed. "I took riding lessons from Piper."

Kai finally wound up in the saddle, scowling, but clearly a little bit happy to be on a horse.

Bowman moved subtly in the saddle and Jorge took long, slow strides. "Let's ride."

Midnight stepped in behind Jorge, eliciting a glimmer of a smile from Kai. The rest of the horses followed and, slowly, they began to ride.

THERE WERE NO sweeter sounds than car doors slamming shut and gravel crunching as cars left the property. The day was over. All the kids weren't completely miserable, and a couple of them even waved.

One day down, fourteen more to go.

Bowman pulled off his hat and ran a hand through his hair. He couldn't remember being this exhausted. His work in the fire department and his pastime of outdoor adventuring often left him physically depleted, but on the tail end of an adrenaline rush that made him uncharacteristically talkative and social. Spending the day with kids was another ball game. No, not another ball game—an entirely different sport. For the last few hours all Bowman could think about was crawling onto a stool at his brother's restaurant, eating delicious food and returning home to the silent bunkhouse to sleep. And now that the kids were gone, nothing stood in his way.

"Where's Kai?" Maisy asked, for probably the sixteenth time since noon.

Bowman glanced up to see Maisy spinning around in search of their most unhappy camper.

"Hasn't his dad picked him up?"

She held up the clipboard with the list of

kids, neat check marks and parent signatures next to the ones who'd been picked up.

Bowman let out a sigh as he scanned the property. The kid had been a determined headache all day long.

"Kai?" Maisy called. "Kai!"

Bowman waved a hand to quiet her. "He's hiding."

"How do you know?"

He gave her a dry glance, reminding her of who they were talking about.

"Good point."

"If he's hiding, calling him isn't going to help. I'll find him."

Maisy checked her watch. "His parents should have been here by now."

Bowman nodded, remembering how Kai had been dropped off a half hour early by someone who hadn't waited to get the orientation. Nothing could excuse Kai's behavior all day, but Bowman could imagine a number of things that might explain it. He trotted down to the stables, where he himself had hidden hundreds of times as a child. If there was a world championship of hiding in the Wallace Ranch stables, Bowman would be a sure bet to win. Under horse blankets, behind hay bales, even up in the exposed rafters. Kai, despite having disappeared numerous times during the day, was still a novice. It didn't take long to find him under the repair table in the tack room.

"Hey."

Kai tucked his head tighter against his knees and didn't move.

"I can see you," Bowman said.

"You can't make me come out."

Bowman sat down on the ground and hooked his elbows over his knees. "Yeah, you're right. You gonna sleep there?"

"Maybe."

Bowman nodded. He was so exhausted, sleeping here didn't sound like the worst idea. But he was still hungry, and Hunter was making his famous posole at Eighty Local. "Didn't realize you had so much fun today."

That got Kai's attention. "I didn't. I hate camp. I didn't even want to do it."

"Me, neither," Bowman mumbled, leaning back against the wall.

Kai lifted his head. "What?"

"I don't want to be here, either. My family's making me do this."

Kai narrowed his eyes. You could practically see the adult lie-detector antenna rising up out of his head. "Really?"

"Do I look like I volunteered?"

Sighing, Kai crawled out from under the

worktable and sat next to Bowman with his back against the wall.

Bowman figured this was the time a capable adult would give some speech about rising to the situation, but it didn't feel right. Kai wasn't the type of kid who liked listening, and he sure didn't feel like talking.

They sat together, the comfortable sounds of horses munching hay and the breeze rustling the leaves outside filtering around them.

"I like this barn," Kai said.

"Yeah. It's nice when it's quiet like this."

"The kids at this camp don't like me."

Bowman was tempted to point out Kai's role in all this. Instead, he said, "They'll get used to you."

"That's not what you're supposed to say. Grown-ups always tell kids to be nice, and then they'll have friends."

"Oh. Sorry. I guess I'm not a very good grown-up."

"Kids in Outcrop don't like me." Kai made his point a second time, giving Bowman the chance to respond like an adult should.

"Well, there aren't *any* kids that like me," Bowman said. Kai made a sound that could be interpreted as a chuckle. "But as my brother Ash would say, it's my fault because I don't try hard enough."

Kai picked up a stick and began drawing in the dirt. "You looked like you were trying today."

"I don't want to make this worse for Doc Martin than it already is."

Kai kept drawing. Bowman leaned his head back against the wall. Maisy had been incredible all day. She kept so calm and moved forward even when chaos rained down all around them. She really was going to make the best doctor.

"I like Midnight."

"You're good with him."

Kai startled with the positive feedback, as if it was the first time he'd heard he was good at anything in a long time.

"Look," Bowman said, "neither of us want to be here. Neither of us fit in. Maybe we can 'not fit in' together. Sound like a deal?"

Kai kept focused on his drawing, but nodded, then smiled. "Deal."

They sat in the quiet barn for a few more minutes before Kai asked, "Do I have to do all the healthy stuff?"

Maisy had presented the Healthy Lives curriculum so sincerely, and for the most part the kids indulged her by half-heartedly joining in the discussion and scrawling a few words on the worksheets she'd brought.

"I think we have to. For Doc Martin's sake, we should."

"Barf."

"I'll tell you what, let's both pick one healthy thing to do from that chart Doc handed out. Then tomorrow when she asks us about it, we can say we did it."

Kai groaned.

"It won't kill us."

"Oka-a-ay. Fine." Kai poked his stick at the ground. "What are you gonna do?"

"I think I'll eat a vegetable with dinner."

Kai grinned. "Me, too."

Bowman held his hand out and Kai shook on it. He was surprised by how easy it had been to connect with Kai, and how good it felt.

"Can I ride Midnight again?"

"Sure."

A car horn honked. "That's my mom."

"Okay. See you tomorrow?"

"Yeah." Kai stood, then gave Bowman a sympathetic smile. "I won't leave you here on your own."

"Thanks, man."

Bowman stood, then stretched, watching Kai head out of the barn. He chuckled to himself. He may have found the one kid in Oregon that he could do some good for.

CHAPTER SIX

MAISY WAS EXHAUSTED, hungry, disheartened and on the verge of tears when she discovered that Outcrop, Oregon, didn't have Uber Eats.

Eyeing the gift basket she had received the other day, Maisy rifled through it and pulled up a menu from Eighty Local, which was, of course, the only restaurant in town. At least she could get a nice, healthy meal there. She'd seen some great-looking salads and soups when she'd been in a few days ago. She leaned her forehead against the wall, blinking back tears as she pressed the numbers into her phone.

It had been *such* a rough day.

Leading the kids took one-hundred-percent focus every single minute they were together. With her medical training Maisy was used to hyperfocusing for long periods of time, but not like this. And it seemed like every plan she made was problematic for at least one, if not all, of the children.

Thank goodness for Bowman's ability to pivot and redirect a failing activity. She could still picture Liya's bright smile beneath Bowman's hat as she rode safely with him on Jorge, and the begrudging respect in Kai's expression when he walked out of the stables at the end of the day.

But while Bowman kept it together for everyone at camp, he bolted the minute Kai got in the car with his mom. There would be no friendly banter and recap at the end of their days, just a fast escape. It was probably for the best. Her heart was responding to Bowman in a way that her brain took serious issue with. This was not the time to get involved with anyone, and he was certainly not the guy.

The phone continued to ring. Maisy's stomach growled. It was interminable, ring after unanswered ring. Maybe no one would ever pick up the phone. She'd be here forever, sad and alone and hungry—

"Eighty Local. What's up?"

Maisy bolted upright. She knew that voice. Had he gone to work for his brother after this awful, horrible day? "Bowman?"

The man chuckled. "Naw, this is Hunter."

"Oh. Sorry. I just called for takeout and I thought—"

"What do you need?"

Right. Eighty Local probably got several

calls a day from women trying to get a hold of Bowman.

"I'm calling for takeout?"

"Okay."

She could hear chatter in the background, and it was clear by his tone that Bowman's brother didn't have time to talk.

"Um, could I have…" The menu fluttered out of her hand. Maisy grabbed at it. She had no idea what she wanted, and she was so tired it was hard to read the menu, much less make a choice. An unreasonable amount of time passed as Hunter was silent, waiting.

"Could I have the special?" she finally blurted out.

"Burma Mile burger. Good choice. You want sweet-potato fries with that?"

All thoughts of salad and vegetable soup evaporated. "Yes. Yes, I want the fries."

"Name on the order?"

"This is Maisy Martin."

"Oh, the new doctor!" Hunter's tone changed. "How'd camp go?"

"Fine?"

"You must be exhausted. I'll shoot this order up to the front. See you in twenty minutes?"

"That sounds wonderful. Thank you."

Maisy hung up the phone and grabbed her jacket. A nice walk up to Eighty Local would be a healthy choice to share with the kids tomorrow. She would get her big, delicious dinner, bring it back to the peace and quiet of her home and enjoy it. A burger would be the perfect accompaniment to some season-four *Grey's Anatomy*.

She made her way to the square, down Main and into Eighty Local, feeling almost positive by the time she got there. The bells on the front door jangled as she stepped into the crowded restaurant.

"Welcome in! Doc Martin, right?"

Behind the counter was Bowman, but...not Bowman. He had the same green-brown eyes, athletic build and shaggy brown hair, but this guy was chatting with several people, manning the tap and directing workers all at the same time. Where Bowman focused on one thing at a time, this guy seemed to have every iron available in the fire, while maintaining conversations *and* greeting her.

"Grab a stool. Your order will be right up. I'm Hunter, Bowman's twin."

Sweet merciful heavens, there are two of them.

Maisy cautiously approached the bar, then perched on a stool. Hunter grinned at her, and while he was every bit as handsome as Bowman, he didn't have a little gap between his front teeth. She gave a sigh of relief, as this one difference in their appearance rendered him significantly less attractive in Maisy's eyes. Clearly, not in anyone else's eyes, if the three women talking to him about renting his events center for a gala were any indication.

"Holly, give me a quick sec. I want to check in on Maisy here. But the short answer is yes, the events center will be open by Christmas." Hunter stepped away from the women and trotted over to Maisy. "Great to have you here. You make it through camp with Bowman okay?"

Maisy nodded. "It was…quite a day."

Hunter laughed. "If it makes you feel any better, Chief Hanson and his daughter stopped by after camp for some lemonade, and Sami gave me the full rundown. She had a great time."

"She did?" Maisy asked, remembering how Sami had fought with other campers, questioned nearly every activity she and Bowman tried to run and burst into tears less than an hour into camp.

"Told me all about riding Cricket in the arena and gave me several suggestions on how I could eat healthier."

Maisy laughed. "Did she tell you the two adults running the camp barely had their act together and nearly lost it with each other more than once?"

"Nope. That didn't make the initial rundown."

Food appeared on the counter behind Hunter. Burgers, chopped salads, a huge dish of mac and cheese. The room was stylish, alive with energy. She remembered Bowman's words at OHTAF. *Eighty Local, where you'll have the best food in central Oregon. My brother built it from the ground up.*

"Bowman said you built this place yourself," Maisy said. "It's fantastic."

Hunter glanced around, as though nervous it might all evaporate in seconds. "I had a lot of help from my family. Particularly Bowman. None of this would exist without his help. And now I've mortgaged the property we own to add on an events center. But—" he leaned across the counter, speaking quietly "—I think these women are going to book it for the Bend Equestrian Society gala, which would be huge."

Maisy smiled at Hunter. "Then get back to it. I'll be here, trying not to eat other people's orders."

He chuckled. "Your burger will be up in a few."

IT FELT LIKE a lifetime had passed since Bowman had waved goodbye to Maisy after their final camper departed. After a day like today, he needed to be near his family. But Ash wasn't home yet, Clara was off somewhere with Jet, and Piper still hadn't returned his call. Hunter would be busy at Eighty Local, but that was fine. He didn't have to talk to his brother, he just needed to be in the same room with someone who understood him.

Bowman pushed open the door, then froze. Maisy was at the counter, her pretty shoulders sagging with what must be the same exhaustion he felt. She stretched her arms over her head, then laced her fingers at the back of her neck. He knew he needed to walk up to her, say hello, ask how she was doing. Instead he kept his hand still on the door, ready to bolt.

"You guys, he's here! Bowman Wallace!" a young woman said excitedly.

Bowman didn't need to look to know a table of young women were now staring at him. The thought propelled him away from the door, to the counter.

He pulled out the stool next to Maisy and sat, startling her.

"Hi?"

He opened his mouth to return the greeting but nothing came out. It was like his vocal chords had shut down for the day after speaking more in eight hours than he had in the previous month. He nodded at her, then connected with his brother.

"I knew you wouldn't be able to resist the posole," Hunter said, ducking into the kitchen, then returning with a big, steaming bowl of soup.

Bowman flickered his brow in thanks and grabbed his spoon. The recipe had been explained to him, but he still didn't understand how his brother managed to make soup taste this good. He pointed at Maisy, to make sure someone told her she needed to order this if she hadn't already.

"You want to try some?" Hunter asked her.

"Oh. I'm fine. Just the to-go order is good."

Bowman placed a hand on her forearm and nodded at Hunter. He disappeared into the kitchen, returning with a cup of the posole. Bowman took big, satisfying mouthfuls of the soup, pausing only to watch Maisy's reaction.

"Oh! Oka-a-ay." She savored a second bite. "I get it now. Wow."

Bowman nodded, but kept eating. A basket of house-made tortilla chips and green salsa appeared between them. Then a plate of fish tacos. At some point Hunter tossed him an avocado. Bowman sliced it open and picked up a spoon.

Maisy eyed him. "Are you going to eat that whole avocado?"

He glanced down at it. There were so many things he should be saying to Maisy right now. *Thank you. You were fantastic today. Can you believe we made it out of there alive?* He owed her a world of words after all she'd done today. Instead, he held up the avocado and said, "It's my healthy choice for the evening."

Her laugh rang out, warming him. It gave him a little energy back. Feeling better, he held out the avocado. "You want half?"

She shook her head. "I've got a big dinner coming."

As though on cue, Hunter slid a massive Burma Mile burger her way, and what looked to be two orders of sweet-potato fries.

"Good choice." Bowman nodded at the plates.

Instead of accepting this evaluation as a fact, Maisy looked around the restaurant, a red flush creeping into her cheeks. "This was supposed to be to-go," she said, searching for Hunter. He was talking with a few of the ladies from the Bend Equestrian Society, and the rest of his waitstaff were slammed. "I—I intended to eat this at home."

"Why?"

She gestured to the food, then around at the

crowd. Bowman could acknowledge that his disinclination to speak made *him* hard to understand from time to time, but Maisy was making no sense right now.

"It's better when it's hot," he said.

She eyed the plate again, then glanced around, like she was afraid of being seen.

"What?"

"We're supposed to be leading kids and inspiring them to make healthy choices." She gestured at her meal. "Kinda hard to do when I'm facedown in a pile of sweet-potato fries."

"We have a whole avocado."

She pressed her lips together, then caught his gaze and grinned. "Truth. Want some fries?"

Bowman grabbed a handful of fries, and in return set half an avocado on her plate.

Maisy picked up the burger, which was almost as big as she was, and bit into it. Bowman watched her eyes expand as she experienced the culinary masterpiece that was a Burma Mile burger.

"That bite of hamburger just made up for the last ten hours of my life."

Bowman was feeling a lot better himself. "It was rough today. Taco?"

Maisy seemed to finally realize Hunter's cooking had the power to rejuvenate even the most exhausted soul. She grabbed a taco and refilled his plate with sweet-potato fries. A Brothers Osborne ballad played over the speaker system. Bowman's body responded to the music, shoulders giving in to a brief sway.

"You like this song?" she asked.

He nodded. He liked this song, he liked this meal, he liked a lot of things right now.

Maisy reached over and grabbed another tortilla chip. An explosion of giggles drew her attention away from the meal. He could feel phones snapping pictures of him, all because he'd made the mistake of letting his body react to the music.

"Those women are staring at you."

He nodded, then pressed his palms to his forehead. "It's really weird."

She studied him, then turned back to her burger. "I bet."

He didn't respond. What was there to say? Unfamiliar packs of women showed up and tried to get his attention in all the wrong ways. He didn't blame them; they were young and seemed to be having a lot of fun at his expense. But there was no way he was going to chat with them, or pose for the pictures they wanted to post to their social-media pages. He certainly wasn't going to go out with any of them.

Piper and Clara had all sorts of theories about the type of woman he *should* date and were relentless about trying to set him up. They called him a lightning-bolt client, something about being the type of guy who would start to fall for someone and not even know what was happening until he was deeply, irrevocably in love. But Bowman didn't trust their matchmaker lists and rules—he'd be able to tell when the right woman came along. It would be someone who shared his interests and didn't expect him to be something he wasn't. And a woman who shared his interests would never, ever stalk a guy because there was a picture of him saving a puppy plastered all over town.

"You like the sauce?" he asked, gesturing to her burger.

"Yes. I like everything in this place."

Hunter appeared before them and pressed his palms against the bar, grinning as he said, "Booked it!"

Bowman dropped the taco he'd planned on demolishing. "Whoa! Seriously?"

"The Bend Equestrian Society just walked out of here with a contract for their holiday gala, which, Holly Banks informs me, is 'one of the three major social events of the season, according to *Central Oregon Living*.'"

Bowman held his hand up to high-five his brother. "Nice work, man." He turned in his seat to gaze out the front window, where the women were climbing into a massive Escalade. "You gonna have any trouble getting the events center finished before then?"

Hunter's expression fell.

Why do you always have to say the wrong thing?

"I can help out," Bowman amended.

"I got it," Hunter said. "You're busy with the camp, then you'll be gone a lot during wildfire season."

"I know you have it under control, but I can work my days off. I want to."

Hunter looked tired. Bowman had long suspected his brother was pushing everything a little too hard. He was glad he'd booked his first event, but it would be nice if it was for a group less exacting than the women in the Bend Equestrian Society.

"I wish I could have it ready for Clara's wedding," Hunter said.

Bowman set down his avocado. "Clara's getting married before December?"

"Clara's getting married in October."

"When was someone going to tell me?"

Hunter looked baffled. "Clara sent the entire family an email detailing the schedule."

Bowman rolled his eyes.

"You *do* check your email?"

Bowman didn't answer that. He looked down

at his plate, trying to put words to the complex feelings running through him. He was happy for Clara, thrilled. When she and Jet finally got together, he'd even suggested the family propose to Jet rather than wait for him to propose to her. Turned out he hadn't been quick enough. But they were getting married in two months? Clara had never handled change well, and this was major.

A gentle hand on his shoulder offered solace in his confusion. He glanced up to see Maisy looking at him, her blue eyes bright with concern. Could she understand?

"When *was* the last time you checked your email?"

Bowman huffed out a breath and returned to his tacos. Hunter laughed, then asked Maisy, "Did you send him an email?"

"I sent him five!" She gestured to Bowman. "I thought he was ignoring me."

Bowman shifted away as Hunter and Maisy laughed at his expense. How was he supposed to know Maisy was emailing him? And why, after having to communicate with people all day, was he expected to stare at a screen and communicate a little more?

It didn't matter. He was going to upset Maisy no matter what, that'd been clear from the start. Maybe one day he'd put out a fire in a building she cared about, and then she might have a modicum of appreciation for him. But there was no way she'd see the best side of him in the current situation.

"What's the plan for the wedding?" he asked.

"It will be at the ranch. Clara invited the whole town."

Bowman nodded. People loved Clara, and his sister would never want to leave anyone out. Bowman picked up his glass of root beer and drank.

"And she wants you to sing."

Bowman nearly choked. The root beer went fizzing down the wrong pipe in his throat and he started coughing. He shook his head. He didn't want to grace the statement with an answer, and fortunately for everyone, he couldn't physically speak.

"Come on. We'll all sing backup for you."

Bowman shook his head, trying to swallow and clear his throat at the same time.

"You should see him," Hunter said to Maisy. "You wouldn't know it, but Bowman—"

"No," Bowman choked out. "Stop. I'm not singing in front of a bunch of people I don't know."

"Exactly, you'll be singing in front of everyone in town. You've known these people since you were born."

"I'm not singing at a wedding."

"You sing?" Maisy asked.

"No," Bowman said, just as Hunter, the traitor, said, "All the time."

They were both right. Bowman did sing all the time. He loved music, could feel the beat and melody deep within his soul. He'd been singing along with the radio since before he was old enough to form the words, belting out pitch-perfect garbled nonsense. He sang for the horses, with his family and for himself. And he liked to dance. It was an extension of all the intuitive physical activity he enjoyed.

But if music was one of the great pleasures in life, attention was not. He had no interest in performing, unless it was at karaoke night with his family.

Bowman finally cleared his throat. "You tell her I said no."

"*You* tell her," Hunter countered. Then he turned to Maisy. "Our sister is impossible to say no to."

"Not impossible," Bowman said. It had better not be, because there was absolutely no way he was singing in front of anyone other than his close family members. There was nothing that could make him sing in public. That was *never* going to happen.

CHAPTER SEVEN

"HEY, PIPER." Bowman kept his voice low as he left a message for his sister. "Camp's happening. Three days in and none of the kids have quit yet, so that's good, I guess." He glanced up into the rafters. Around him the horses stood, expectant, as he readied them for camp. "There's a kid named Kai who's pretty good with horses. Anyway, call me when you can. Or come home." He cradled the phone against his ear with his shoulder as he straightened the saddle on Cricket. "Yeah. Do that, actually. Come home this weekend, if you can."

Bowman pulled the phone from his ear and examined the screen for a moment before disconnecting the call. Something was up with Piper. She never missed a chance to boss him around, and right now, when he really needed someone to tell him what to do, she was MIA. He was always the one his siblings chastised for not showing up, not the other way around. But now, with Clara planning her wedding, Hunter expanding the restaurant and Piper flat-out not being here, it was like he was responsible for getting everyone together.

He rounded the corner into the tack room, then stopped. There was one thing that never failed to get all his siblings together. He pulled out his phone and sent a group text: *Mom and Dad are home next week. Celebrate with karaoke Wednesday? I'll get the barn set up.*

The phone was vibrating with positive responses before he could slip it back in his pocket. He pulled Alice's saddle from the rack, grinning.

Kids' voices came drifting through the half wall into the tack room. His stomach tightened but not as badly as it had the last few days. Things were going…okay. The camp was not a complete disaster. He was a wreck every day when it ended, but after the first day there'd only been a few tears and a manageable amount of fighting.

"Bowman?" Maisy called from the arena. "Time for circle!"

"Bo-o-owma-a-an!" Sami echoed her, other kids joining in.

He chuckled, throwing the saddle over his shoulder. "Be right there!"

Technically, it would have been possible for him to have all the horses saddled up by the time the kids got here. But then he'd have to attend morning circle with the Healthy Choice check-in, and that was almost more than he could handle.

Bowman led Alice out of her stall, and Dulce immediately came to the front, ready to ride.

"Ms. Dulce, you're in no shape to hang out with the kids."

She gave him a look. Bowman rubbed her ears and tried not to let his concern show. This was Dulce's first pregnancy, and way later in the season than he would have liked. All the other breeding mares had birthed in the spring and early summer, but Dulce had taken longer to conceive.

"What's wrong with her?"

Bowman glanced down to see Kai. "Shouldn't you be in the circle?"

"Shouldn't you?"

Bowman placed his hands on his hips and stared down at Kai. In the background they could hear the kids playing a name game where they had to name a fruit starting with the first letter of their name, then repeat everyone else's name and an alliterative snack.

"Hand me that saddle blanket," Bowman said.

Kai picked up the blanket and brought it over. Bowman draped the blanket over the horse, then set the saddle on her back. With few words, he showed Kai how to buckle the girth and check for stability. They worked in silence as the voices from the circle drifted toward them.

"Liya, lemon, Ava, apple, Maisy, mango..."

"To answer your question, there's nothing wrong with Dulce. She's going to have a baby."

"Cool. Will she have it during camp?"

"I hope it'll come in the next couple of weeks, but it'll probably be in the middle of the night."

"Can I see it after it's born?"

"Yeah," Bowman said. "Of course."

"Bowman! Kai!" Sami called. "Come say your fruit!"

Bowman gave Kai a questioning glance. Kai shook his head. While he agreed with Kai, he didn't want to let down Maisy any more than it was likely he would that day already.

"Let's go do it. It's not gonna kill us."

Kai didn't move. Over the last few days, Bowman had observed that everything was a negotiation with Kai. He extracted a price for each piece of good behavior. It was annoying, but Bowman imagined Kai had to feel pretty powerless in other aspects of his life, so he tried to exercise some power here. He wasn't sure how to handle the kid, but he went with his gut and it seemed to be working.

"If I go in the circle, can I help lead the horses in?"

Bowman glanced up at the rafters, then back at Kai. Kai had hung around during lunch the day before as he put away the tack, and Bowman let him lead Midnight back to his stable. "I'm counting on you to lead in the horses, either way."

Kai looked startled, then reached up and ran his hand along Alice's neck. He didn't move toward the arena.

"But we're not the type of guys who make a big deal over something like saying a fruit. Let's save our fight for something that matters." Bowman took long steps toward the arena, gratified to hear Kai's tennis shoes crunching on the earthen floor as he followed behind.

"Bowman, blackberry," he said as he entered the arena. Liya pushed Ava aside to make room for Bowman. When Kai tried to move in next to him, Liya closed the gap. Bowman felt the unfairness of the move and urged Kai into the circle next to him.

"What was your healthy choice last night?" Maisy asked. She was paler than normal, her freckles standing out in contrast. It was weird. They were finally getting the hang of things around here, but Maisy was extra tense today. Had something happened?

"I took a walk after dinner, and ate at least two servings of vegetables," he said.

"And those vegetables were?"

"Sweet potatoes." Bowman was unable to repress a wink.

Maisy didn't take the bait. She turned to Kai and asked the same question.

Kai was still stewing over being shut out of the circle. "I can't remember."

She opened her mouth to prompt a better response, but Bowman intervened with a slight shake of his head. Everyone was silent, waiting for Kai. Maisy's frame was alert, and he could tell she was trying to stay cool. Maybe he should be better about getting in for circle on time. Was that what had her upset?

Finally, Maisy smiled at Kai, a real one that rearranged the freckles on her nose. "Let us know if you do."

Bowman nodded, then turned to the kids. "Helmets on, everybody. Kai and I will lead the horses in. Today we're going to head out onto the trails."

Kai shot back to the stables, and Bowman trotted after him. Maisy blocked his path. She was very close, the floral scent of her hair wiping out their surroundings for a minute. "Is it safe for Kai to lead the horses in?"

Bowman bristled. He'd spent a lot of time dealing with Kai this week and leading the horses in was way safer than the trouble the kid would be getting into if left to his own devices. He forced himself to calm down. Maisy was different this morning—something was up, obviously, and keeping steady was probably the best way to help her relax.

"Yeah." The kids were milling about, starting to get a little restless as they waited on Maisy and Bowman to finish a pointless discussion. "Look, I'm trying to include him in a positive way."

"I see that, but if he gets hurt—"

Out of the corner of his eye he saw Kai watching them. While Maisy was only looking out for his safety, Kai would interpret not being allowed to lead in the horses as a vote of no confidence for his abilities. Bowman didn't want to upset Maisy, but he had no intention of going back on his word with Kai.

"It's fine." He stepped past Maisy, gesturing to Kai to follow him.

"How come Kai gets to help?" Marc asked.

Bowman let out a sharp breath. It was only eight thirty in the morning. They had a long day ahead of them and he needed to keep his temper in check. "Kai got here early to help."

"Don't get kicked in the head!" Marc yelled at Kai's back.

"Marc!" Maisy turned on the kid, heat rising to her face. "That's not funny. We don't joke about head injuries."

"We don't?"

Bowman jogged back to the stables, leaving Maisy to deal with Marc. Kai was waiting, kicking the toe of his tennis shoe against Dulce's stall. Bowman unclipped Cricket from the crossties.

"Walk slow, like you see me doing." He handed the reins to Kai, then went back to get Alice and Hopper. Kai moved deliberately; the horses could feel his apprehension. Maisy was tense, Kai was tense and that could set off all the kids and horses. Bowman sang an old Stevie Wonder song quietly under his breath to ease the tension. The horses always loved Stevie Wonder. Kai glanced at him but didn't comment as Bowman kept his voice low.

"Sami, here you go." He directed Kai to walk Cricket over to her. Kai kept cool, depositing the reins with Sami, then ran a hand down Cricket's nose, like Bowman did. Bowman specifically didn't comment, just ushered Kai back to the stalls to grab another horse.

Maisy looked like she was about to snap in half, she was so tense. Bowman moved on to whistling Neil Diamond, because who could be tense when hearing "Sweet Caroline"?

"I get to ride with Bowman!" Liya cried as he led Jorge into the arena.

"You about ready to take on a horse of your own?" he asked.

She shook her head. He'd noticed how Liya was happiest when an adult was paying direct attention to her. He didn't mind the job, but figured she'd do well to branch out on her own.

"All right, then." He swept up Liya, giving her a spin before landing her onto his horse's back. Liya giggled, then grabbed Bowman's hat.

"Me, too!" Sami yelled, startling Cricket. The horse shuffled, but quickly regained her equilibrium when Bowman spoke in a low voice to her.

"Okay, Miss Sami, up you go!" He lifted Sami, giving her a spin before setting her on Cricket's back. Sami laughed, and Bowman moved on to the next camper who wanted a lift up. He might not be good with kids, but they always responded well to being picked up and spun through the air.

"I'm gonna do it again!" Liya cried, turning in the saddle and getting ready to drop to the ground. Jorge, already fed up with all the action, neighed and tossed back his head. Liya slipped, but was holding on to the saddle horn. Her feet dangled along Jorge's flank, inadvertently kicking him.

"Whoa there." Bowman sprinted across the arena, catching Liya in one arm and grabbing Jorge's reins in the other hand. He spoke quietly to steady the horse, keeping Liya tucked up under one arm.

Everyone, and every horse, settled. Bowman opened his mouth to tell Liya she needed to be more careful with Jorge when Maisy's voice cut across the arena "That's it. Everyone, off your horses and out of the arena. Now."

"EVERYONE OUT. Let's go. Bowman, you can stay and put away the horses, or get your brother to do it. Everyone else, out." Maisy could feel the blood pounding in her temples, knew she was a deep shade of red. But right now, the only thing that mattered was getting these kids safe, and away from the horses.

"What's wrong?" Bowman scanned the arena.

What's wrong? He had Kai leading horses, a task the child was completely unprepared for; he was swinging the children around, getting them riled up and upsetting the animals.

Then, Liya had fallen, and rather than get her to safety, Bowman just stood there, holding her like a feed sack while he focused on the horse. It was a miracle no one had gotten trampled.

Bowman set Liya *back* on the horse, then crossed to Maisy. He stood in front of her, looking into her eyes as though trying to read each of her thoughts and coming up short. "What are you worried about?"

She gestured around the arena. "This is out of control."

He drew back his head, baffled. "This is fine."

Maisy lowered her voice. "Liya could have gotten seriously injured."

"Anyone could get seriously injured at any time."

"You know what I mean."

"I don't, really. Maisy, everyone is fine. In fact, everyone was having fun."

It felt like her mind was imploding. Bowman stood there, unreasonably attractive, intentionally obtuse. Meanwhile, Kai was heading back to the stalls to get another horse, and the other children were scampering up on the animals like it was nothing. Maisy's breath shortened. All she could see was Elliot's still form lying in the street, the red pool of blood expanding below his head. Bowman reached out a hand

and rested it on her arm. She flinched it off and he stepped back, raising his hands in surrender.

"How can you be so cavalier about this?"

"Maisy, what's wrong?"

She felt trapped, panicked. The sound of her mother's sobs echoed through her head. "We can't ride if it's going to be dangerous like this."

"It's not dangerous." He glanced around at the kids, then lowered his voice as he stepped close to her. "This is Cowboy Camp. I'm sorry, but we're gonna ride whether you like it or not."

The anger and fear coursing through her blurred her senses. If the kids were reacting to their argument, she had no idea.

"Why don't we just let them loose with the horses on their own? Let them run wild while we kick back at the house."

"You're being ridiculous."

"I'm trying to keep them safe."

"What do you want to do then? Roll them in bubble wrap and lecture them about vegetables all day?"

"This week's theme is *fruit*."

"Do we get to play with bubble wrap?" Marc asked. "Yes!"

Maisy closed her eyes. Of course, the children liked Bowman's reckless, crazy ideas. It was no problem to Liya if she slipped off her horse, so long as Bowman was there to catch her. None of them had any idea how serious this was.

"I can't do this, Bowman."

"We don't have a choice."

"What's going on in here?" Ash strode into the arena. Clara, all smiles and flashing a diamond ring, followed.

"Bub-ble wrap!" Marc chanted.

Kai joined in with him. "Bub-ble wrap! Bub-ble wrap!"

Ash turned to Bowman. "I thought you were taking the kids out on the trails today."

"Trying to," Bowman muttered.

"Well, git. We've got Clara's wedding to plan." He looked down at Kai, completely unaware of the complex behavioral time bomb he was addressing. "You want a lift up?"

Kai, who normally argued with every little thing, looked shocked at Ash's blunt offer. Then he lifted his arms. Ash picked him up and spun him through the air, like Bowman had done with the others, and set him on the horse.

The next several minutes passed in a blur for Maisy. She was aware of Bowman speaking to her, of getting on her horse. Bowman led the group out of the arena, across the pasture. She rode at the back, waiting for someone to fall off, trying to wrap her brain around what had happened.

How had she lost control of herself so quickly? Self-discipline and self-restraint were traits she took pride in. Yet she'd completely lost it in the arena.

Light filtered through the leaves of the aspen trees as they rode onto one of the paths. Her mom had called the night before, and as much as she didn't want to accept it, she had to admit it was a big part of the problem.

Her mother didn't remember much about the days in the wake of the accident, but Maisy recalled every second in sharp detail. The wailing, the sirens, the ugliness in her mother's face when she'd spun around and screamed at Maisy, "Couldn't you keep an eye on him for two seconds?"

Maisy had blinked, stunned and horrified. No one had told her to watch Elliot. She'd never been expected to keep an eye on him. She didn't know his safety was her responsibility.

Over the decades, Maisy had come to terms with the accident. Her mom was in shock, she didn't know what she was saying. She'd never intended to foist the blame on her daughter. But Maisy had taken the blame nonetheless.

Logically, as a scientist, Maisy knew the accident wasn't her fault. But she never could shake the feeling that if she'd been watching him for those two seconds, their lives would have been irrevocably different. She thought becoming a doctor would finally absolve her of that guilt. But here she was, with a medical degree, and a clinic she would run entirely on her own, still afraid it might have been all her fault.

When Marc made a comment about Kai getting kicked in the head, it had sent her over the edge.

She glanced up to the front of the line. Bowman was riding with Liya, instructing her to hold the reins with him. Kai, anxious for his attention, kicked Midnight with his heels in an effort to get the horse running. Midnight wasn't having any of it. The horse ambled pleasantly, as though Kai was no more of a bother than the white clouds floating across the blue sky.

The group followed Bowman and Jorge along one of the many barked paths leading up the wooded hillside. Sunshine warmed them, and there was no hint of danger anywhere. Maisy was embarrassed, and mad. Was this what she was going to be like as a doctor? Constantly losing it every time she sensed a child was in danger?

She'd been an excellent student and resident. But now that she'd met her goal, and was embarking on her life as a doctor, she kept second-guessing herself. She had to find a way back to her confidence.

Two more minutes of self-pity. Then I'm back in the game.

"Gross!" Juliet called out.

"What is it?" Kai twisted in the saddle, wanting in on anything disgusting.

"There's, like, a billion ants."

Bowman pulled up on the reins and turned his horse. "Probably best to leave it alone."

Maisy couldn't see what they were looking at along the side of the trail, but Bowman's advice was sound.

"Are they fire ants?" Kai asked.

Maisy cleared her throat. "No."

The group looked back at her. Kai clearly wanted these to be fire ants. "How do you know?"

Maisy tried to negotiate her horse forward, a skill she didn't seem to be able to conjure at the moment. She stood in the stirrups, trying to look over everyone's heads. "Fire ants aren't often found in Oregon. If there's a mound, it's probably thatching ants, or maybe harvester ants."

Bowman swung out of the saddle and approached the mound, leaving Liya, once again, alone on a massive beast. "Can you tell?"

"Um, yeah. Sure." This was a good time to pretend she hadn't lost it earlier. She pivoted to get out of the saddle, then remembered that the ground was a long, long way down.

Bowman trotted over. Without a word, he placed his hands on her waist and pulled her from the saddle. The movement was easy; being in his arms felt like the only place she was ever interested in being. He set her down, keeping his hands on her waist for a few seconds longer than she expected, but not nearly as long as she would have liked. "Are you okay?"

She made the mistake of looking into his eyes. For a moment she wondered if he might spin her around like the kids.

"I'm sorry I upset you back there."

She shook her head. "I overreacted."

"Maisy, come see the anthill!" Juliet cried.

Bowman spoke low enough so no one else could hear him, leaning in toward her ear. "I should have listened to you." Then he smiled crookedly. "I might not have understood what you were talking about, but I could have listened."

And that was the Bowman she was used to. Maisy slugged his arm and headed over to the anthill, which turned out to be more like an ant mountain! The structure was at least three feet tall—a mass of twigs, decomposing leaves and pine needles.

"Oh, wow! You guys, these are thatching ants! These are like..." She gestured, trying to find the right words. "These are my favorite ants!"

"You have a favorite ant?" Liya asked, as Bowman gave her a questioning look.

"Okay, can everybody see this? It looks like there are at least a thousand ants here, right? But my guess is under the ground—" she spread her hands to indicate the area all around them "—there are hundreds of thousands! They make networks of tunnels, and little alcoves, and all the ants work together."

The kids looked down at the ground below them, as though they could see the colony beneath their feet.

She continued. "Every single ant has a job to help the colony as a whole. Some are gathering food, some are helping with the babies, some are protecting others. The queen keeps the whole group together. How cool is that?"

Sami slid down from her horse and stood next to her. "They're all helping each other?"

"Yep. Aren't they awesome?"

Bowman crouched down next to her, keeping his eyes on the ant colony. "So they thrive by working together?"

"Yep."

"And each ant does what it's best at." He grinned at her. "And over time they make something cool like this."

Maisy caught his meaning and managed to smile back at him. "They play to their strengths."

He nodded. "Sounds like a healthy habit to me."

"Maybe cooperation should be our theme this afternoon," she said.

He nodded. "I'll circle up for that."

CHAPTER EIGHT

"Bye, Doctor Maisy!" Liya called, then ran back to hug her a second time. Maisy relished the brief moment, letting the affection wash through her as it chased away some of the exhaustion and fear.

Liya kept her arms around Maisy's knees as she looked up. "Can we go visit the ant mountain again tomorrow?"

"Absolutely!"

Leave it to thatching ants to save the day. This morning had shaken her, but she'd recovered and Bowman didn't hold it over her.

She waved as Liya headed off to a car with her mom. Working with kids was as hard as she'd expected it to be, but significantly more awesome than she'd anticipated. They were eager to forgive her shortcomings, as well as Bowman's, and just move on to the next activity if things went sideways.

"Hey, Sami!"

Maisy looked up to see Josh Hanson exit the fire chief's truck and wave. Sami waved back but was intent on finishing her conversation with Juliet before leaving.

Josh walked over to Maisy, shaking his head. "I swear she's been about thirty years old since the day she was born."

Maisy laughed. "Nature or nurture?"

"It's just Sami. I'd like to take credit for her, but she's always been this way."

"Well, she's fantastic at camp. It's like Bowman and I have a third adult to help us out."

Josh nodded, then scanned the property. "He still around?"

"He's in with the horses."

Josh arched his brows. "They provide about the right level of conversation for Bowman."

"Actually, they do communicate." Maisy twisted, nodding toward the open bypass door into the stables. "Have you seen him with the horses? He's got all these conversations going on in the barn. I think he expects the rest of us to understand them the way he does."

"I can see that. Where most of us use our heads, Bowman leads from the heart."

Maisy brushed her hair off her forehead. "How so?"

"It's hard to explain. Bowman can assess a situation and *feel* the right thing to do. It's what makes him a great firefighter. Where I've been trained to analyze patterns and apply correct action, Bowman just seems to intuit what to do next."

Maisy nodded. She'd seen it in his work with the kids and the way he was able to gently nudge Kai in the right direction.

"That makes sense."

"Yeah. It's cool to see him in action at a fire. The funny thing though is he's good about letting his intuition guide him, but if you ask him to explain it, he's got nothing. It's like the feelings are so intense he can't put words to them."

"But this tendency to shoot from the hip is also the same trait that got him suspended, right?"

Josh lifted his brow. "I could suspend Bowman once a week, every week he's working. The problem isn't that he goes with his gut, it's that he doesn't factor in his own safety. Bravery, when you consider the risks and move forward, is necessary as a firefighter. Bowman doesn't know he's putting himself at risk. Or rather, he knows it but since he doesn't label the emotion as fear, he reacts differently than most people. He's more focused when he's in danger."

Maisy shuddered. Josh looked down at her, eyes full of sympathy. "He would never put someone else at risk, though. If that's what you're thinking."

She shook her head. It was all so complicated. She knew she overreacted when kids were involved, but Bowman had such a different definition of safety than she did. "Sometimes it's hard to tell."

"Dad," Sami called, checking the little watch she wore, "it's time to go."

Josh gave her a smile. "Thirty years old," he muttered.

"Bye, Maisy!" Sami called, climbing up into the truck.

Maisy waved back. The last few campers departed with their families, and now she could take off, too.

Josh's assessment of Bowman was astute.

But it occurred to her that Bowman's fearlessness was confined to physical risks. Socially and emotionally, he kept things locked down.

Maisy stretched her arms over her head, basking in the sunlight for another moment as she contemplated whether or not to say goodbye to Bowman. It was important to finish up the conversation from this morning. Yes, she'd overreacted, but he needed to communicate better about things. If he thought Kai was ready to help with the horses, he should've let her know ahead of the game. Maisy headed toward the stables. She may have royally lost it earlier, but she had the grace and intelligence to talk it out and make it right.

Should she tell Bowman about her brother? It would help both of them, and the kids. If he understood where she was coming from, he might not get as frustrated by her.

Maisy stepped into the shadow created by the stable, where the air cooled immediately. She could tell him. The pain and loss she locked up would ooze out, pooling around every interaction with Bowman. What would he say? If Bowman didn't have the right words in a situation, at least he didn't bother trying to spew out the wrong ones. In his interactions with the kids, he was deeply empathetic, but would he even get this?

Maisy inhaled. It made sense to let him know, but she didn't have to tell him right now. Maybe Friday.

Maybe never.

She did, however, want to clear the air before she left for the day. Maisy took decisive steps toward the bypass door. A snippet of a song floated out. Was he listening to Otis Redding?

BOWMAN PLACED HIS palms against Dulce's stall door and listened. A family of barn swallows chattered in the rafters above, horses shuffled, snug in their stalls after a day in the pasture.

The breeze whistled through the arena, stirring the Oregon state flag Ash had hung over the main entrance. Light shifted, and everything seemed to soften in relief as another day at camp ended.

There was a lot rambling through Bowman's mind and he needed to let it filter through before he headed out.

Kai had come a long way today. The kid wasn't perfect, but he'd done great. When they'd come across the anthill, Bowman had been on alert, because Kai was the type of kid to grab a stick and smash it, just to watch the chaos. But he'd been interested in all Maisy had to say. He'd settled in as she spoke, taken his cue from the others and watched the fascinating order of the ant colony instead of destroying it.

And Maisy. *What had happened there?*

Images from the day flickered through his mind: the gray pallor chasing the color from her cheeks, the mix of fear and anger in her eyes, the expression of determination when she'd set out on the trail ride, the complete joy in describing the ant community to the kids.

Helping her down from her horse. The feel of her waist under his hands.

Bowman shook his head. He needed to work to understand Maisy. Dwelling on how pretty she was and giving in to this urge to get close to her wasn't going to do either of them any good.

Bowman felt a nudge at his pocket. Dulce pressed her nose against him, hoping for a treat. He rubbed her ears. "I don't know what to do about her. Feels like one minute everything's okay and the next… Well, you saw what happened."

Dulce blew out a breath.

"Yeah. That's about all I got, either."

He pulled his phone out to see if Piper had texted back. She hadn't. He set the phone on the railing and engaged his music app. Otis Redding's "Try a Little Tenderness" poured out through the little speakers.

Bowman tapped up the volume, allowing the music to move through him. He sang along with Otis. The man was right: a little tenderness could make things easier.

The tempo of the song picked up. Bowman shook out his shoulders, then spun. He cruised down the aisle as Otis urged the listener to "never leave her." Learning to moonwalk in boots, on the earthen floor of the stables, had been difficult, but he'd had years to get good at it. Bowman jumped, pointing at Dulce as he and Otis moved into the *na-na-na-nas* of the song. She munched her oats, watching with polite attention. Bowman slid down the aisle, then realized he was dead in front of Bella's stall. Bella glared at him. *Sheesh. Leave it to the lead mare to take issue with Otis Redding.* Spinning quickly, he sang to Stan, who was old enough to really appreciate the classic. Music filled the stables, lifting the heaviness from him. Bowman sang, settling the horses and settling himself. The day, the kids, the pressure released.

Bowman kept dancing, singing, letting the music be the only answer he needed.

MAISY STEPPED UP to the bypass door and stopped.

Um, whoa.

No, not whoa. More like, *giddyap!*

When Hunter had mentioned Bowman's talent for singing, Maisy imagined a reasonably good voice with a bit of bopping around. Every family had someone who liked to sing. But this was unlike anything she'd ever witnessed. The music and movement seemed to come from somewhere deep inside him. He watered and fed the horses, all while grooving and singing at the top of his lungs. Maisy wasn't sure she'd ever seen anything as free.

The horses didn't seem to think this was anything out of the ordinary. Most of them watched the beautiful man singing with mild interest.

Maisy couldn't take her eyes off him.

And she really needed to.

She leaned against the old pine of the door, letting the understanding move through her. This was Bowman. He felt things deeply and responded accordingly. He didn't need, or want, attention. He wanted the freedom of moving through the world without the censorship of those around him.

And he hadn't invited her here to watch this performance. Maisy pressed her forehead against the bypass door, gathering the strength to leave. Then she pushed away, taking a few steps backward, and spun around.

And nearly tripped over Clara.

"Oh. Hi. Sorry, I..."

Sorry I was staring at your singing brother like a lovesick puppy?

"No worries. It's a little shocking when you first see it." She gestured to Bowman. "But amazing, right?"

Amazing. Riveting. Heart-stopping.

"He's good."

Clara's eyes narrowed slightly as she glanced from Maisy to Bowman and back again. "How are you two doing, working together?"

The implication was clear. Clara suspected Maisy had a crush on her brother and was trying to suss it out.

"It's good." She reached back and rubbed her shoulder, trying for a casual vibe, like, *I'm more interested in a twinge in my shoulder than your gorgeous brother singing soulfully in the background.* "Speaking of work, you're a matchmaker, right?"

Hello, world's most awkward transition.

"I am. Very satisfying work." She glanced from her to Bowman a second time.

Maisy needed to clear this up. Sure, she had a crush on Bowman. Everyone in central Oregon had a crush on Bowman right now, so it was no big deal.

"I've been meaning to call you about that. About matchmaking, getting matched up. I got your card in the basket."

"My card in the basket?"

"The Outcrop welcome basket. Michael and Joanna Williams brought me a basket when I arrived and there was a card from Love, Oregon."

Clara's brow furrowed slightly, then she smiled. "Of course. Are you interested in meeting someone?"

"Sure. I'd like to meet someone steady. Sensible. I'd like to meet a guy who's really…steady and sensible."

The song in the stables changed and Bowman joined Ed Sheeran in "Thinking Out

Loud." Maisy fought the urge to sprint into the barn to witness this.

A slow smile spread across Clara's face. "As it happens, a few men on my list have already asked about you."

"They have?"

"Yep. If you're interested, I'd love to have you as a call-in client. That means you and I would have an initial meeting, and if I think you're a good fit, I'll set you up with a client of mine who has already expressed interest in you."

"Oh. Um. Yeah." Maisy used all the core strength she'd developed over the years to keep her torso facing Clara and not turn back and look at Bowman. "Yes, actually. Sounds perfect."

"Unless there's someone you're already interested in?" Clara had two dimples that flexed as she smiled.

Maisy let out a breath. "Nope. No one at all. I'd love to meet new people I haven't met before. Sensible people."

Clara gave a little chuckle, then pulled out a planner and made a note. "Okay. Let's get together and talk about finding someone sensible."

They agreed on a time and meeting place, then Maisy exhaled a breath as she passed

Clara. This was going to be fine. Better than fine, it was going to be fantastic. Clara would set her up with someone completely suitable and she wouldn't spend one more minute thinking about the beautiful man singing in the barn behind her.

CHAPTER NINE

"WHAT'S WILD IS how fast the days go. We get back from the ride, then it's lunchtime, and then we circle up again and boom, it's four o'clock. The day's gone."

Clara stared at Bowman, then slowly tilted her head to the side. "That's literally the longest sentence you've ever spoken in your life."

Bowman rolled his eyes and hauled a saddle off the rail of Hopper's stall. Clara just smiled.

Morning sunlight poured through the open bypass door. Bowman hadn't expected his sister in the stables so early on a Friday morning, but with all her wedding planning, Clara spent a lot of time at the ranch these days. It was nice to talk about camp with her.

"Speaking of long sentences, how's Maisy?"

He glared at her over Hopper's saddle. "The complete randomness with which you switch topics is impressive."

"So she's good? You two are doing well?"

He stalked back to Cricket's stall and coaxed the mare out with a slice of apple from his pocket. Not that Cricket needed the coaxing, but a bite of apple never hurt any horse.

Clara was still grinning like one of Jet's emus.

"What?"

"Nothing."

"Maisy's fine. Camp is going pretty well. She's great with kids, and I'm not completely messing it up."

"I'm sure you're great, too."

A long shadow appeared in the aisle from the bypass door. Bowman glanced down to see light pouring in around Maisy's silhouette. He waved, feeling better knowing she was here.

"Good morning." She stretched, stifling a yawn. "Are you as exhausted as I am?"

He nodded and called back, "It's Friday, though."

"I still can't believe we've nearly made it through one week."

Bowman held a hand up for a high five, even though she was still a good thirty feet away. She responded, pretending to slap him five from the door. At the sound of car wheels on the gravel, she turned back.

"Maisy, are we still on for tomorrow?" Clara asked.

Maisy shifted, looking from Clara to Bowman, then back again.

"Yes? I mean, yes. I'm looking forward to

it." She glanced over her shoulder to the parking area. "Kids are arriving. See you in the circle."

Bowman nodded, then threw a blanket over Cricket. He didn't look at Clara as he asked, "You're hanging out with Maisy tomorrow?"

"Is that a problem?"

"No."

It wasn't a problem. It was curious, but not a problem.

The sound of another car approaching alerted them to more campers arriving. Clara stood and gave Cricket's ears a scratch.

"I'd better get out of your way." She gave Cricket a kiss on the nose, then ran her hand along Midnight's neck before she turned to leave. "Have fun today!"

"Hey." Bowman stopped her. "You heard from Piper recently?"

"Of course." Clara tucked her hair behind her ear. "Why do you ask?"

Bowman shrugged. Good to know Piper was at least still talking to Clara. It'd be nice if she'd return his calls.

Clara drew the toe of her boot through the dust on the ground. "She's got a lot going on with work."

"I know. But it's weird. She didn't stay for

the family dinner last weekend, and she hasn't been in touch."

Clara fiddled with her necklace, pulling the clasp to the back of her neck. "Our business is exploding in Portland right now. It's probably time for us to hire an assistant to help her out, but Piper likes to handle everything herself. She's busy."

Bowman didn't respond. Piper'd always been busy. She was born busy. But she'd never had so much going on that she didn't take the time to weigh in on his life.

"I'm sure she's fine," Clara said. "She's literally the only one of us I don't worry about."

Bowman raised his brow. Clara was hiding something about their sister and he didn't like it one bit.

"You don't want to tell me, you don't have to. Just let her know I'm thinking about her."

Clara's gaze connected with his, and it was apparent she didn't have authorization to speak about whatever was bothering Piper. "She'll be home Wednesday for family karaoke night," Clara said softly.

Bowman nodded. It would have to do.

The feeling in the stables shifted, and he felt, rather than saw, Kai slip in.

"You ready to get to work?" he asked Kai.

Kai shrugged. He'd come into the barn early

the last three days in a row. Bowman always managed to find something for him to do.

"All right then, start hauling the saddles in. Think you can remember which one goes with each horse?"

"'Course I can."

Kai scuttled off to the tack room. Clara grinned at her brother. "You *are* doing a great job."

"Kai's a good kid."

"A little young to be carrying a big ol' saddle on his own, though."

Bowman glanced down the aisle. Clara had a point. Five days in and he still didn't even know the basics about kids.

He did, however, know the basics about Kai. "He'll get it."

Bowman led Midnight out of his stall and clipped him into the crossties. He had most of the horses ready to go, but saved Midnight and Cricket so Kai could help. Clara leaned against a post, settling in to watch him work with Kai.

"If you're gonna hang around, you could at least help the kid with the tack." He nodded to where Kai was struggling with determination under the weight of a saddle.

"Cowboys aren't great at accepting help."

Was it impressive or annoying when his sister made astute observations about his character?

"Don't you have a wedding to plan?"

That got her moving. "So excited!" Clara clapped her hands and jumped. "Okay, I'm getting out of your hair. Still planning on having you sing, with the rest of the guys backing you up."

Bowman shook his head. "Still not gonna agree to it."

"I hate to go all Ash on you, but you haven't agreed to sing...*yet*."

"Git outta here!" he said, unable to keep from laughing.

"I'll send you a few song proposals!" She ducked out of the barn before he could respond.

He shook his head and got back to work. Kai returned, bent under the weight of the saddle. Bowman threw a blanket over Midnight's back, then took the saddle from Kai and set it on the horse.

"You're here extra early."

"Yeah. My stepdad has to drop me off on the way to work."

"That's cool." Bowman gestured for Kai to pass the girth to him under Midnight's belly, then he let Kai buckle the billets.

"I thought you could use the help," Kai said.

"I can. This is better with two people." It

felt strange to say it, but it really was easier to get the horses ready with a helper. And Kai clearly wanted to help.

"Like the ants," Kai said.

"The ants?"

"They work together."

Bowman smiled to himself. "I'm glad you're here. And the rest of the group, too. We make a pretty good anthill."

"Greg thinks this is good for me."

Bowman looked up at Kai, then refocused on the saddle. "Greg is your stepdad?"

"Yeah. He thinks I need to get outside."

"Everyone needs to get outside." Bowman caught Kai's eye and grinned. "Probably even Greg."

Kai smiled.

"He a cool guy?"

"He's okay." Kai started to say something more, then pressed his lips together. "I get to ride Midnight again, right?"

Bowman nodded. Kai had deliberately brought up his stepdad, then deliberately changed the subject. Seemed like the kid wanted to talk about whatever was going on at home. It was probably best to let him open up in his own time. "Sure."

"What about when Liya finally stops being such a scaredy-cat? Are you going to make me give up Midnight?"

"Naw. You work well with Midnight. I'll find another horse for Liya." Bowman realized he'd been wrong with his original assignment of horses. It was Kai who needed the gentlest, sweetest horse in the herd.

Kai focused on straightening out the stirrups, then ran his hand down Midnight's side, gazing up at the horse. Bowman pulled an apple slice from his pocket and handed it to Kai.

"Hold your hand out flat."

Kai placed the apple slice in his hand and stretched out his palm. The horse dipped his head, his lips scooping up the slice, sending Kai giggling. It was the first time Bowman had heard the kid laugh. Midnight swallowed the treat, then immediately began nosing around Kai for another, making him giggle even harder.

Bowman had a funny feeling, like he wanted to cry it felt so good to hear Kai laugh. Maybe it *was* good that Kai was here, and he was here to help him. Maybe this camp might just do everyone some good, including him.

"AND THAT'S WHY fruit is so important to our diet," Maisy said, glancing around at the group.

The day had gone *so* well. In fact, it was going a little too well. She'd led the morning circle, which was as fun and engaging as she'd imagined it could be. They'd taken the horses out on the trails again. As she, and the kids, gained confidence on the horses, she was finally able to relax. Liya still rode with Bowman, and while they hoped she'd ride on her own eventually, there was still time.

No, camp was going well. The afternoon was perfect, a brilliant eighty-five degrees with a sage-scented breeze. The Healthy Lives lesson was fun and informative.

And now the kids stared back at her expectantly, waiting for the next activity.

Unfortunately, there was no next activity.

Things had improved so much over the week that this lesson plan, which would have taken her the better part of the afternoon to wrangle through on Wednesday, was now finished in thirty minutes. The kids had participated, had fun, learned a little…and they still had an hour and a half to fill.

Bowman trotted over and leaned in close to her. His breath brushed her ear as he said, "Is that it?"

She gave a barely perceptible nod.

"Could we start the next lesson?"

She shook her head. "Next week is vegetables. There's a whole big introductory thing."

Bowman glanced back at the kids, who were all staring at them. "What are we going to do?"

"Make something up?"

"Okay." Bowman put his hands on his hips and glanced up at the sky. "We could have a race. Maybe—maybe everyone pretends to be a fruit, and they have to… I don't know, run like their fruit would run?"

Maisy furrowed her brow.

"What? I'm trying to brainstorm."

"A race where everyone pretends to run like a fruit?"

"Okay, it's more of a brain drizzle," Bowman admitted. "What have you got?"

Maisy drew in a breath, almost ready to suggest the bubble-wrap idea.

"What's next?" Sami asked.

Kai shuffled a few steps to the left, and Bowman could feel he was about to make a break for the stables.

"This is boring," Juliet said.

"Just a minute!" Maisy said. "Bowman and I are deciding which of the top-secret fun ideas we want to end Friday with."

"Not to add any pressure," he muttered.

"I'm trying to buy us time."

"At a hefty price, Doc." His pre-grin appeared beneath his Stetson. Suddenly, Maisy could think of all sorts of things she'd like to do this afternoon. Unfortunately, none of them involved the children.

"Is there something active and outdoorsy you used to do as a kid?" Bowman raised his brow, as though to ask if she was serious. "I mean, not the trampoline and not the swimming hole, but something…healthy we could do with the kids?"

Bowman met her gaze. "You're trusting me to come up with an activity?"

Maisy paused, letting herself get a little lost in his brown-green eyes. Was she going to trust him? He'd been fantastic this week, but he was still a daredevil at heart. He shifted, his gaze probing hers, wanting her trust.

"Y-yes? Yes."

"Okay. I've got an idea. But you've got to promise not to lose it on me."

Maisy bit her bottom lip. "Can I promise to try?"

His full smile broke out under the rim of his Stetson. For the sake of his smile, she was going to try very, very hard.

"Hey, gather up, everybody." Bowman indicated that the kids should circle around. "We're gonna go to one of my favorite places. But when we get there, we have to talk about safety."

Maisy was unable to hold back a snort. Bowman glared at her. *Sorry*, she mouthed.

"Today, everyone is going to learn to be responsible for their own safety. Sometimes that means backing down when something feels wrong, sometimes it means asking an adult for help and sometimes it means having an escape route if it gets sketchy. We're going to practice having fun and keeping ourselves safe."

Bowman took off toward the west. The kids scrambled to keep up as he led them across the open fields. Sami ran back to Maisy and grabbed her hand, tugging her along.

"Where are we going?" she asked.

"Somewhere special. Let's go!"

They arrived at an outcrop of rock, and Bowman's intentions materialized instantly. He was going to let the kids climb this thing. Maisy immediately scanned the rock, imagining all the ways a kid could get hurt playing on it.

"This is Fort Rock," he said. "My brother and I played here when we were little."

Marc ran up to investigate a little cave in the outcrop. "Awesome!"

Bowman caught him by the shoulder. "Before we explore, we're going to set some parameters. You climb up as tall as you are, and you can go inside any cave, but you have to be able to see me or Maisy at all times."

Marc made another break for the cave, and Bowman scooped him up and threw him over his shoulder. "And you have to stay on the east side of the rock, over here, where all these pine trees are."

Maisy took a peek around the outcrop. Whereas this side of the rock was shaded by pine trees, and fairly low to the ground, on the other side the rock gave way to a creek bed. The climbing looked significantly more difficult and soared up fifty feet over a shallow creek with boulders sticking up out of it. She shivered as she noticed climbing chalk on the west side, indicating that these safety rules didn't apply to Bowman."

"We get it!" Marc cried. "Let's go!"

"First, I want you to notice a few things." Bowman directed his gaze significantly at the ground. "What's at our feet?"

The kids looked down into the cushy bed of pine needles.

"Pine needles?" Juliet asked.

"The perfect landing spot," Bowman said. He scaled the rocks a few feet off the ground. "If you're climbing, and you want to jump off, this makes for a cushy landing." He demonstrated, launching himself onto the pine needles.

Kai didn't need any more encouragement. He scaled the rock and jumped off, rolling through the pine needles and getting back on his feet to try it again before most of the other kids made it to the rock.

"Notice the people around you. You don't want to jump off the rock and land on someone else."

The kids climbed up a few feet, then experimented with jumping into the soft landing.

"Keep low. I don't want anyone going up higher than they are tall."

Bowman watched the kids launch themselves off the rock, helping them learn how to land correctly, and laughing with them as they rolled onto the soft pine needles.

"Now, if you get too high, and jumping down doesn't seem fun anymore, what else can you do?"

"Climb down?" Juliet asked.

"If you feel comfortable. Or you can ask me or Doctor Maisy to come help you down. But, you need to always be aware of how high you're climbing. If it doesn't feel safe, come on back down."

Bowman showed the kids how to use the nubbins and pockets in the rock to climb, all while complimenting good climbing form. He also reminded them to be thoughtful of their surroundings, who was climbing near them and to ask for help if they got up too high.

"Maisy, are you going to climb with us?" Kai asked.

It was the first time Kai had spoken politely to her. Most of the time he stuck by Bowman, and while he hadn't been rude to her for the past few days, he hadn't been friendly, either.

"Sure. It looks fun."

Maisy placed her hands on the sun-warmed rock and climbed up next to Kai.

"Now you gotta jump!" he told her.

Maisy launched off the rock into the soft pine needles.

It was really, really fun.

"Bowman! I'm too high up!" Juliet called.

Bowman reached up and plucked Juliet from the rock, spinning her around before he set her down.

"Me, too!" Liya said.

"I bet Maisy gives some good spins." Bowman nodded at her. "She can help, too."

Maisy helped Liya down, imitating Bowman's motion as she gave a child a spin through the air for the first time in her life. Liya's laugh resonated through her and Maisy was surprised to find herself blinking back tears.

"You okay?" Bowman asked.

Maisy nodded, pressing her palm against the tears. "Yeah."

He reached out, paused for a moment, then ran his hand along her back. The strength and warmth in his touch resonated through her.

"That's the first time I've ever spun anyone through the air," she admitted, keeping the second part of the sentence to herself. *And I was never spun around as a child.*

"You did a..." He pointed, cleared his throat and nodded at Liya. "You did a good job."

Maisy fixed her gaze on Juliet, who was piling up pine needles. "What are you working on?"

"I'm making a home for some thatching ants, in case they want to live here."

Maisy kneeled next to her and pushed more needles into her pile. "That's thoughtful of you."

Bowman took a few steps away, then turned back to her. "I mean it." He gestured to the tumble of kids around them. "You're good at this."

Maisy let the warmth of his gaze filter through her defenses. She never would have gotten this far with camp if it hadn't been for Bowman. And she knew, deep down, she had to put a stop to her crush, since it was starting to get mixed up with respect and genuine care for this man. But it was Friday afternoon. She was meeting with Clara tomorrow to get matched up with someone more suitable. Today, she was going to let herself be a little bit in love with Bowman Wallace.

"You know what else I'm good at?" Maisy asked, scooping up some pine needles.

Bowman, immediately alert to her intentions, backed away. "Oh, no, you don't."

She jumped up with the pine needles and advanced on Bowman.

"Pine-needle fight!" Marc yelled, launching himself off the rock and scooping up pine needles. Maisy threw her handful at Bowman, who skillfully dodged the needles and rallied with an attack of his own. Marc threw an armful of needles at her, squealing with laughter. The rest of the kids joined in the fight, climbing and showering pine needles down on each other, then jumping off the rock and gathering more.

It was so fun Maisy forgot to be scared. In that one, brilliant moment, all she could feel was laughter and possibility.

"Hello, there!"

Maisy twisted from where she was standing over Bowman, her hand on the collar of his T-shirt, poised to shower him with pine needles. A woman in a pantsuit with a clipboard and epically inappropriate footwear waved as she approached.

"Hello?"

"You all are a tough bunch to find! But then I heard laughter, and decided to follow the joy. And here you are!"

Maisy released her handful of pine needles. "Yes. We are here."

Wow. Glad we cleared that up...

Maisy moved on to the real question. "And you are?"

"I'm Linda Sands. From the Healthy Lives Institute." She smiled and held up the clipboard. "I'm here for the first assessment."

THE COLOR DRAINED out of Maisy's face. Bowman was used to her going red by now, but when she lost all color it was far, far worse.

"There's an assessment?" she asked.

"Just the first one." The woman waved the clipboard, not specifying how many there would ultimately be. "Go ahead with whatever you're doing. I'll take a few notes."

Bowman couldn't get a full view of the clipboard, but it was full of boxes, and each box was full of words. It was a safe bet that *rowdy pine-needle fight* didn't correspond with anything Linda Sands might be rating them on.

"I didn't get the rubric," Maisy said, with

what Bowman could recognize as a fake smile. "Was it in the curriculum?"

"Oh, we don't include a rubric. We want to see how people implement the curriculum on their own."

Maisy looked like she was about to pass out. The kids had gone silent, alert to the intruder in their midst. They were a ragtag mix of imperfect humans, but they'd all learned to work together. With his lack of experience, Maisy's hesitation to get out of her comfort zone and the various issues the kids brought to the table, Bowman had assumed they were all in for a miserable three weeks. But the opposite had turned out to be the case. The kids had relaxed in a place where it was clearly okay to be imperfect. And right now, none of them liked the idea that they were being graded.

He needed to say something—anything—to help Maisy. Fifteen bad jokes knocked around in his frontal lobe but not one helpful comment.

It was Kai who broke the silence. Hanging from one arm halfway up Fort Rock he said, "You know what I like? Fruit. It's…good."

The silence continued another beat. Liya coughed.

"And very healthy," Marc said.

Sami snuck up beside Linda and peeked at

the clipboard. "I like the *nature walks* we go on." She walked deliberately over to Maisy and took her hand.

Some of the color returned to Maisy's face. Bowman gestured to Clara's running path, hoping Maisy could feel his intention.

"Are you all ready to finish the *nature walk*?" she asked.

The kids reluctantly climbed down off the rock and shuffled after Maisy, making loud comments about fruit as they did so. Bowman felt a tug at his sleeve and looked down to see Juliet. "We're coming back here next week, right?" she whispered.

Bowman nodded.

"I like it here."

"Me, too," he told her.

She smiled, then asked, "Piggyback ride?"

Bowman crouched down and she jumped up on his back, then he trotted to catch up with the group.

Linda Sands spent the next hour with them, her evaluation ending as the last kid hopped into a car and headed home. Maisy kept it together until Linda's car crested the ridge of Wallace Creek Road. That's when she fell apart.

"They didn't tell me she was coming! There was *nothing*. No forewarning, no heads-up."

Bowman took a deep breath, but it didn't matter how much air he took in, he couldn't breathe for Maisy.

"My whole agreement with the Healthy Lives Institute is on the line here. Two hundred and fifty thousand dollars. If I mess this up—"

"You're not messing up."

"You don't know that! We can't see the rubric."

"Maisy—"

"I need to know what's expected of me." Her bright blue eyes filled with panic. "I don't want to be held responsible for things I didn't know I was supposed to be doing."

Bowman took a few steps toward her. He hesitated, searching for the words to help her, then rested his hands on her shoulders. She stilled.

"What's the worst thing that can happen?"

"I could lose the loan-repayment program."

"Yep. You could." Bowman connected with her gaze. "That would be awful. It's a whole lot of money."

"Your family could lose the funding from HLI and you'd have to find another way to get insurance for camp in the future."

"I don't want to let down my family. We were relieved when we found this solution, and I'd hate to have to find another. What else?"

Maisy finally took a breath. Bowman adjusted his breathing to match hers. "What else could happen if we fail this assessment?"

Maisy blinked. "They might think they made the wrong decision in awarding me this position."

Bowman lowered his head to meet her gaze. "That's another possibility. They won't fire you, or pull funding from us. They just won't realize you're brilliant."

She let out a dry laugh.

"Anything else?" he asked.

She gazed up at him, her sharp mind running through all the possibilities. "We might get a bad score."

He smiled, waiting for her to come to the logical conclusion.

"Yeah, I get it." She gave him a rueful smile. "There are worse things than an imperfect score on a grading rubric."

"It could be a lot worse."

"I guess that's it, then. I'd have to pay back the loans. You'd have to find someone else to fund the insurance on camp. I'd have to accept that I made a bad impression on people I wanted to impress."

"You'd still be a doctor—they can't take your medical degree away. You'll still have this job if you want it. It would be inconvenient to have to pay back those loans, but if you stay here, the cost of living is low. You'll be okay."

She pressed her lips together and nodded. "You're right. It's not the end of the world."

Bowman removed his hands from her shoulders and took a step back.

"It's not."

Maisy crossed her arms over her chest and raised her chin. "But this is literally my stress nightmare, getting graded on a rubric I'm not allowed to look at."

Bowman couldn't quite think of what to say. He nodded and put his Stetson back on. Maisy took a couple of steps toward her Jeep. He wanted to say something. One more thing to let her know he appreciated the stress she was under, but also knew she was going to be okay. But all he could come up with was "Sounds like you've earned yourself a batch of sweet-potato fries, then."

She laughed. "Oh, yes! The silver lining." She opened the door to her Jeep, then glanced back at him. "Should I save you a seat at the counter?"

He shook his head. "I got a thing I have to work on tonight."

Something like disappointment flickered across her face, then she shook it off and climbed into the car. "See you Monday!"

"See you." He touched his fingers to the tip of his hat as he watched her drive away.

Once her Jeep was out of sight, he pulled out his phone and opened up his pictures. He tapped the one he'd snapped of Sami explaining the thatching ant colony to Linda. He enlarged it until the words came into focus, smiling to himself. This picture of the rubric, and his plan on how to nail it, would be the gift Maisy deserved for putting up with him.

CHAPTER TEN

THE LAST BOOTH along the front window at Eighty Local was apparently the Wallace family office. Maisy tried to keep her thoughts to herself as she sat across the table from Clara, but after ten minutes of working with the matchmaker, she finally blurted out, "You're *really* organized."

Clara looked up from the leather notebook, slipped a second sticky note at the top of a page and smiled.

"I am. It helps me in a job where I deal with a lot of big feelings. There's literally nothing more important in the world than my work as a matchmaker, and I like doing it well."

Maisy appreciated Clara's dedication, but she wasn't going to let the statement slide. She shrugged and grinned at Clara. "Except for maybe my work as a doctor?"

Clara pressed the tip of her pen to her lips and considered. "Of equal value."

"I'll take that. My work keeps people living

long lives in healthy bodies—your work makes them happy."

"And this is why I like you already." Clara flipped to a new section of her notebook and grabbed a violet-colored gel pen. "Now, let's talk about who you're looking for."

Maisy, no slouch when it came to being prepared herself, had pored over Clara's website as she sat at the counter alone the night before and enjoyed her sweet-potato fries. She knew what to expect from this meeting, and had her answers prepared.

"I'm looking for a good man who is sensible. Because my work is unpredictable, I think it would be best if he had a stable, nine-to-five profession. I'd like him to be polite and sociable. I see us going to parties, spending time chatting with lots of other people."

I'm looking for the anti-Bowman.

Clara glanced at her. "Do you go to a lot of parties?"

"Um, not yet? I've been in school, and then residency. Not much time for parties."

"But you've made time for hiking, running marathons." She checked her notes. "It says here you biked across Oregon. You made time for all those things."

Maisy sat back. *Is it normal to feel like you're getting called out by the matchmaker?*

"Well, I have to take care of my health, right?"

"Of course." Clara grinned, tucking her hair behind her ear. "And since you've logged over two hundred miles on the Pacific Crest Trail, I'd like to add you're looking for a man who enjoys outdoor adventure, if it's okay with you."

"Sure. But those big trips were mostly celebrations. Like, I did the bike trip with a friend after we graduated from medical school. And the marathon training was a gift to myself when I got my residency."

"Hmm. That's amazing. I love how you mark milestones with adventures." Clara wrote down a couple of notes. "Because most people would be inclined to celebrate by throwing a party."

"I *like* parties."

"I believe you." Clara moved a paper from one section of her notebook to another. "But you have to admit there's very little evidence to back up your statement."

"Well, I do. And I'd like to be with a guy who is pretty social."

"Fantastic." Clara made a note, then looked up at her. "We're having a family karaoke night on Wednesday. It's just us Wallaces and a few close friends, but it's definitely a party. You'll come?"

Maisy blinked. Family karaoke night with the Wallaces?

"It's superfun. Piper will be there, so you'll get to know my sister better." She grinned, like it was already decided, then flipped topics before Maisy could argue. "Let's talk about physical attributes. I've found over time that when my clients fall for someone, looks don't tend to matter much in the end. But it's good to have a sense of who you find attractive."

Maisy opened her mouth to give a thorough description of Dr. McDreamy but found she wasn't able to speak. Or even close her mouth as her gorgeous, maddening coworker emerged from a door at the back of the dining room, joking with a tall, dark-haired cowboy. Bowman had on his standard worn jeans and work boots. An old leather tool belt was slung across his hips, various hammers and whatnot weighing it down. His simple white T-shirt was a little dusty. His smile landed on her, creating an atomic-strength reaction in her gut.

"Hey!" He crossed the room. "What are you doing here?" His eyes ran to his sister, to the paperwork, then back to Maisy, and finally fixed on Clara. "Are you serious? She's only been here a week."

Clara didn't respond, as she was completely focused on Bowman's companion. "Hi, babe." He bent to kiss her cheek, then traced his steps back a few paces, grabbed the flowers off a table and offered them to Clara as he sat down next to her. "You hard at work?"

"I am." Clara gazed at him, the air around the two of them seeming to pulse with energy.

"Too bad someone's taking so long to finish up your office." The man brushed a lock of Clara's hair from her face.

"My landlord's really busy these days." Clara placed a hand on the side of the man's face. He leaned in to kiss her.

"Enough!" Bowman said. "Clara, you got a client here."

Clara shook her head, dazed. Then she beamed at Maisy. "Oops! Sorry."

"Jet, put those flowers back," Bowman directed. "You know what Hunter said."

"I'll get Hunter some new flowers."

Bowman glowered at the man, who reluctantly rose and put the flowers back in their vase.

Bowman dropped into the booth, next to Maisy, and ran his hands through his hair. The scent of the woodsy, sage soap she'd come to associate with him wafted around her. "It's a sad day when I'm the responsible one around here."

"You're plenty responsible," Clara said.

Bowman turned to Maisy and pulled a face. Maisy laughed, even though she really didn't want Bowman to be the one who made her laugh like this.

"What are you up to?" she asked, hoping to distract from the fact that she was sitting here with his matchmaker sister, trying to find anyone in central Oregon other than him to focus on.

"We're helping Hunter with the addition. Jet and I—" He gestured to the man across from them, who now had one hand behind Clara on the booth and the other on her arm, pulling her back into the magical love cocoon. "Knock it off." Bowman picked up a napkin and threw it at Jet, then shook his head in exasperation. "We're helping Hunter finish up the events center. Did you hire my sister to set you up?"

She scrunched her brow. "Not exactly?"

"She's a call-in client," Clara said, somehow managing to move even closer to Jet.

The man, presumably Jet, and clearly the person who'd slipped the ring on Clara's finger, asked, "What's that?"

"I have three clients who've asked me about Maisy. This is a preliminary, get-to-know-you meeting, and if I think she's ready for a relationship, and a good fit with any of my clients, I'll set her up free of charge. If none of these dates work out, and she wants to hire me, we'll talk more later."

"Three guys?" Maisy asked, as Bowman said, "Can I guess who?"

"No," Clara snapped at her brother, then she smiled at Maisy. "And, yes, you've created quite a stir in our community."

Bowman rested his elbows on the table and looked into Maisy's eyes. Maisy gave herself a hard, fast reminder that Bowman was *not* one of the guys who was interested. But he *was* currently gazing into her eyes.

"You gotta set her up with someone cool," Bowman said.

Okay, he's definitely not interested. Which was good, because she wasn't interested, either. She was all about healthy choices. Clara would set her up with the male equivalent of a well-balanced meal. Bowman was a basket of sweet-potato fries.

Clara inclined her head. "Of course."

"No one fussy."

Clara glanced between her and Bowman, bemused. "Shall I put that down?"

"Sure." Maisy managed a weak laugh. "I'm probably fussy enough for two people."

"You're not fussy. You're careful. Fussy is when people get all upset over nothing."

Should she remind Bowman that less than twenty-four hours ago he was trying to talk her off a ledge over a rubric from the Healthy Lives Institute?

"You're the new doctor, right?" Jet asked.

"Yes, I'm Maisy Martin."

"Jet Broughman." He held out a hand. "Michael Williams told me all about you."

Maisy opened her mouth, hoping to steer the conversation away from her potential dates and toward the nice doctor who'd been her greeting committee, but Jet said to Clara, "Someone smart. Maisy's got to have someone who can keep up intellectually."

Clara laughed. "Thank you both for your help but I think Maisy and I can handle this."

"And no dry guys," Bowman said.

Clara tilted her head to one side. "Dry guys?"

Maisy understood the reference perfectly. "Dry guys, like the type of guy who drives four and a half hours to get to the coast, then doesn't get in the water when he gets there."

"Or even leave the hotel observation deck."

Maisy giggled. "The guy who won't join in a pickup basketball game, because he's afraid of scuffing his expensive basketball shoes."

Bowman turned to Maisy. “Or the type of guy who wouldn’t join in a pine-needle fight, because he’s worried about getting pine needles down the back of his shirt.”

“You *so* deserved that.”

“Just wait ’til next time, that’s all I’m saying.”

Clara raised her eyebrows. “Seems to me, brother, you have a pretty good sense of what Maisy likes.”

Bowman sobered quickly, looking a little confused.

Which was probably better than what Maisy looked like at the moment: way-over-the-line confused, verging on downright baffled. She gave herself a mental slap upside the head.

So what if Bowman knew her pretty well by now? They were friends. Over the last week she’d discovered a lot of things she liked about Bowman, and they *did* work together well. But he was, and would always remain, reckless. Gorgeous, funny, intuitive and kind, but likely to get himself seriously injured or worse the minute he went back to firefighting. She couldn’t live with the pressure and fear. She *wouldn’t.* To get him off her mind, she needed a nice, sensible man. She needed a good match. Not a match held next to a gallon of gasoline, in a stable full of tinder, and a smile that threatened to ignite it all.

"Did she tell you about the love rules yet?" Jet asked.

"There are rules?"

Bowman grinned at her. "Think of it like a rubric."

Okay, he knows me very *well.*

"Rule number one—never waste time on someone who isn't in to you," Jet said, beaming down at Clara.

"I feel like that one should be printed on fliers and posted on every door across the nation."

"My sister and I have considered it."

"Love rule number two—to find love, love yourself first," Bowman said.

"Aw! Bowman, you remember your love rules!" Clara grinned at her brother.

"Because you repeat them over and over," he muttered.

"Number three?" Clara asked, looking from one man to the other.

"Know your core values—" Bowman began.

"And find someone who shares them," Jet said, finishing for him.

"These are really good." Maisy turned to Clara, impressed. "Did you make them up?"

"More like my sister and I gave voice to the truth," she said sagely.

"Then typed it up in a fancy font and printed it out on pastel, premium-grade paper," Bowman said.

"Number four is my favorite," Jet said. "Know your love chemicals. Choose when, and with whom, to release them."

Maisy thought back to her biochemistry classes. "Like oxytocin and vasopressin?"

Clara nodded. "Exactly."

The chemicals were released with human touch. Something as simple as a hug, or as complicated as a kiss, could get a person feeling like they were falling in love. Clara had found a scientific reason for urging her clients not to jump in too far, too fast. "I'm impressed."

"I get all the rules except for number five," Bowman said. "Look good, feel good—what does that even mean?"

"You'd know what it means if you'd ever spent more than half a second getting dressed in the morning." Clara turned back to Maisy. "It has to do with taking time to care for yourself. I want my clients to put energy into caring for themselves as they open up to caring for others."

"Not everyone gives a rip about clothes," Bowman said.

"But a lot of people give a rip about showering."

Bowman rolled his eyes and turned to Maisy. "My sister is great, but don't let her get involved with your wardrobe. She's relentless."

"Maisy is perfect." Clara waved a hand in her direction. "You're the problem child around here."

Maisy couldn't imagine one thing her coworker could do to be more attractive. Sure, he might look nice in a button-down shirt, or even a suit. But in jeans and a T-shirt, he looked like Bowman.

And now he was grinning, which only made matters worse. "Good thing you're not setting *me* up, then."

BOWMAN WAS STILL smiling as he pushed through the front door and headed for his truck. He couldn't pin down what he was feeling. It was happiness, but with something like trepidation. It'd been fun talking with Maisy, Jet and Clara. He was glad Maisy was willing to let his sister set her up with a few guys. It meant she wanted to stay in Outcrop. That was good. He wanted her here.

But something about the whole exchange felt weird, too.

Bowman shrugged off the feeling. Maisy was complicated, and while he didn't want Clara to send her out with a bunch of guys who didn't get her, he also knew his sisters were incredibly good at what they did. So good that he'd resisted every attempt they made to set him up. He wanted to find someone on his own, someone who liked him for who he was, and wouldn't try to change him. He knew himself—he wasn't social, could be focused to a fault and truly didn't care what other people said about him.

Except for one person. Maisy thought he was too reckless, and he found himself wanting to change that opinion.

He glanced back into the restaurant, where Maisy and Clara were still in the booth. *Reckless* wasn't the right word. He knew when he was in danger and took risks based on potential reward. He didn't plot it all out with charts and graphs the way some people did, but that didn't mean he wasn't aware of what he was doing.

It didn't matter. Maisy wasn't here in Outcrop to understand him. She was here to get her loans paid back and start her career as a doctor. He pulled out his phone and looked at the picture he'd snapped of the rubric again. He grinned to himself. They were gonna crush this.

It had taken quite a bit of time to shift through

the language and figure out what the Healthy Lives Institute actually wanted out of this camp, but he'd done it. Maisy hadn't been too far off the mark at all. In fact, were Linda Sands to be there all day on any given day, Maisy would get top scores in every category without his help. But since they didn't know when Sands would show up next, they needed to be ready to hit all the points on the rubric when she did arrive.

Over the weekend, he'd write up the plan so they could pivot at any given moment and nail the rubric. That way Maisy wouldn't have to worry.

"Wallace."

Bowman tucked the phone in his pocket and looked up. The fire chief was standing directly in his path. He paused, waiting for his body to react, to get angry. But he didn't feel anything particularly strong. He still felt good.

"Hey, Josh."

Josh Hanson was a steady, reasonable guy. If he was fazed by how rude Bowman had been the last time they spoke, he wouldn't say anything. "How's it going?"

"Great." Bowman was as surprised by the word when it came out of his mouth as Josh seemed to be. But he really *was* great. It had been a fun morning working with Jet and Hunter on the addition. Seeing Maisy and his sister talking felt right, and now he had the afternoon to do something he'd never been interested in before—make a plan. "Yeah. Things are good. You?"

Josh gave Bowman a sidelong glance but kept up the conversation. "Sami's loving camp."

"She's awesome. All the kids are. Sami's the one who keeps us all in line."

"That's my girl. She tell you she's planning on being a doctor now, just like Maisy?"

"There's a lot worse than just like Maisy," Bowman said.

"That's the truth." Josh glanced at Eighty Local, then back at Bowman. "I'm glad to hear it's going well."

Bowman nodded. It was the first good conversation he'd had with Josh in weeks. He felt somehow more centered. It was like he could see Josh's side of things, and even though he still stood by the decision to break protocol during the Jansen fire, he also understood why Josh had to suspend him.

"We got a lot coming up next week. Vegetables, that's the theme."

"I'm sure I'll get the full rundown," Josh said.

Bowman nodded, then took a few steps toward his truck. "See you later."

"Two weeks," Josh said.

Bowman stopped and spun back around. "I've only got two more weeks?"

Josh laughed, like Bowman was making a joke. But he'd honestly forgotten his suspension would be up so soon.

"I've got a meeting right now—" Josh gestured to the restaurant "—but let's talk this week about your return."

"Sure." Bowman waved, then continued on to his truck. He absolutely looked forward to getting back to his old life, but in the meantime, he had a plan to make.

CHAPTER ELEVEN

"You Are the Sunshine of My Life" by Stevie Wonder filled the barn, calming the horses and Bowman. He sang along as he fed Dulce an apple slice. Kai gave him a suspicious glance but Bowman continued singing, promising the horses he'd always be around.

Kai kept his head down as they saddled Midnight. Bowman was pretty sure he heard the kid join in on the "yeah, yeah, yeah" with him and Stevie. It was Monday morning, and Bowman was gratified when Kai picked right back up where he'd left off on Friday, helping with the horses.

A copy of the Healthy Lives Institute rubric was burning a hole in his pocket. He wanted to show Maisy the minute she got here, but couldn't quite get the words out. It was like, after having a quiet Sunday all to himself, he had to warm up to conversation again. Maybe he'd get the chance before they circled up.

"You want to hear something?" Kai asked.

"Sure."

"My mom and my stepdad had a big fight yesterday."

Bowman paused, then forced himself to continue getting the saddle on Midnight as he thought about how to best encourage Kai to keep talking. "That's no fun."

"They fight a lot."

Bowman shuddered. He'd always felt deeply, and hated it when other people fought. "I imagine it's gotta be pretty tough."

Kai kept his eyes on Midnight, testing the waters as he spoke. "He and my mom met on the internet. And then Mom divorced my dad and we moved to Outcrop."

Bowman let the words settle, then responded carefully. "Sounds like a big move."

"Yeah. Now I have a brother and a sister, too."

"Is that good or bad?"

Kai was quiet for a long time, then finally said, "They're all right. I just don't know if we're going to be family with them for very long."

Bowman settled the saddle, then crouched down so he was at eye level with Kai. "That's hard."

Kai nodded.

"I'll tell you what. I don't know what's gonna happen with your mom and Greg. But I do know you're real good with horses, and that's a gift that comes from the inside. You can always come here and be with the horses when things get hard."

Kai shrugged. "If my mom and Greg get divorced, I'd have to move and I'd never see Midnight again. Or you."

Bowman shook his head. "If your mom and Greg get divorced, and you move away, you won't see me or Midnight until you're old enough to come back here on your own."

Kai focused on Midnight as he asked, "I could come back?"

"Anytime."

They worked in silence, getting Midnight saddled, then Cricket, as Stevie Wonder sang in the background. Bowman wanted to say the right thing, but really didn't have any idea of what that was. What would his dad say in this situation?

"Look, you can't control what your parents do. But you can control what *you* do. If you want to be around horses, you need to be the type of guy people can trust with their animals."

"I was thinking I could be a doctor, like Doc Martin, but with horses. Like a veterinarian."

"I like that idea."

"Guess I'd have to do good in school."

"Guess you'd have to."

"Hmm."

They worked in silence. Bowman knew Kai needed a lot right now, but if the kid was anything like him, he wouldn't want platitudes. He'd want time in the stables and steady friends that had his back.

Bowman felt Maisy enter the stables. He turned around to find she'd gotten even prettier over the weekend. He stared at her for a minute, trying to figure out what was different. The hair was the same. The jeans and T-shirt fit her athletic frame in the same way they always had. She seemed…brighter.

"Mornin', Doc."

"Good morning. Are you two ready for circle time?"

Kai met his gaze, questioning the necessity of circle time. Bowman tried to communicate that since it mattered to Maisy, they ought to do it.

"We're finished up here."

Kai rolled his eyes, but headed on down the aisle, toward the arena.

"How was the rest of your weekend?" Bowman asked.

"It was good. Fun. Your sister's no joke when it comes to matchmaking."

Bowman chuckled. "That's the truth." He

reached into his back pocket. "You still worried about the HLI assessment?"

Maisy glanced around, as though Linda Sands was hiding in the barn. "Yes? Yes. I'm trying to take what you said to heart. And I did take it to heart. I just really want to nail that rubric."

"Then I got a present for you." Bowman held out the folded piece of paper.

"You do?" She moved closer; the floral scent of her hair was faint, but managed to push out everything else. She took the paper, her blue eyes connecting with his before she looked at it. Her smile glimmered in the dusky stables, and the long hours he'd put into creating the gift vanished. He could unpack a rubric once a week for a smile like that.

MAISY UNFOLDED THE piece of paper, baffled by what Bowman could possibly have in store for her. It took her a moment to make sense of the document. A picture of words and boxes had been blown up, and Bowman had written notes in the margins. Visually, this piece of paper was the antithesis of Clara's notebook, but way more powerful.

Her hands began to shake. "Where did you get this?"

"I took a picture of it on Friday."

She allowed herself to glance up at Bowman. "When?"

"When Sami was showing Ms. Sands the anthill and explaining how healthy it is for everyone to work together."

Her gaze returned to the paper. For every point on the rubric, Bowman had made notes about how they could meet the criteria, no matter what stage of the day they were at. He'd made plans, backup plans and contingency plans for all the different activities they did.

"Bowman… I don't know what to say. This is incredible."

He shrugged as if it was nothing.

A lump formed in her throat. She swallowed. "This may be the nicest gift I've ever been given."

"Figured you deserved something for putting up with me."

Maisy finally gave in to the urge and slid her arms around his waist. She hugged him, leaning her head against his chest and breathing in his warm, woodsy, sage scent. He startled at the action, then wrapped his arms tightly around her. Along the stalls, horses shuffled, and from the arena she could hear the kids' voices floating toward them, but right now all she wanted was to be here.

Unfortunately, she could only hug her co-worker for so long before he got suspicious. Maisy forced herself to step back, then she pointed an accusatory finger at Bowman. "So you *can* make a plan."

"Yeah." He glanced up at the rafters, then around the barn. "Guess you make me feel like planning."

Maisy resisted the urge to read all kinds of things into that statement. Which was good, because Bowman's pre-grin appeared and he said, "I can *make* a plan. I might not follow it..."

She hit his arm with the paper. "Shush, you. This is the best plan, and we're following it."

He grinned down at her, warming her to the core with his mischievous smile. "Two hundred and fifty thousand dollars." He held out his fist for a bump. "We're going to crush this."

She tapped back with her fist, letting herself smile up at him.

And that was a terrible idea because now all she could think about was hugging him again. She looked back down at the rubric. He had a number of activities listed that they could start up at any time, in case Linda arrived when they were doing something nonhealth-related.

"What's 'The Veggie Song'?"

"I just rewrote "Single Ladies" to make it about vegetables. So instead of singing about all the single ladies, it's—" Bowman gave a brief groove of his shoulders and started singing. "All the vegi-tables, all the vegi-tables."

Maisy cracked up as he continued to channel Beyoncé and the produce market simultaneously.

"The kids are going to love it."

"I hope so."

She tried to keep her voice neutral as she said, "You like to sing, don't you?"

"Sometimes." He gazed down at her, and some big emotions that she couldn't define—and knew he wouldn't bother to define—passed between them. Then he kept walking. "You're gonna have a big week. You'll nail camp, and my sister will probably have you married off by Wednesday."

Maisy shrugged. "I wouldn't be so sure about that. Clara's got her work cut out for her."

Bowman turned his focus on Jorge. "You go out on any dates this weekend?"

"I guess? I mean, yes. I was in the company of two different men at Clara's suggestion."

"Was it fun?"

Maisy shrugged. "It was fine. It's a little weird, being set up."

"You don't have to let her do this. I know how she gets, but you don't have to go out with these guys. Or you can wait until you've settled in."

Maisy snuck a glance at Bowman. She *had* to go out with these guys. She had to find someone to distract her as quickly as possible.

"No, I want to. I like meeting new people."

"That's my idea of a nightmare," Bowman said. "Stuck with someone I don't know, havin' to talk, all kinds of expectations."

"So…camp, basically."

He laughed. "Now that I know you and the kids, it's not so bad."

"Not so bad? I'll take that compliment."

"Maisy! Bowman!" Sami's voice called out from the arena. "Circle time!"

"We're coming!" Maisy quickened her steps toward the arena, but Bowman remained still. She turned back as he spoke.

"I mean it. I can run interference with Clara if you want me to. She wants to set up the whole world, and if someone's not ready for a relationship, she takes it on as her personal mission to get them ready. You don't have to do this if you don't want to."

Maisy gazed at Bowman. Since the moment she'd set eyes on his picture, she'd been half in love, half horrified by the danger he put himself in. She could not live her life in fear of him getting hurt. He would always be rushing into fires and swinging kids around and brushing up against danger. Her brother's death had destroyed her parents' lives, and she'd never put herself in a position to let that happen to her.

"It's fine. Who knows, maybe tonight's date will be the guy I'm destined for."

"Maybe. Let's go circle up."

"It's veggie week," she reminded him, skipping ahead toward the arena.

"Can't get much more exciting than veggie week."

Maisy laughed, letting her shoulder bump up against his as they jogged into the arena. She might not be able to let herself fall in love with this guy, but it was hard to think of anyone she liked more.

BY FIVE O'CLOCK that evening, it was apparent her date was not going to provide sufficient distraction from Bowman. Even the first day at camp had been less awkward than this guy, and significantly more exciting.

She shouldn't have let Clara set her up on a Monday. She was exhausted after camp, and wished she was at the counter awaiting another Burma Mile burger, rather than sitting across from the legal counsel for the town of Madras in an incredibly stilted conversation.

"If you're wondering if I always wanted to work for the state, the answer is maybe."

Jeremy sat back and nodded, like he'd rehearsed the phrase carefully, and it came out just the way he intended it to. Maisy had half a mind to congratulate him.

He beamed at her expectantly.

My turn to talk, I guess.

"That's cool. I'm glad you wound up doing work you…might have wanted to."

Okay, that didn't come out right at all.

"It's good work."

"Oh, absolutely." Maisy's eyes drifted to the poster of Bowman on the door of Eighty Local. He'd described firefighting as a calling. There was no *maybe* with Bowman. He was either all in, or all out.

"What about you?" Jeremy had established a predictable conversational pattern. Offer a piece of information about himself, explain it, then ask her for a similar piece of information. It was like they were taking turns on the world's simplest jigsaw puzzle.

"I knew I wanted to be a doctor in high school."

"Why?"

Maisy stirred the glass of iced tea, the clatter of ice cubes abnormally loud. She had her standard answer ready to go, but over the last week, hiding her brother's death had become exhausting. Being with kids all day brought the accident to the forefront of her mind. She wanted to spew out the whole horrible story and see what happened. But Eighty Local was not the place, and Jeremy was definitely not the man.

"I've always loved science, and I wanted a job where I could give back to the community. I chose to become a general practitioner because of the lifelong connections I'll be able to create with my patients."

It was all she could do not to lean back in the booth and nod with satisfaction at *her* answer. She'd offered enough information to satisfy her listener, and it was hopefully dull enough to keep him from asking more.

"That's really interesting." Jeremy seemed to have an incredibly low threshold for entertainment. "I have a dog. And if you're wondering, she's a golden retriever."

Movement in the parking lot got her attention. Bowman's long strides carried him across the gravel to the front door. She waved and caught his eye. He nodded, then stopped and backed up so he could see who was in the booth with her, his smile promising mischief.

Maisy drew her eyes away from the reckless, gorgeous man and refocused on the sensible guy who might be very nice once she got to know him.

"I love dogs," she said. "What's her name?"

The bells on the front door jangled as Bowman entered. Rather than head to the counter, where he normally took his meals, he ambled over to the booth next hers, then sat so she could see him over Jeremy's shoulder.

Fun date? he mouthed.

She gave him a barely perceptible glare, then leaned toward Jeremy, trying to focus on whatever he was saying about his dog. Bowman reacted with mock fascination as Jeremy let her know that Cookie was really sweet, but also shed a lot of fur.

"How about you? Do you—"

"How did you come up with the name *Cookie*?" Maisy interrupted before they could get into her thoughts on animal companionship.

Jeremy startled as she broke the conversation code but managed to recover. "She likes cookies. So do I."

Bowman slowly closed his eyes, his head nodding like he'd drifted off to sleep.

She bit down on her lip, hard. She was *not* going to start laughing.

"What kind of cookies?"

"Well..." He paused, like he was revving up to make a joke. "Not chocolate!"

Maisy laughed, not because the quip was at all funny, but because Bowman was holding up his hands making bunny ears behind Jeremy's head.

Jeremy chuckled. "This is fun," he said, as if a pleasurable evening had in no way been an expectation of his. "We're getting along well."

Bowman mugged an expression debating that statement, then bent over and scribbled something on a napkin.

Maisy cleared her throat, determined to focus on Jeremy and continue with this date. The guy was nervous, and she intended to give him a solid chance. Bowman had been awkward the first time she met him, and once she got to know him, well...

Okay, best not to think about that.

"I don't have a dog," Maisy said, giving her date a sincere smile, "but I always wanted one."

Bowman raised two napkins, one on either side of Jeremy's head. Maisy kept her eyes on Jeremy. But the harder she stared at him, the less attractive he became. *Fussy* felt like the only adjective she could put to the button-down shirt he wore. Her eyes flickered over to the counter, where Hunter was laughing. Against her better judgment, she glanced at Bowman, who was patiently holding up two napkins, on which he'd rated the date like a figure-skating competition.

5.3 and 4.9.

Maisy choked back a laugh, nearly spewing iced tea all over the table. She grabbed a napkin, covering her face as she tried to stop laughing. While she knew it was unlikely she'd choke to death on iced tea, she felt like it was an imminent possibility.

"Are you okay?" Jeremy asked, with the same intonation he'd used for every question he'd asked for the last hour.

She stood abruptly. "I'm sorry. I'll be right back."

Maisy marched over to Bowman, who was now innocently studying a menu. She grabbed it out of his hands and whispered, "You knock it off, Bowman Wallace."

"I was trying to help!" he insisted.

"You've got a twisted sense of help."

"You've got a twisted sense of fun." He lowered his voice and imitated a robot as he quoted Jeremy. "This is fun. We're getting along well."

Maisy couldn't stop herself from laughing with him. "You are *impossible*."

"You're making bad decisions, encouraging

him. You need to put this date out of its misery." Bowman glanced at Jeremy with concern, making Maisy laugh even harder. He was right. It didn't matter how many second or third chances she gave him, he was not the man for her. She wanted stable and safe, but not this safe.

Maisy let out a breath and wiped the tears of laughter from her eyes. "You are *so* going to pay for this."

He glanced back at Jeremy. "I kinda feel like Clara should have to pay for this."

"I'm just a call-in client. I agreed to go out with anyone who was interested and fit my list of expectations."

"What'd you put on the list?"

Maisy glanced back at her date. She'd asked for the anti-Bowman, and she'd gotten it.

"I'm going to get back and try to salvage this."

"Rearranging deck chairs on the *Titanic* if you ask me."

"I didn't ask you." Maisy spun on her heel and pulled up a big smile as she approached her booth.

Then her eyes landed on Jeremy.

Yeah, Bowman was right. It was time to put this date out of its misery.

"Well, this has been fun—"

"That's the firefighter guy, right?" Jeremy interrupted.

"Um, yeah. Firefighter of the Year."

"Is he your ex?"

Maisy startled, then glanced back at Bowman. "Oh, God, no. He's my…"

What was he? Her friend, her nemesis, her antithesis?

"Your what?" Jeremy asked, with uncharacteristic interest.

"He's just my…Bowman."

BOWMAN MOVED OVER to the counter to let Maisy have her date. He shouldn't have interrupted, but this was obviously *not* the guy for her.

He pulled out his phone and sent another quick text to Piper: Got a question about call-in clients.

He set the phone on the counter, and for once she texted right back: Coming home for karaoke Wednesday. Check in about it then?

Bowman stamped a like on the text and slipped his phone away. This was weird. Normally Piper couldn't wait for an opportunity to educate him, or anyone else, on the minutiae of her business. Something was definitely up.

Hunter set a bowl of elk stew in front of him. "How's she doing over there?"

Bowman twisted in his seat to look back at Maisy, who was now standing and holding her jacket.

"That guy's a dud."

"Clara must have had her reasons for setting up the date."

"The only reason I can think of is she wanted Maisy to spend the evening bored and miserable."

Bowman felt Maisy move to the exit, the guy following close behind. A twinge of regret unsettled him. He shouldn't have made fun of her date or interrupted them. His terrible habit of making bad jokes at the wrong time was probably going to get him slapped sooner rather than later. He swiveled toward the door.

Maybe I should run out and apologize.

Before Bowman could slip off the stool, Maisy stiff-armed the door and came marching back into the restaurant.

"Hit me with a root beer," she commanded, popping onto the stool next to Bowman's. She buried her face in her hands and groaned.

Bowman caught Hunter's gaze. "That bad?" Hunter asked.

Maisy kept her face tucked in her hands and nodded. Bowman lifted a hand and slowly, carefully, patted her on the back.

Her head shot up. “You were *not* helping.”

“But wasn’t I?” She gave him a dry look. “You weren’t laughing at all until I showed up.”

Hunter placed the pint of root beer in front of Maisy. She picked it up and drank deeply, then set the glass on the counter. “You are impossible. You’re the least…possible person.”

Bowman laughed, feeling strangely light at her words. He couldn’t articulate the feeling, but it was a mix of freedom and anticipation. For the first time in a long time, he was excited about things to come.

“I’m sorry. You looked really bored.”

“I *was* bored, that’s not the point.”

Bowman gazed down at her. If she was bored, wouldn’t she want out? It was confusing, but then he’d never been good at dating. “I gotta give you props for getting out there to date at all. I hate it.”

She gave him a sideways glance. “That’s funny, because it seems like there’s six billion women who want to date you right now.”

Bowman shrugged. “It will all be over as soon as the posters come down.”

“Are you sure about that?”

He nodded. “I’m not for everyone. Or even for most people.”

Maisy kept her gaze on Bowman, calling his bluff.

"No, seriously. Most people can't put up with me. I'm an introvert in a noisy world. I go with my gut when everyone wants me to follow the rules. I've never met a woman who didn't want me to change, and I'm *not* going to change. So that's that."

"Do you want to be in a relationship?"

"Of course I do."

"How are you going to fall in love if you don't date?"

It wasn't something he'd totally thought through. "I dunno. I'll meet someone?"

"I approach it like science. I can't meet someone if I don't get out there. It's a numbers game. The more men I meet, the more likely I am to find the right one."

"You're gonna line up all the frogs? Evaluate 'em and pick the best one?"

"Something like that."

Hunter leaned across the counter toward Maisy. "I hate to break it to you, but frogs don't stand in line very well."

She rolled her eyes.

"He's right," Bowman said. "We've definitely tried to line up frogs."

Maisy gazed at him. "By the pond?"

Bowman nodded. Hunter reached under the

counter and pulled out a picture of the two of them, age seven, covered from head to toe in mud, standing on the banks of the big pond on Wallace Ranch.

"You must have had so much fun together." A reluctant grin flickered across her face, as though the picture made her both sad and happy. Hunter seemed to notice it, too.

"We did."

Maisy sighed, then handed the picture back to Hunter. "You're right. Jeremy's not the guy for me. So, yes, thank you for helping me end the date sooner than I might have."

"Anytime. And if you want me to tell Clara to back off, I'm happy to."

Maisy gazed at her hands for a moment, then drew in a deep breath. "No, I need to do this. It's good for me."

"Suit yourself," Bowman said. "But I sure wouldn't let either of my sisters set me up."

"Why not? You're not just going to stumble across the love of your life."

"Maybe I will," Bowman said. "I'll meet someone, and I'll just know."

"Well, I'm not going to let life happen to me. I'm going to get out there and find the right guy. That way I won't fall in love with the wrong guy."

"But if you fall in love with someone, how can he be the wrong guy?"

Maisy gazed at Bowman, then turned back to her root beer. "Leave it to me to do exactly that."

CHAPTER TWELVE

KARAOKE NIGHT WITH the Wallace family was a huge mistake. Possibly the worst mistake Maisy had ever made, including taking an accelerated summer class in organic chemistry.

A breeze stirred, echoing her unsettled emotions as she stood outside the open bypass door. The whole Wallace family had congregated inside the big red barn. Fairy lights hung from the rafters, glowing against the encroaching night. Long tables held a selection of delicious-looking Eighty Local offerings. Old chairs had been brought in, and even a few bales of hay, but no one was sitting. They were too busy connecting—laughing, helping out, getting in each other's way. The family couldn't look happier about being right here, right now.

She never should have accepted this invitation. There'd been an inkling of trepidation when she went home to shower and change. The inner voice she should learn to listen to warned against switching out her usual jeans and tank top for a red sundress. When she'd picked up a bag of baby carrots at Manny's grocery on the way over, her entire system was on alert.

But had she listened? Nope. So here she was, way overdressed, clutching a subpar bag of veggies, about to be the only person with divergent DNA at a party that required singing.

Way to get yourself locked in, Doc.

But, of course, the carrots weren't the real problem, and neither was the dress. It was that she'd chosen both with Bowman in mind. Her eyes were drawn to him as he bounded across the room and wrapped a fiftyish woman in a bear hug, then lifted her off the ground. The woman laughed, brushing a piece of straw off his T-shirt. Bowman exchanged an animated greeting with the man at her side. She couldn't hear them, but the pattern of interaction looked well-established and easy. These must be his parents?

As a group, they turned toward a young man, fifteen or sixteen, in a sweatshirt declaring him to be a member of the Outcrop Eagles football team. Bowman grabbed a soda and launched it through the air as the teen ran to catch it, nearly crashing into Jet.

Unperturbed, Jet complimented the kid on his technique, then seemed to be explaining something related to catching a fast-moving object in the air. Clara took the soda from the boy's hands and replaced it with one that hadn't been shaken up. Hunter called Bowman over to where he was arguing with Ash about the karaoke machine. Ash continued to give directions and Hunter rejected them as Bowman silently set up the machine.

The family worked together as one unit. Over their days at camp, she'd watched Bowman open up and even enjoy himself, but it was nothing like this. He was truly in his element here.

And she'd be standing around all evening trying not to fall any more in love with him than she already was.

"Pinot gris?"

Piper joined her at the bypass door and pressed a chilled glass of white wine into her hand.

Too late to escape now.

"Thank you." Maisy accepted the glass and took a sip. "How's Portland?"

A glimmer of stress flickered across Piper's face, then she smiled brightly. "It's fine. You look amazing." She gave Maisy a once-over. "Like Taylor Swift, 2012."

"That's the nicest compliment... Well, it's literally the nicest compliment. Thank you. You and Clara always look so perfect, I wasn't sure what to wear."

"You always look beautiful. We love your vibe. But, if you're going to dress up, I'm always in favor of using T-Swift as an inspiration. You can't go wrong."

Maisy felt about a billion times better. Maybe she could hang out in the doorway with Piper, discussing Taylor Swift looks all evening. They had a bottle of wine and a bag of baby carrots. The warm August air was dry, alive with the smell of juniper. It would be fine to just park herself here for forty minutes, then head home.

Piper gestured to the frenetic hive of activity that was her family. "You want to know how all this goes down?"

"Yes, please. Clara kind of roped me into this."

"Of course, she did. But I'm glad you're here. Okay, that's all delicious." She pointed to the food. "But it's going to be an odd assortment. It's what we call 'Family Special.' Eighty Local food Hunter made too much of during the week, baked goods he won't put out for a second day, open bottles of wine that didn't get finished. It's good, but if you're wondering why he's serving hazelnut scones alongside beef brisket, that's why."

"My carrots aren't too out of line?"

"The carrots are perfect."

Maisy held up her glass. "Is this from Eighty Local, too?"

Piper scoffed. "I brought my own wine, and glasses, because Hunter seems to think it's okay to serve family members beverages in mason jars." Piper grinned at her. "Not that there's anything wrong with jars of wine, I just want what I want."

Maisy nodded as Piper continued, "Those are my parents. Dad's a science teacher and when he finds out you're a doctor he's going to talk science at you all night long, so be warned."

"Fine by me."

"But Mom is literally the nicest person on earth, so she'll swoop in and save you as needed. The karaoke rules are that everyone has to sing, and no one is allowed to sing more than one Elton John song."

"E-everyone?" Maisy asked.

"*Everyone*. And I hope you like Elton John."

Maisy drew in a deep breath. "And if I were to sneak out now?"

"You'd become the doctor who refused to sing karaoke. We'd all repeat the story at every family gathering for the next twenty years." Piper winked at her, but Maisy didn't get the sense that she was actually joking.

Piper took a sip of her wine then switched topics abruptly. "How's it going? I mean—" she gestured to Bowman "—how's that working out?"

"Um?" A flush started at Maisy's neck. She willed the heat to recede before she was the same color as her dress.

"With camp," Piper clarified.

Maisy desperately wanted to step back into the twilight, back into her car, and slip out of here.

"Not bad. We're actually, kind of succeeding."

Piper raised her eyebrows, then clinked her glass to Maisy's. "Well done. I think you may be the only person capable of getting Bowman to work with kids."

As though on cue, Bowman looked up from the karaoke machine and saw them. His brilliant smile broke out, and he stood and trotted over.

"Hey!" He delivered his normal greeting, then stopped short a few feet away and stared at her.

"Hi." Maisy brushed her hair from her face,

then held out the woefully inadequate contribution. "I brought—"

"You're wearing a dress," he interrupted.

Maisy blinked. Then nodded. Heat burned at her neck. "Yes, I am."

He stared for another moment before Piper huffed out a sigh. "Way to state the obvious, bro. She looks gorgeous."

"I know," Bowman replied, defending himself. "I've just never seen her…in a dress."

Maisy dredged up images to cool the heat rising up her face. Oceans, snowfall on the tundra, teachers with erratic grading processes.

Piper grabbed the carrots from Maisy's hands and thrust them at Bowman. "Take these over to your brother. And make sure Maisy meets Mom and Dad."

Bowman rolled his eyes at Piper, then took another look at Maisy. "I like your dress."

She let out a breath. "Thank you. I didn't know what to wear."

"It's just the family."

She nodded slowly. *It's just* your *family.*

"Come on." Bowman's smile was back. "Come say hi to everybody."

Maisy followed Bowman into the barn. Everyone was happy to see her, and she *did* know most of the family by this point. Plus, she had a point to prove with Clara. She *liked* parties, and standing in the doorway all night would not give credence to her assertion.

The parents, Bob and Lacy, were as wonderful as she might have expected. Ash was more relaxed than she'd ever seen him. It was as though having all his family members together in a barn was the end goal and he could let down his guard while they were here. Clara and Jet spent much of the time completely focused on one another, but when they did emerge from their bubble, they were fun to talk to.

"Did you get some of the quinoa salad?" Hunter asked her as she walked along the table. Her tin plate was piled with pretty much everything he had to offer, so it was likely.

"I think so."

"It's a new recipe," he said. "I need opinions."

"I have opinions!" Piper called out.

Hunter chuckled and yelled back, "I want a nonfamily member opinion."

"She's literally here every day running kids' camp," Clara said. "How is that not family by now?"

"Yeah. And Bowman talks to her. Pretty sure they'll issue adoption papers any day."

"Or some other legal document binding her to the family," Piper quipped.

Maisy searched real hard for the quinoa salad on her plate and took a bite. She closed her eyes as the Mediterranean seasonings and the South American grain melted together. "So good."

"You want more?" he asked.

Maisy contemplated her plate, which was not going to withstand the weight of one more serving of anything. "Can I have the bowl?"

"It's Doctor Martin!" a familiar voice cried out.

Maisy turned to see Michael and Joanna Williams. Nonfamily members! These were her people. It was all she could do not to wave her arms in the air with joy, but that would have sent a lot of good food flying through the barn.

"So nice to see you!"

"I was hoping you'd be here," Joanna said.

Bowman nodded at Michael and Joanna, then took a step back. It wasn't impolite, more like they hadn't cracked the shell yet. Maisy surprised herself by placing a hand on Bowman's arm and steadying him next to her side. "We can't thank you enough for the planning guides. They've been a life saver at camp."

"Those guides are gold," Joanna said. Bowman cleared his throat and glanced up at the rafters. "How's camp turning out?"

She looked up at Bowman, hoping he'd answer. He met her gaze, politely suggesting she take the conversation from here.

It was strange, how Bowman had come so, so far with her and the kids, but still couldn't find the words to chat with these family friends.

"Camp's great," she said. "I think it far exceeds our original expectations."

"Do you have a kid named Kai Larsabal?" Joanna asked.

Bowman reacted quickly, but it took him another moment to answer Joanna. Finally he said, "You know Kai?"

Joanna exchanged a quick, surprised look with Michael, then said, "He attends the school where I teach. I'll have him in class next year. How's he doing?"

"He's a great kid." Bowman glanced over his shoulder, then back at Joanna. "Real good with the horses."

Joanna let out a sigh of relief. "I'm so glad to hear it."

"I mean, he's still Kai." Bowman's half smile landed on Joanna, and she laughed out loud.

"I hear he can be a handful."

"Kid's two hands full, but…" Bowman lost his words for a moment, then wrangled them back. "I'm glad he's in camp."

Joanna widened her eyes, communicating that Kai had perhaps been more than even two handfuls in school. "Sometimes a kid needs to be in the right setting with the right person to find out what they're capable of. Sounds like he landed in a good place."

Bowman shrugged, but he clearly understood what Joanna was saying. Most people weren't able to connect with Kai the way Bowman had. Maisy rested her free hand on his back for a moment. Warm and strong, she felt him pull in a breath as Joanna acknowledged he'd done something extraordinary with Kai.

Then he completely shocked everyone by continuing the conversation. "Do you know Liya Patel?"

"Oh, she's a great kid."

Bowman nodded. "She is, but we haven't been able to get her to ride on her own. She's fine riding with me, but I'd like to see her get out on a horse by herself. I feel like that'd be good for her."

"Give it time," Joanna advised.

"Tryin' to, but we've only got a week and a half left."

A week and a half? That's all they had?

Since learning about camp, she'd looked forward to it being over and out of the way. But right now, she felt like she was going to miss these kids terribly.

And this ranch.

And this Bowman.

"You know her dad is deployed with the National Guard. He's in Poland right now. I think her mom's pretty nervous and that filters on down to the kids."

"Makes sense." He looked Joanna directly in the eye. "Thank you. That's helpful. I thought she was just being clingy."

"She probably is being clingy." Joanna smiled at him. "But with a good reason."

"Everybody, find a seat," Ash instructed. "It's karaoke time."

Piper patted the spot next to her on a hay bale and Maisy jumped at the opportunity to join her. If she spent one more second next to Bowman, she was going to start snuggling him, and that could get awkward for everyone involved. Piper refilled her glass. Clara sat on the next bale and pulled Jet down to join her. Lights twinkled above, and jokes flew back and forth between family members.

Okay, fine. Karaoke night wasn't the worst

idea she'd ever had. In fact, it was a blast. Maisy wasn't sure she'd ever laughed so hard. Everyone really did sing, and not everyone was a particularly good singer. The choices ran from Beyoncé to Buddy Holly. Jet tried to beg off, saying he didn't know any songs, but the family wasn't having it. Finally, he stood up and started singing the high-school fight song, and everyone in the room joined in, loudly. Clara sang a song from a Muppets movie, earning her a standing ovation from her fiancé. Ash surprised Maisy by tuning up an old guitar and singing a Hank Williams tune. Bob started off with an Elton John classic, "Rocket Man," then was denied the chance to sing a second and had to settle for Billy Joel's "Uptown Girl."

But nothing compared to Bowman.

Most of the family had taken turns, and at some point Maisy forgot to be nervous.

"Bowman!" Hunter called out as he finished up a country ballad.

"Bow-man!" Piper stomped her feet on the floor.

"Bow-man!" the family kept yelling until he finally stood and stretched.

"What's it gonna be?" he asked, loping up to the machine.

"Cat Stevens!"

"No! Bon Jovi first!"

Bowman fiddled with the machine, then a smile lit up his face. He glanced at Maisy as he selected a song. His shoulders grooved in anticipation.

A warm summer night's breeze wafted through, lifting pieces of straw, pulling the hem of her skirt to tickle her calves, stirring anticipation.

The first few heavy beats of the song pounded through the speakers and Bowman spun, eliciting cheers from his family. Maisy recognized the tune but couldn't quite place the song.

Then he started singing.

"Stuck in the Middle with You," a joyful, playful song about being surrounded by clowns and jokers, trying to figure things out, summed up their camp experience perfectly. If the two of them ever did have a song—which they didn't, and wouldn't—this would definitely be it.

There was nothing more fun than watching Bowman sing. All that he was—physical, soulful, impulsive—shone through in his performance. His voice was rich, full of feeling, like he was channeling the emotions of the original songwriter. He moved with the intention of the music.

He was so free, completely in his element. This performance was like the smile everyone reacted to on the poster. This was the Bowman he didn't let anyone else see, save his family and his horses. This is who he was when he wasn't exhausted by not fitting into the world's expectations.

Maisy leaned so far forward on the hay bale she probably looked like a sprinter at the starting blocks. She felt the privilege of being here, with his family, in this moment. All she wanted was for Bowman to keep singing, and to be sitting on this bale of hay every time the Wallace family broke out the karaoke machine.

But that wasn't an option. All the things drawing her to Bowman were the very reasons she couldn't fall for him. He would always be the first to rush a fire, the last to leave a burning building if there was anything left to be saved.

A life in love with Bowman would be a life of constant fear. His need to live on the shining edge of physical danger would result in her lurking in the shadows of life.

The family burst into applause as Bowman set down the mic, not even bothering with a bow. People heckled him for another song, but he walked back to the hay bales, a satisfied grin on his face.

Maisy turned to Clara, intent on asking her to set her up with as many men as she saw fit, and discuss bumping her up to a real client.

Clara beamed at her, like she might understand, then called out, "I think it's Maisy's turn!"

"Mai-sy! Mai-sy!" Piper stomped her feet again.

"Maisy's turn!" Bowman jogged over and offered her his hand, his reckless smile racing through her like a high-speed car chase.

It took an abnormally long time to answer. "I…"

"What would Taylor do?" Bowman asked.

What would Taylor Swift do in this situation? Jump in, fall in love, get hurt, get mad and wind up with a number-one hit song about Bowman's smile. Scratch that, she could write a whole album about this evening.

Bowman tugged at her hand. "Come on. It's fun."

One thing was absolutely certain—Taylor would never understand if she didn't take this chance.

Maisy shook her head, then gripped Bowman's hand and stood.

BOWMAN STOLE MAISY'S seat next to Piper. He felt a little bad for the way Maisy dragged her feet up to the karaoke machine. But as he'd gotten to know her, he'd learned that when offered a nudge, she often thrived when trying something new. Piper gave him an appraising glance.

"You looked like you were having fun up there."

He nodded. This was fun, and it was good to have Maisy here. She flipped tentatively through the song list, with the baffled expression she got when faced with too many choices she didn't like.

"Do you think she needs help?" he asked Piper. Without waiting for an answer he stood. "I'm going to help her out."

He got two steps away from the bale when Maisy turned to Ash and asked, "May I use your guitar?"

Ash brought it to her, then positioned the stool he'd used for her.

"You play the guitar, too?" Michael asked.

"No." Maisy flushed as she gave the instrument a tentative strum. "I only know four songs."

"How do you only know four songs?" Ash asked, as Piper yelled out, "'Teardrops on My Guitar'?"

Maisy flushed, grinning as she dropped her

head and nodded. Piper, Clara and Joanna got really excited about this, and Maisy started laughing.

"Every true Swiftie has to at least *try* to learn Drew's song," Clara said.

Maisy strummed the guitar. She opened her mouth to sing, then flushed completely. "I don't know if I can do this."

"You have to!" Piper cried.

"She doesn't have to do anything," Ash said.

"But we one-hundred-percent want to hear this song!" Clara insisted.

Maisy cleared her throat. "I got it. If I can work kids' camp, I can sing in front of you all."

"If you can put up with Bowman at kids' camp, you can do anything," Hunter quipped.

Maisy strummed the guitar, familiar chords Bowman couldn't quite place. Then she started singing about being in love with someone who only saw her as a friend. It was a pretty song, and Maisy was, well, really pretty.

It felt like the music wrapped around him as she sang. Like all he needed was the comfort of this voice, and the simple, imperfect chords strummed on the guitar. The same feeling of freedom and anticipation he sometimes got with Maisy swept through him.

And then, with a thud of disappointment, it

was over. Maisy tried to return the guitar to Ash, but he wouldn't take it. "Sing one more."

"I think one's my limit."

"You said you know four songs."

Maisy laughed, her head thrown back, a soft flush running up her neck. Again, she tried to hand off the guitar to Ash, but his brother held up both hands and shook his head. It felt good to see her here, having fun, laughing with his family.

Feelings swirled in his chest, things he couldn't identify. He felt better than normal, better than he ever had. Bowman nudged Piper's shoulder, trying to communicate all this. Piper glanced up at him, a slow smile growing across her face.

"She's good." Piper gestured to the guitar.

"At everything," Bowman added.

"Everything?"

"Like working with the kids. All the detail stuff. Dealing with me."

"You know there are a lot of women who would enjoy dealing with you?"

Bowman laughed, his eyes drawing back to Maisy. "But would they be good at it?"

"I doubt it."

Maisy was back on the stool, guitar in hands.

"Do you know 'Picture to Burn?'" Piper asked.

Maisy scoffed. "Of course, I know 'Picture to Burn.'"

"Best Taylor Swift song, ever!" Clara cried out.

Maisy shook her head. "There is no best Taylor Swift song. The canon stands as a whole." She strummed a few chords, then looked up. "Sing with me?"

Bowman could kick his former self for not knowing the words, or even having heard this song before. But his sisters and Joanna, who had all been indoctrinated into the TS fan base, jumped up to join her.

Bowman rested his forearms on his knees, leaning into the music. Maisy didn't know the chords to this song as well, but everyone felt passionately about the lyrics. The air around her seemed to shimmer. Her voice, while quieter than her compatriots', hit him straight in the solar plexus and moved through him.

Everything finally, clearly, clicked into place.

Maisy.

She was why camp was so fun, and why every day felt like an adventure. He'd gotten less angry about having to move through a world that didn't value him, and more adept at making the adjustments needed to fit in. She was smart, and seemed to get prettier by the minute. She was everything.

How had he not realized this? Could a guy fall for someone without even noticing? It was like everything was fine, good, fantastic even, but then tonight it was like…

It was like getting hit by a lightning bolt.

Bowman pulled in a breath as he ran his fingers through his hair. His sisters had been right about him. *Dang it.*

Whatever. He felt so good it didn't matter if they were right.

Bowman caught Maisy's gaze. Could she be thinking what he was thinking? Bowman had been in a number of relationships, but most of those consisted of women pursuing him and Bowman going along with their plans, until their plans included changing him. Then he was out and had never felt much regret or remorse about anything. If someone didn't like him the way he was, there was no use trying to make her like him.

He hadn't ever really tried to woo a woman.

Maisy dropped eye contact, keeping her focus on the guitar for a moment. Bowman had half a mind to walk up and take away the guitar so she'd look at him again, but that would make the song over, something he was completely uninterested in having happen.

But happen it did, just like the last time she came up to the final chords and stopped. The family burst into applause. Maisy stood and forced the guitar into Ash's hands.

"Your turn," she told him, with the same finality in her voice that got kids, him and probably all her patients to do what she wanted.

Bowman stood and made his way to Maisy. Would it be weird to tell her right now how much he liked her? Because she could cancel the whole dating thing with Clara and be with him. He couldn't think of any good arguments to convince her of this—he just felt it.

He stepped over a hay bale, not noticing the beer Hunter had left sitting on it, or the fact that he knocked it over. Ash was strumming a Lyle Lovett tune, and under other circumstances he'd be tempted to jump in and sing anything Lyle wrote. Right now, he wanted to be near Maisy.

"Okay. You are amazing and I love you," Clara told her.

Bowman swirled those words around in his head. Could he use that same sentence?

"If you're serious about setting her up, Clara, you should have an open-mic night and everyone would fall in love with her after two songs."

Bowman froze in his tracks. Why was Piper suggesting this? Had he not made it clear five minutes ago he was interested?

"I don't even have to do that," Clara said. "I have plenty of suitors for Doctor Maisy."

Maisy glanced at him, then back at Clara. "Set me up! I have a 'Blank Space.'" Everyone laughed, and Bowman assumed she was referring to another Taylor Swift song. "Seriously, I appreciate being a call-in client, but I feel like I should start paying you for this service."

"No." It was all Bowman could think to say. His sisters and Maisy turned to stare at him. Bowman placed his hands on his hips and looked up at the rafters, willing the words to come. "You've got…school debt."

Maisy's clear blue eyes connected with his for a moment, then she smiled, but it wasn't one of her real, freckle-rearranging smiles. She seemed nervous. "Thanks to you, I think I'm good with the student loans. Did Bowman tell you guys about the plans he made to ace the HLI scoring rubric?"

"Bowman made plans?" Clara asked.

Piper clarified, "Wait, are you telling me he actually read a scoring rubric?"

Bowman felt anger rumble through him. He'd just experienced a moment of clarity around his feelings for Maisy. His sisters were all about people falling in love and had been bugging him about dating for the last eight years. Why were Piper and Clara making this so hard?

"He did." She fiddled with the straps on her pretty sundress, then gave him a real smile. "It's impressive. And probably the most thoughtful thing anyone has ever done for me."

Bowman melted a little, taking a step toward Maisy. Women probably didn't like men declaring their feelings at family karaoke night, but the feelings were not going to stay inside much longer.

"So, yeah. I'm set for the loans. I start making pretty good money in another few weeks, so I can pay you," Maisy told Clara.

The air washed out of his lungs, leaving him unable to tell her she didn't need to get set up with anyone. He was right here.

"Totally appreciate the intention," Piper said. "But from what Clara's told me you're doing great as it is. Do you have any more dates set up this week?"

Clara started talking, but Piper wasn't able to hear the answer because Bowman grabbed her arm and walked her several paces away. "Whose side are you on here?"

"Are there sides?"

"I don't know. I just realized that Maisy is—" Bowman drew in a breath. He couldn't quite put the words together. *Maisy is it* was all he could come up with.

"So get in there," Piper encouraged. "If you and Maisy are a good fit it shouldn't matter if she's got a million guys lined up. You want help planning a date for her?"

"No." Bowman had held off his sister's attempts to "help" his love life for years. He wasn't going to cave in now.

"Oh, sorry." Piper feigned confusion. "I thought you wanted me on your side."

Bowman glanced at Maisy, who was now cheering on Ash as he sang.

"How many sides are we talking?"

"According to Clara, Maisy is very popular. There are any number of sides. Maisy will pick the guy who's right for her." Piper fixed him with the bossy gaze she'd been perfecting since she was two. "You're going to have to step up."

Bowman let that idea settle around him.

"You've always let women do the work in your relationships. They pursue you, and you stick around until it gets hard."

"I stick around until they get to know me, and then try to change me," he corrected.

"Whatever. Point is, if you're serious about Maisy, get in there."

He knew Maisy was right for him, but was he right for her?

But if the way she'd described some of her recent dates was accurate, Clara didn't have much of an idea of what was right, either. He could compete with those guys. In fact, he was going to plan the perfect date for Maisy. She wanted to line up guys and rate them on a rubric? Fine. He could ace that test.

CHAPTER THIRTEEN

"This date didn't work out either, huh?" Bowman asked, leading Alice out of the stall. Maisy took the reins, allowing herself one small glance at Bowman as she shook her head. She *was* trying. But finding likable characteristics in anyone but Bowman felt impossible. Images of him joking with his siblings, so happy and free as he basked in their company, looped in her head. His easy laughter, the way he enfolded her into his family. The way his eyes met hers as she sang.

It was like she'd gotten caught in a dangerous storm at sea. A really fun, beautiful, dangerous storm.

Maisy shook her head. The horse nibbled at her ear and she playfully pushed his nose away. She was proud of how much more comfortable she'd gotten around horses in the last two weeks. She might drown in heartache, but at least she could ride now.

"Better or worse than static-conversation man?"

"Oh. Not much could be worse than Jeremy," Maisy said quickly. But then, as she thought through the grueling evening she'd spent with a prosecuting attorney the night before, she amended, "Except for maybe this guy."

Bowman knit his eyebrows together, then imitated Jeremy's speech as he said, "If you're wondering, would I like to know how it could be worse, the answer is yes."

Maisy burst out laughing. Bowman had a funny kind of smile on his face, like he was pleased he'd made her laugh.

He shook his head. "My sister is generally a lot better than this. She won't send someone out on a date unless she's pretty sure it's going to work out."

"No, it's my fault. I told her to send me out with anyone who asked."

He stopped walking right in front of her, his scent blocking out everything else. "Why?"

Why? *Because I'm gonna be in a world of hurt if I fall for you.*

"I guess I want to see who's out there."

"But if you met the right guy, you'd know, right? At some point you have to go with your gut. I'm sure you've got a rubric, but in the end won't you just know?"

How to even answer that? She was doing her best *not* to go with her gut here. She'd basically forced Clara to set her up with anyone within a decade of her age that wasn't Bowman.

All the same, it felt hopeless. Every date had been laughably bad.

Except one.

Sami's dad, Fire Chief Josh Hanson, had been the first to ask Clara about her. He'd been a Love, Oregon client for a while, but was more selective than most because of Sami. He referred to the situation as "dating for two." He wasn't desperate to fall in love, but was open to meeting someone. Clara had told her that for the most part, firefighters were barely able to stay single long enough to need matchmakers, they were such heroes in these days of wildfires. Josh hired Clara to help keep him from making a bad decision that might wind up hurting his daughter. He was nice, smart, interesting. As the fire chief, Josh wasn't in constant danger on the job, like Bowman was, and he approached the work with a scientific methodology that mitigated danger. His smile didn't disrupt her respiratory system, but that was okay, wasn't it? Maybe a relationship should be planned with the head, and with a good foundation, the heart could follow?

"I think so. Yes? I haven't been in love before, so I don't actually know what to expect."

Bowman's pre-grin glimmered. "According to my sisters, being in love makes you feel free, like you can do anything."

Like running a kids' camp with no experience?

He stepped around Alice and joined Maisy as she scratched under her mane. "What are these guys doing wrong?"

"I don't know that anyone is doing anything wrong, necessarily." Except for not being Bowman. "Maybe just trying too hard."

"Can't blame a guy for trying."

"No. And I'm trying, too. Maybe the problem is me?"

"I doubt it." His smile broke out in full force. "Unless some guy thought you were *actually* asking questions all evening."

Maisy laughed, then really wished she could kick herself in the behind without anyone noticing. Why couldn't Bowman be a nice, safe guy? Like an accountant with a passion for playing bridge?

Because then he wouldn't be Bowman.

"When's the next date?" he asked.

"Um, Saturday. Two on Saturday."

He nodded. A flash of attraction, or whatever it was when she was feeling attraction and Bowman was feeling whatever he was feeling, ignited between them.

"So you're free tonight?"

Maisy blinked. Free for…what?

"Because it's Outcrop Outside. All the businesses set up outside, and Hunter has a booth. There's music. It's fun."

Maisy exhaled. He wasn't asking her out, just alerting her to a town festival.

"Are you going to sing?"

"No," he scoffed.

"What do you mean 'no'? You're—" Maisy bit down on her lip, hard, to keep herself from finishing the sentence.

"You gonna sing?" he asked.

She imitated his scoff.

"We got that settled, then. Leave the singing to the band." He cleared his throat. "I'll swing by around six thirty?"

His green-brown eyes shone, a hint of mirth and a hint of…well, she didn't know what the other hint was.

Okay, she really didn't want to be staring at Bowman, but what was that nonmirthful hint and what did it mean?

Tires crunched on gravel and car doors opened and slammed. No one called out, and the car drove away.

"That'll be Kai," Bowman said. He didn't walk away but continued waiting for her answer to a question he hadn't really asked.

"Yeah. Yep. That's Kai."

"So, six thirty?"

Maisy gazed up into his hazel eyes. This wasn't a date. This was a friend, showing her around town. "Sounds great."

His eyes sparkled, his lips pressed together in a smile she hadn't seen on him before. He looked happy and somehow shy at the same time. Then he nodded and headed for the bypass door.

"Captain Kai!" He saluted.

"Reporting for duty." Kai held out his hand for apple slices to feed the horses. Maisy slipped past them and headed into the parking area to greet the rest of the campers as they arrived.

If she had more self-control, she might have kept herself from spinning back to take one last look.

Then she never would have seen Bowman, turning back to take one last look at her.

He smiled. It was the same smile she'd fallen in love with on the poster, the one shining as he sang at the family karaoke two nights ago. That smile landed deep in her chest, exploding like fireworks, setting off a chain reaction through her body.

Then Kai slipped his hand into Bowman's, commandeering his attention as the two disappeared into the barn.

Maisy had no idea what his smile meant, but she was pretty sure she'd just agreed to a date with Bowman Wallace.

BOWMAN TRIED TO keep his focus on the kids. That was tough when every cell in his body felt like leaping into the air and yelling *yes!* Even circle time, where they had to tell the group what vegetable they identified with and why, was fun.

Piper was right. He'd been lazy when it came to relationships. No one had ever inspired him to much more. Maisy inspired all sorts of things, as evidenced by the fact that he was willingly surrounded by children as he described how much he had in common with a jalapeño pepper. He was so excited about planning this date for Maisy he was having a hard time restraining himself from telling his friend and coworker—also Maisy—about the date.

"Why are you smiling so much?" Kai asked as they led the horses into the arena after circle.

"I'm in a good mood. Why are you smiling?"

"I'm not smiling."

"You sure?"

Kai fought against a grin. Bowman furrowed his brow theatrically.

"I'm not smiling!"

"Of course not."

Kai led Jorge into the arena, then called back, "Now I'm smiling because I feel like it. Not because you said I was smiling."

"Me, too." Bowman grinned, following with Alice.

He walked the horse to Maisy, who was looking a little flustered. "You think Linda Sands will be here this afternoon?" She took the reins, scratching the horse at the base of her neck.

"It's likely."

Alice leaned into Maisy's attention. "We're all set, though. It should be fine."

"We *are* fine," he reminded her.

She was particularly fine, but this wasn't the time to let his mind go there.

"Bowman!" Kai came tearing into the arena, without Midnight. "Dulce's acting funny."

"What did you notice?"

"She keeps rolling on the ground. Really hard."

He laughed. "That's great. She's getting ready to have her baby."

Kai looked suspicious.

"I'm sure that's what it is, but let's go check her out." He trotted back toward the stalls and explained, "The momma will roll on the ground to get the baby in the right position."

They arrived at Dulce's stall to find her rolling aggressively on the ground. Bowman was thrilled to see her move into this first stage, but Kai's brow furrowed in concern. "It looks like it hurts."

"Probably does."

Dulce stood, looking uncomfortable, but focused. She'd get through this just fine.

"When's she gonna have it?"

"Hard to say with a first-time mom. Most horses give birth in the middle of the night, though." He glanced down at Kai, who clearly wanted to be in on this. It was unlikely the kid's parents would be up for driving out at 2:00 a.m. for a birthing. "There'll be a foal when you return on Monday."

Kai winced as Dulce dropped to the ground again. Bowman hummed one of the Taylor Swift songs he'd streamed that morning, trying to keep everyone calm. "Let's grab Cricket and Midnight and head back into the arena. I think the Healthy Lives Institute lady is probably going to come back today, so we should take our trail ride while we can."

"Will Dulce be okay?" Kai asked.

"She'll be fine, and she'd probably prefer a little quiet. I'll let my brother know what's happening and he'll check in on her."

Kai nodded, reluctantly moving away from

Dulce's stall gate. Bowman broke into the actual lyrics of "You Belong with Me," as they led the horses into the arena…where he stopped abruptly. Liya had led Jorge over to the steps and was currently using those steps to climb up on Jorge. On her own. Wearing her helmet.

He released Cricket's reins to Sami and took long strides toward Liya. Maisy held out her hand, stopping him. Her powerful look instructed him to let this play out.

Which was a little funny, coming from Maisy.

Kai tightened his grip on Midnight's reins. "I'm riding Midnight, right?" The kid had come so far but was still worried about the horse he loved being ripped out from beneath him. His need for stability was palpable.

Bowman signaled for him to settle down. He wouldn't be switching out horses at this point, but Jorge would not be his first choice for anyone's first solo ride.

Maisy crossed to him and said quietly, "She just climbed up, saying she wanted to ride on her own."

Liya's face was determined. Curls sprung out around her helmet and her little hands clenched the reins. Maisy's face was also determined, like she had to work past her own fears to let Liya take this step forward.

Bowman drew in a deep breath for all three of them, then squeezed Maisy's arm and walked over to Liya. "Hey, there."

Liya didn't take her eyes off her horse. "I'm going to ride by myself today."

"You're going to ride Jorge?"

Liya nodded.

He ran a hand under the horse's mane, checking in with him about the situation. Jorge blinked nobly, insulted Bowman would question his willingness to provide steady transportation for the young human.

"Okay. You know what to do." Bowman readjusted the stirrups, then double-checked the saddle.

"I can do this," Liya said, more to herself than anyone else.

"You've had good practice over the last couple of weeks." Bowman grinned at her, then stepped back. "Jorge's gettin' tired of hauling me around, anyway."

Liya loosened her grip on the reins and gave the horse a gentle tap with her heels. The arena was silent as Jorge took one long step, then another. Liya's eyes were bright, her lips pressed together in concentration. The massive, stately horse carried her around the arena slowly, one step at a time.

"Liya, you're doing so good!" Juliet cried.

Marc said, "You've got this!"

Kai's scowl loosened, and he said, "Relax your hands, like Bowman does."

"I'm brave," Liya told them, and herself, "like my dad."

The campers broke into encouraging cheers. Liya cracked a smile that grew with each long, careful step.

Bowman wanted to join the celebration but there was too much pressure building at the back of his throat. He glanced at Maisy, who wiped at tears as she watched Liya overcome her fear. And that was more than Bowman could handle.

He spun back toward the stables just as the emotion threatened to turn into a messy cry. He cleared his throat and croaked out, "I'm gonna saddle up another horse for me to ride."

He pressed a hand against the warm ache in his chest as he entered the tack room. Through the half wall, he could see Liya make her slow, steady progress around the arena. It made everything—his suspension from the fire department, the trepidation about camp, the exhaustion of actually running camp—all worthwhile.

As it turned out, Liya's ride was only the first big break of the day. The second took place when the representative from the Healthy Lives Institute showed up at a quarter past one, just like she had the week before.

This time, they were ready.

When they heard her car, they calmly abandoned a horse-grooming lesson and made their way into the arena for a rousing game of nutrient ball.

"Vitamin C!" Bowman yelled, launching the ball at Juliet.

"Um, oranges! And spinach!"

"Nice work!" Maisy whooped, offering a high five to her teammate.

Juliet stared down the other team, then threw the ball toward Marc and hollered, "Clasium!"

"It's calcium," Sami corrected.

"That's what I said."

Marc caught the ball and called back, "Milk!"

Linda Sands made an approving grunt and marked off several boxes on her chart. Bowman clenched his fist in victory, but not for calcium. He and Maisy had gotten another box marked off on the rubric.

Also, he'd asked her out and she'd said yes.

His phone buzzed in his back pocket, but he wasn't going to check it. Piper, who'd been incommunicado for weeks, was now texting constantly, urging him to call her for help planning this date. He wasn't gonna do that. He'd made a plan to ace the rubric and it was going brilliantly. What did he need Piper's help for?

The afternoon sped along to the sound of the kids' laughter and Linda's appreciative grunts as she checked off boxes on her rubric. She was particularly pleased with "The Veggie Song." Who knew representatives from the Healthy Lives Institute were such Beyoncé fans?

The closer they got to the end of the day, the harder it was to keep his head in the game. By the time four o'clock rolled around, it was all Bowman could do not to yell *"Scat!"* and herd everybody off the property, so he could take a shower and get ready for the evening.

But, as usual, the kids hung around, their parents chatted, all while Bowman tried to keep from staring at Maisy.

"What are you going to name him?" Kai asked.

He didn't have to ask who they were talking about. Dulce's foal was pretty much the only topic of conversation Kai was interested in today.

"I don't know. My mom does most of the naming. She's got a whole system that helps us track which year a horse was born, and who the parents are."

"I could think of some good names."

"I bet you could. I'll let my mom know you're interested in helping out."

Kai scowled. "I wish I could be there to help when he's born."

"The middle of the night's kinda late to stay after camp."

Kai kicked the dirt. Bowman got it. He'd be reacting the same way.

"Well, I'll be taking off," Linda announced.

Bowman waved absently, keeping his focus on Kai. Maisy tugged at his sleeve.

What? he asked, not bothering to say the word because it was clearly implied. Maisy gestured to Linda, suggesting something about stopping what they were doing to throw a farewell parade for this woman neither of them was particularly fond of. Bowman didn't heave a sigh. Maisy had been cool when she arrived, he could be cool when she left.

He approached Linda and nodded, prepared to force out the words *nice to have you here.* But Maisy spoke first. "So great to see you, Linda! Will you be back next week?"

"I'll come for the closing presentation from the kids. You two are doing fantastic. As a rule, I don't give people mastery marks on the second-round observation, but you earned four."

Maisy's brow furrowed, like she was going to argue about when and where a person should be allowed to get a check in the mastery box. Bowman put a hand on her arm, subtly reminding her that two weeks ago she was in a complete panic about this and was pretty sure they were going to fail.

"Thanks," Bowman said. It took strength to draw up the next few words, but if it kept Maisy from talking right now, it was worth it. "We're having a great time."

Linda nodded, like Bowman had said the right thing. "Speaking of a great time, I have an offer for you both."

Bowman prayed this offer had nothing to do with spending one more minute in Linda's company.

"Maisy, we know you'll be very busy, starting up with the clinic. But we've been so impressed by the way you connect with children."

Bowman placed a hand on Maisy's back. She'd been so stressed about working with kids, and here she was, two weeks in and already impressing others with her skills.

Linda then gestured to him. "And Bowman's just a natural."

Maisy turned a mischievous grin on him. "That's our Bowman. A natural with kids. And everyone, really."

At that comment he intended to remove his hand from her back and playfully tap her arm, but somehow he wound up running his hand along her shoulders instead.

"There's funding at the HL Institute to continue working with some of these kids. If you're interested, we would be willing to fund an extension onto camp with weekly horse-back-riding lessons. We'd ask you to identify about five of these kids who, for whatever reason, might benefit from more time on the ranch and with the two of you. Maybe kids who have shown a lot of growth this week, or who have specific social or emotional needs."

Bowman glanced down at Maisy.

Kai, Liya, Juliet.

But working with the kids, once a week? Was he ready for that? At the beginning, he couldn't wait for this to be over. Now he was dreading the end.

This wasn't his life, though. He was a fire-fighter, and free time was spent with his family, or rock climbing. Could he sign on to spending more time with these kids? That was a big commitment.

Of course, it would also mean getting to spend a lot more time with Maisy.

Kai was slowly backing away from the group, likely trying to slip back in the barn in hopes that Dulce was having her baby right now. That was one kid who could seriously benefit from more time on the ranch.

Bowman didn't know what to say. Maisy, of course, said the exact right thing. "Thank you, Linda. That's a wonderful offer. We'll think about it."

CHAPTER FOURTEEN

BOWMAN PARKED HIS truck under the locust trees in front of Maisy's cottage and pulled the scrap of paper off the dashboard.

> Take Maisy to the chocolate shop.
>
> Get a family special from Hunter.
>
> Show her Second Chance Cowgirl and introduce her to Christy Jones.
>
> Go to the yarn shop.
>
> Dance with Maisy as the band plays in the park.

He grinned. This was going to be so much better than the bad dates Maisy had been on since arriving in Outcrop. A slam dunk, red point, home run.

He hopped out of the truck and jogged up the steps to her front door.

At which point he realized that while he'd put considerable energy into planning this date, he hadn't given any thought into what he was wearing. He looked down at himself. His jeans were pretty old, but they *were* clean.

There was a stain on his T-shirt. Did he own a not-stained T-shirt? There was a full drawer of nice clothing his sisters bought him that he didn't wear. He really should have looked in there. But it would be fine. Maisy didn't care about stuff like that.

Or did she?

Bowman reached up to knock on the door, just as Maisy opened it.

She was wearing another sundress.

Bowman grinned as he took in the sky-blue dress that echoed the color of her eyes. She always looked good, but this was beyond pretty. *How often did she wear dresses?* When he thought of her, which was a lot of the time these days, he pictured her in the jeans and tank tops she wore to camp. But she was a doctor, too. Would she wear a white lab coat over her jeans and tank top? Or did doctors wear jeans? He'd never noticed. But Maisy would look great in a lab coat, too.

"What?" she asked.

Bowman shook his head. "Nothing. Hi. You ready?"

She eyed him suspiciously but nodded. "I guess so?"

Bowman opened his mouth to tell her how pretty she looked, but she probably already knew.

He gestured for her to walk with him up

her street to the town square. Music floated down from the festival. Bowman moved with the music. It inspired him to reach for Maisy's hand.

Or was that a first-date thing? He couldn't imagine why it wouldn't be, but he literally didn't know. His hand was hovering out in space between them, not taking hers, just failing around in indecision.

Maybe he should have consulted Piper about hand-holding.

Maisy solved the problem by putting her hands in the pockets of her dress.

"A group of teachers at the high school have a cover band," he told her, waving in the direction of the music. "They cover Eagles songs."

"Just the Eagles?"

"Pretty much."

"Why?"

"Because—Eagles."

"Eagles?" she asked.

"Right. Eagles. Like the Outcrop Eagles." The beat thrummed in the sultry evening air, matching the beating of his heart. It was difficult to come up with anything to say, or even think, for that matter.

They reached the square. A crowd had gathered on the lawn, and booths lined the street, running up Main all the way to OHTAF. A line of people stood in front of the Eighty Local stand.

Maisy paused in the middle of the crowd, taking in the people, the lights strung overhead, the cheerful noise. Bowman felt eyes on them, which made sense because Maisy was so beautiful.

He gazed down at her, ready to say just that, when a phone snapped in his face.

"OMG! You're Bowman Wallace!"

Bowman blinked, turning to two women, one of whom held up a phone and was recording a video of him. Frustration, like a swarm of gnats, enclosed around him. He put a hand on Maisy's back, like she was the one who needed protection from these women. He started to speak, but one of the women spoke first.

"Can I take a selfie with you?"

Bowman lashed around in his brain for the right words, and came up with "No."

The woman had already positioned herself with him and had her phone out. "No?"

Bowman shook his head. When she didn't budge, Bowman pressed his hand on the small of Maisy's back and walked away.

"You're right," the woman told her friend, "he is super rude."

That felt unfair. He'd been minding his own business, or rather trying to mind Maisy's business, when they'd approached him. Was it rude to not want to be interrupted on what he was hoping was a fantastic date?

Bowman stopped walking. What should he do? Turn around and tell them he wasn't rude? Try to be nice about people taking pictures of him without asking?

He shook out his shoulders and returned his focus to Maisy. He had a plan and should probably stick to it. "Want to go to the chocolate shop?"

"Sure." She didn't start walking, but kept her blue eyes focused on him as she gestured back to the women. "Is that normal?"

He shrugged. "It's just the posters. It's been weird."

She looked confused, and that made him even more frustrated. He was finally on this date and ten minutes in something had gone wrong. But if he'd learned anything from Maisy over the last few weeks, it was that when things go sideways, you just push through.

"Chocolate?"

"Yes. Yummers." She bit her bottom lip as she glanced up at him. "Are we going to save the chocolates for dessert?"

"No, this is predessert. Then we'll have dinner. Dessert is ice cream."

She laughed. He hadn't intended the suggestion to be a joke, but it still felt nice to hear her laugh. He held open the door and Maisy stepped into the shop.

It was really crowded. Uncomfortably so. Maisy said something to him, but he couldn't make out her words. The customers jostled against one another, yelling orders to the women who ran the shop.

Maisy turned to him, saying something else, a smile bright on her face. Unfortunately, Bowman couldn't understand her over the din. There were too many people in this shop. When he'd written "take Maisy to the chocolate shop" in his plan, he'd imagined they'd have the place to themselves. This felt more like a trendy city nightclub than Outcrop.

"You know what you want?" Georgie asked from behind the counter.

Bowman looked down at Maisy. "Do you want some chocolate?"

"Um...are *you* having chocolate?"

Bowman glanced around him. What he wanted right now was out of this store. "It's really crowded in here."

"It is."

He pointed to the door. "Do you want to just...go?"

She looked confused, but she nodded. They

could come back here later, when it wasn't such a zoo.

Bowman felt better as they headed out of the shop, but the town was still packed. People kept talking at him. At camp, when he was talked out, Maisy would often sense his need for a break and pick up the slack. Unfortunately, he knew these people and she didn't. And tonight, everyone was relentlessly social. Why people kept talking to him when he was clearly on a date was beyond him.

"Want to go see what Hunter's got for us?"

"Yeah, that sounds great." Maisy took a few steps toward the line, but Bowman grabbed her hand and pulled her back. She glanced at her hand in his, then up into his eyes.

"Come on." He tugged her hand, leading her to the back of the booth.

His brother broke into a smile when he saw them approach. "I hope you're hungry."

"Yeah. Whatcha got?"

Hunter picked up a few random baskets containing other people's messed-up orders. Bowman held them out to Maisy so she could choose first. His parents were working, along with Jackson. Ordinarily he'd be in the booth, too, but tonight was about showing Maisy around town.

"Where's Ash?" he asked.

"Keeping an eye on Dulce. He thinks she'll be fine but wanted to be there just in case."

Bowman nodded. "I'm planning on heading into the barn once we finish up here." He looked down at Maisy. Would she want to come out and be there for the birth, too? That would make this the perfect date. Great company, Eighty Local food, good music, a favorite horse giving birth.

They chatted with the family while eating their meals. Or Maisy chatted and Bowman enjoyed watching her connect with his parents.

"What have you seen so far?" Mom asked Maisy.

"Hmm. The inside of the chocolate shop? And the back of this booth."

"Literally the two best things in this town," Clara said. "But also, Second Chance Cowgirl."

Bowman consulted his slip of paper. "That's where we're heading next."

"*You're* going into a clothing shop?" Clara asked.

Bowman glared at her. This was a date. He'd have thought as a matchmaker she'd have it together.

"Yep. And then the yarn shop."

Mom and Clara exchanged a look that Bowman chose not to acknowledge. Clara and Jet had spent time in the yarn shop when they were at Outcrop Outside, and they were getting married in six weeks. Women liked yarn, apparently.

The crowd thinned as they headed down Main. Coach was standing outside Second Chance Cowgirl, talking up Christy's products. Bowman didn't know anything about women's clothing, but he knew his sisters loved this place, and his former football coach was in love with the owner. That was enough of a recommendation for him.

"Hey, Coach." Bowman nodded.

"It's Bowman and Dr. Maisy Martin. Enjoying yourselves?"

"This is great!" Maisy gestured to the festival.

"Is Christy in? I thought Maisy should meet her."

Coach opened the door. "Everyone should meet her."

Two steps into the shop, Bowman noticed Holly Banks and several women from the Bend Equestrian Society. His heart sank. He knew he had to be polite to these women since they'd taken a risk and booked Hunter's unfinished events center for their holiday gala. But right now, his sociability was hanging by a thread. On a normal day he'd just exit, but being in Second Chance Cowgirl was part of his plan for Maisy.

"What do you think?" Maisy held up a vintage crusher hat. She flipped it upside down and looked at the label. "It's a Stetson, like yours."

He took the hat from her to examine it. It was a Stetson, but not like his at all. It was a pretty fawn color, smaller than most Western hats, but it would still keep the sun out of her face. Bowman placed the hat on her head. It fit her perfectly; her blue eyes looked up at him from right under the rim.

He grinned. "Now you're an Outcrop local."

She touched the brim, imitating him.

It took his breath away. She was so beautiful, and so…right. Everything about Maisy enthralled him: her humor, her determination, her intelligence. And she was smiling at him.

Piper had told him he'd need to step up if he was interested in Maisy, and he was all in. It didn't matter how steep the steps got.

"Well, that looks nice," a voice said, interrupting his thoughts.

Bowman managed to take his eyes off Maisy to greet Christy Jones.

"Hey, Christy. This is Doc Martin."

Maisy sighed patiently.

"Doctor Maisy Martin," Bowman amended.

"It's lovely to meet you." Christy was good at talking to everyone. Bowman relaxed and let her chat with Maisy. He didn't track their words, just watched with pleasure as the women connected.

They were discussing something—second-hand dresses, the clinic, he wasn't really sure. Bowman reached up to Maisy's hat and untied the ribbon holding the price tag. He checked it, then pulled cash out of his wallet and handed both to Christy.

"You're taking the hat?" she asked, smiling first at him, then Maisy.

Bowman wasn't sure how to respond. Obviously, they were going to take the hat. Had she not noticed how stunning Maisy was in it?

Maisy touched the hat tentatively, then glanced at him. "Thank you."

He looked into her eyes, feeling himself start to flush. He didn't know what to say but tried to tell her, anyway.

"Hi, Bowman."

He looked up to see Holly and the other women from the Bend Equestrian Society approaching. He took a half step in front of Maisy. "Hi, Holly. Shawna." He nodded at the third woman but could not remember her name for the life of him.

The gnats of frustration swarmed again. It

was taking all his energy to be social, and he needed to focus that energy on Maisy, not on every other person who felt like they wanted to chat today. But he wasn't going to do anything to jeopardize his brother's success. He had to talk to them. Period.

Maisy didn't have to, though. He'd protect her from the chatter of the horse ladies. When he was finished with them, they'd go to the yarn shop, then dancing in the park. His heart beat in anticipation.

Just get through this one conversation.

He moved to block Maisy completely, then tried to smile at the intruding women. "How are you all this evening?"

MAISY HAD NEVER been more confused in her life. This couldn't be a date. If it was, Bowman was the worst person at dating in the known universe. Which was entirely possible, given that the two of them were currently drifting aimlessly through a yarn shop.

She sifted through the data again.

Bowman had asked her out, and met her at her house. *Date.*

He made no comment about how she looked, or that it was nice to see her. *Not a date.*

He took her into a chocolate shop. *Date.*

They left before buying any chocolate. *Not a date.*

He grabbed family specials from Eighty Local. She felt like on any normal scale, buying someone dinner was more romantic than snagging leftovers. But Bowman wasn't to be measured on any type of normal scale. And dinner had been amazing. She'd call dinner *date-neutral.*

Buying her a fantastic hat representative of her putting down roots in Outcrop and staring into her eyes as he set it on her head. *Date, date-y, date-date!*

But then the women.

She couldn't blame him for his responses to the groupies. She wasn't going to blame those women, either. Hadn't she felt the same way when she saw his poster for the first time? In fact, she still had a copy of that poster, uncrumpled and folded up in her living room. She didn't fault the random girls with their phones, and she knew Bowman well enough by now to understand this was exactly the type of situation he didn't handle well. No, the clincher was the women from the equestrian society.

Throughout the evening Bowman had haphazardly introduced her to people. In some instances, like Christy Jones, he'd drawn her into a conversation, but then stepped back as she spoke. But in others, he didn't introduce her at all. The women from the equestrian society looked to be professional women, about her age. Bowman not only failed to introduce her, but he'd also stepped in front of her so she couldn't even introduce herself. Was that weird?

But then there was the way he looked at her. She'd never seen a man's eyes so full of… Well, she didn't know what his eyes were full of. Hope, excitement, more than that?

No, stop. The real clincher, which was going to clinch this decision, no more debating, was that she didn't *want* this to be a date. Bowman was gorgeous, funny, smart and kind. And he was going to get himself killed with his penchant for danger. She'd seen the climbing chalk on the west side of Fort Rock, heard the stories of his daring saves as a member of the fire department. She was already falling for him, and it had to stop, now. They were friends. She was not going to get any more lost in love with him, no matter what his intentions for the evening.

They were two friends, out for a fun evening. And those friends were currently standing in the middle of a yarn shop, neither of them with any sense of what a person did with yarn.

He glanced at her like he sometimes did at

camp, as though she was supposed to know what to do next.

She picked up a soft, yellow skein of yarn. “This one is nice.”

“Yeah.” He nodded.

She set down the yarn and wandered farther into the store. Had she said something to indicate she liked yarn?

“It’s not so crowded in here.”

“That’s true.” Did they come in for some privacy? Maisy glanced around. The store was less crowded, but there were several people milling about, discussing various yarn issues.

Bowman picked up the yarn she’d dropped and placed it across the back of his hand like a wig for a puppet. “Hello, Doc,” he said in a funny voice, hand talking to her. Maisy burst out laughing.

“I don’t think I’m getting enough sleep,” the hand said, twisting like a Muppet. “I can’t stop yarning all day.”

Maisy giggled harder as Bowman’s hand continued to make bad puns. How was this happening? After all her careful planning, good decisions, medical school, successful residency…she was in a yarn shop with the Firefighter of the Year, falling even harder for him as he goofed around with wool.

Leave it to Bowman Wallace to make impromptu puppeteering unreasonably attractive.

Maisy pulled in a breath against the laughter, wiping tears from her eyes as she turned away from Bowman so she could stop laughing while growing even more attached to him.

The door opened, letting in warm air, music and the scent of barbecue, along with Josh Hanson and an older woman.

"Hi, Maisy!"

The laughter washed out of her belly as her system went on alert. She couldn't figure out if Bowman had planned this as a date or not, but Josh had been perfectly clear last weekend. They'd had a nice time, and he wanted to see her again.

And Josh was the type of good, sensible man she wanted to want. Sure, he was a firefighter, but cautiously brave where Bowman was reckless. He considered the risks—Bowman just took them.

"Hello."

"Mom—" he turned to the woman "—this is Maisy Martin, the woman I was telling you about. Maisy, this is my mom, Debra."

As Maisy greeted Debra, Bowman moved quickly to her side. "Hey, Josh."

Josh slapped Bowman on the back. "And this is Bowman."

"The famous Bowman!" Debra said. "Sami can't stop talking about you."

"To be fair, she can't stop talking about Maisy, either."

Bowman grinned. "Sami does like to talk."

Josh and Debra laughed. Maisy glanced around the store for an escape route.

Then she squared her shoulders. This was no big deal. She'd been out with Josh. She might be out with Bowman right now. Confident young medical professional examining her options, that was her. There was nothing wrong with this.

"I like your hat," Josh said, playfully batting the brim.

Bowman bristled.

Okay, there was *technically* nothing wrong with this, but Josh and Bowman had a complicated relationship. It didn't need any more fodder for tension. And her date with Josh was the only date she hadn't told Bowman about.

"Are we still on for Saturday?" Josh asked. "There's a great new restaurant in Bend. I thought we could drive over and check it out."

"I'm babysitting," Debra said, thrilled to be in on the action.

Maisy's face burned. "Yes?" she finally said.

Ugh. I'm pulling out the question mark now? Literally the worst habit.

Bowman turned to her, hurt evident in his eyes. His disappointment spread to her, like flames in a high wind.

"Josh?" was all he said to her, but the implications were clear.

This *was* a date, with her friend, whom she adored and was trying really hard not to get any more attached to.

Bowman felt deeply, she knew this. He didn't express those feelings, but she knew how intense they were. He shook his head, then glanced up at the fluorescent lights.

When he looked back down, his gaze connected with Maisy's and she clearly heard everything he wanted to say.

You didn't tell me about Josh.

I went out on a limb with this, with you, with camp.

Am I one of the frogs, just some guy you're comparing with others?

Fix this. Take back your yes *to Josh and tell him it's me.*

But none of this came out. Bowman took one step back, then another. "Yeah. You know what, I gotta get out of here."

Maisy set a hand on his arm. He gazed down at her fingers, then closed his eyes momentarily. He sighed, pulling away, and took long steps toward the door.

"Hey. Could you—" Maisy batted around for the correct word as she called after him "—stop? Wait."

"I'm sorry." Josh pointed to Bowman. "Were you two…on a date?"

Wouldn't we all like to know?

"I…um. We were just at the festival."

"How many men *are* you dating?" Debra asked, placing a protective hand on her son's shoulder. Several other patrons raised their heads to observe the action. This was probably the most drama the yarn shop had ever seen. Or any yarn shop.

Bowman paused at the door, his shoulders expanding with a breath. Then he jogged back to her and held out a slip of paper. "Here's an outline for the evening, just in case you wanted to use this as part of your evaluation system."

Maisy glanced down at the paper.

A step-by-step plan for their date. The evening hadn't been a haphazard conglomeration of random incidents, but Bowman's attempt to show her the best of Outcrop Outside.

"Guess you make me feel like planning," he'd told her in the stables as he handed her the annotated HLI rubric.

She'd been reckless with Bowman's feelings, assuming that because he was the center of attention for so many women, she couldn't be having an impact on him.

Bowman had been changed by this experience, too. By her.

She glanced up to see him pull the rim of his Stetson low over his eyes, but not before she caught the expression of hurt and disappointment on his face. Then he was gone, disappearing into the crowd. And there was no way they'd be dancing in the park together now.

CHAPTER FIFTEEN

BOWMAN STRODE AWAY from the festival, music and chatter dogging him as he made his way to his truck. This was not the ending to the date he'd had in mind. Emotions, strong and muddy, like boiling currents in the Deschutes River, washed through him, pulling him down. There were no words for this emotion. And right now, he didn't want to articulate his feelings, or even feel them.

He'd left Maisy with Josh at the festival. It didn't matter. She was going to use her superscientific evaluation system and pick the "right" guy, and he wasn't interested in being measured up against everyone else. He liked Maisy. He liked her so, so much. But they didn't fit together. That was obvious from day one. His sisters always said you had to "know your core values and find someone who shares them." That was fine. Josh and Maisy could sit around and discuss protocol and rubrics into their old age together if they wanted. It didn't matter.

Bowman hoisted himself into his truck and started the engine, barely avoiding squealing his tires as he raced away from Maisy's house. The truck started chiming at him almost immediately, coercing him to put on a seat belt. Bowman kept driving.

An inner voice told him things might not be as bad as he thought. Bowman disagreed. The voice, which sounded a lot like Piper, suggested it was okay not to have a stellar first date—sometimes you have to try again.

Bowman mentally crossed his arms over his chest and turned away. The voice started to ramble on about how he'd gotten to know Maisy on his home turf, where he was comfortable. Every time they'd been together it was with the horses or his family, and it made sense he was easier at home than in town with everybody coming up to him all the time. He knew Maisy was dating, the voice said, and Josh was a smart guy, so, of course, he would ask her out.

Bowman turned up the radio to drown out the noise in his head. He loved this Eric Church song, but the music didn't roll through him like it should have.

And when a man doesn't even feel like singing along to "Record Year," that's a problem.

Bowman pulled onto the highway. A passing

car flashed its lights at him. Bowman flipped on his headlights, grumbling at the other car under his breath. The moon was nearly full; he'd driven on cloudy days with less light than there was right now.

It felt like forever before he finally pulled onto Wallace Creek Road. Cresting the hill before the ranch, he waited for his heart rate to steady, and to feel better, like he always did when returning home. Tonight the calm refused to come.

He parked next to the bunkhouse, slamming the truck door behind him. He was sick of all this intense feeling. The last few weeks had been a freak weather pattern of battling emotions—a deluge of rains, spectacularly bright moments and crop-destroying hailstorms.

Bowman approached the bunkhouse instinctively, but stopped before he hit the stoop. These wild emotions would follow him inside, keep him up, as though he had the whole Outcrop Eagles cover band in his head, making noise. He glanced back to where the moon hung in the sky. There was plenty of light, and it was still early. He stalked back to the truck, grabbed his climbing shoes out of the back and threw his phone onto the driver's seat. Fort Rock peaked out through the pine trees. Bowman started at a jog, then broke into a run, relishing the burning in his lungs and the pounding of his blood over the emotions. The grass shimmered in the moonlight. He was alone, and outside on his family's ranch.

Bowman took a wide berth around the rock, avoiding the east side, where he and Maisy played with the kids. He didn't want to think about her, didn't want to evaluate what went wrong, or if things had any hope of going right. He was sick of thinking.

The west side of Fort Rock was open to the night air, each climbing route illuminated in the moonlight. Bowman caught his breath as the routes winked out at him, one after the next. He hadn't been climbing in a while. The movement and focus would absorb him, block out any thoughts other than where and how to move next.

Bowman kicked off his boots and put on the climbing shoes. The easier routes on the rock didn't rise more than twenty feet and were all clustered at the north end. The ground broke away to the southwest, exposing the full length of the rock where it hung over Wallace Creek. At this time of year, water still rushed through the gully, but it was at its lowest point in the year. The boulders that barely poked through the water in spring were fully exposed in August. If he fell, it would be onto those boulders. So he needed to not fall.

Today, everyone is going to learn to be responsible for their own safety—he'd told the kids that the first day they'd come to Fort Rock. *Sometimes that means backing down when something feels wrong, and sometimes it means having an escape route if it gets sketchy.*

He should have made a plan for his safety before asking Maisy out. He hadn't thought through what would happen if the date went wrong. Now he still had to be around her for another week. When that was over, she'd be the doctor in town and he really *did* spend a lot of time in the clinic.

Bowman rested his hands on the rock. It was still warm, even as the air cooled around him. He pressed his palm against the rock, hiking up a foot and reaching for a hold above his head. A gust of wind swept past the rock, reminding him of Maisy's sharp intake of breath whenever she felt like things were getting out-of-hand dangerous. He kept climbing, taking an easy route, and crested the top of the rock quickly. He could imagine her, arms crossed, chin raised, assuming her very posture would make him stop doing whatever it was she didn't like. In response to the memory, he jumped off the rock at the north end and jogged back around toward the creek. He picked a longer, more difficult line that veered over the drop-off. He focused. Each move had to be made with precision. The inherent danger helped wipe Maisy and all the disappointment from his mind. Bowman's muscles tensed as he made one difficult move, then another.

Again, he crested the rock. His breath came out ragged from the effort. The moon was huge, illuminating the land in shades of gray. Bowman wondered if Maisy was looking up at the moon, too.

Which was stupid. She was probably back inside her house, evaluating the traits of various men she knew on a graph, running calculations to see who would be the best fit.

Bowman stalked along the edge of the rock, then launched off the north side. His climbing shoes pinched his feet as he trotted back to the hardest routes. On an arête at the southern tip of the rock was a challenging climb. He'd done it on a rope with Hunter a couple of times. The route was sketchy, but doable. He'd slipped on a tricky move toward the top before, unable to muster the mental and physical intensity at the right moment. But tonight he'd be fine, he could handle it.

Bowman stretched, then approached the rock. There was no space for Maisy, or wondering how he was going to get through the next week of camp, or the rest of his life with her in town. He started the climb. Rock came into sharp focus in the moonlight. The route got harder, the ground receded below. He regulated his breathing to help with the effort of the climb. Muscles in his calves, his core and his forearms engaged, burned against the effort. He shook out a cramp in his hand, found a good foothold to balance on as he rolled a shoulder. Before long there was nothing but rock and moonlight, breath and heartbeat.

MAISY PAWED HER phone off the nightstand beside her.

Was someone honestly calling at 1:00 a.m.?

She bolted upright in bed.

Someone was calling at 1:00 a.m.

"Hello?"

"Maisy. This is Ash. Have you seen Bowman?"

Fear sliced through her, along with a deep sense of confirmation. This was the call she'd been waiting for since the day she'd met him.

Unable to speak, she shook her head. Ash continued, "Dulce is giving birth and she's pretty distressed. I think the foal is positioned fine, but she could use Bowman singing to her." Ash chuckled, like there was nothing out of the ordinary about Bowman having gone missing and the only problem was that he needed to sing to a horse.

Maisy steadied her voice. "He took off around nine. Have there been any accidents reported on the highway?"

"I'm sure he's fine. Sorry to bother you. He was pretty excited about showing you Outcrop Outside this evening and I thought he might have gotten carried away and was still dragging you around town."

Maisy wanted to scream at Ash. It was the middle of the night, he couldn't find his danger-courting brother and he was sure everything was fine?

"I'll come out." Maisy gave in to the impulse. "I'm not a vet but I can probably help."

"We got it," Ash said.

"But what if—" Maisy bit down hard on her lip to keep from finishing the sentence. What if Bowman needed a doctor when they found him?

"Let me come out."

Ash paused, then said kindly, "Maisy, I'm sure he's fine."

Fear whipped through her, pushing tears to the corners of her eyes.

What if he's not?

Ash, who no one could ever assume was

as intuitive as Bowman, but seemed to have a pretty good sense of this situation, finally said, “It would be great if you wanted to come out and check on Dulce. I could use another set of hands.”

Maisy was already stepping into her jeans. “I’ll be there in ten minutes.”

“Drive safe.”

The familiar panic roared in her head as she made her way into her clothes, out the door and into the Jeep. She gripped the wheel to stop the shaking in her hands.

She’d hurt Bowman. That was plain on his face when he’d walked away, leaving her talking to Josh. In truth, she hadn’t known she possessed the power to hurt him. Still, if he’d walked off and done something stupid…

Maisy slammed her palm against the driver’s wheel. This *wasn’t* her fault. If she’d hurt Bowman it was unintentional. She didn’t have the information she needed to act appropriately. He should have told her this was a date, and been clear about his feelings.

Her intuition, long ignored and mistrusted, forced her back to the truth. She should have been honest with him, too. She’d never told Bowman about the date with Josh because she sensed how complicated the relationship was.

No one had to lay that out for her in charts and graphs.

And now Bowman was missing, and probably hurt.

As a scientist, as a thinking adult, she knew that Bowman's actions were beyond her control. If he did something stupid and got hurt, that was on him and him alone. But as a child shaped by trauma, she would take all the blame for this tragedy, just as she had the last time.

You couldn't keep an eye on him for two seconds?

The highway ahead of her blurred and Maisy forced herself to pull in deep breaths. Running herself off the road wouldn't help the situation.

And it was possible there was no situation. Maybe Bowman was out for a hike. Or maybe he went for a drink with one of the women he didn't introduce her to.

Yeah, because Bowman just *loved* going to crowded bars with people he didn't know very well…

No, he had to be at the ranch. He knew Dulce was close to giving birth. Surely, he was just out for a hike. He wouldn't abandon this horse he adored as she was about to give birth.

Unless he was really upset. Because she'd hurt him.

Maisy wiped at her tears as she pulled onto

Wallace Creek Drive. She parked by the barn, drawing on all of her strength as she opened the car door.

Moonlight washed across the property, soaking everything in a milky haze. Maisy stood by her Jeep, afraid to go to the barn, where Ash would have no news of Bowman, and afraid to stay where she was.

Warm, August air blew across the property, bringing the snippet of a Motown song with it. Maisy closed her eyes, letting the air and the song swirl through her.

Her lids popped open.

Someone was singing Motown.

Maisy sprinted to the stables, struggling to open the bypass door. Tears blurred her vision but she could make out two men, one horse and a newborn foal.

BOWMAN CONTINUED TO crouch next to Dulce as Ash shifted the newborn up to her head. Dulce nudged the foal with her nose, then began to lick her. The foal twitched closer to her.

"She's a good momma," Ash said.

Bowman nodded, keeping a hand on Dulce's neck. He was furious with himself for leaving her alone. He'd been worried about this pregnancy for weeks, and on the night she needed him he was out heartbreak climbing? He needed to get it together.

"Bowman?"

He glanced up at Maisy's voice, his eyes meeting hers and all thoughts of getting anything together evaporated. Her skin was mottled red, tears streaked her face. She looked angry and relieved at the same time.

Ash cleared his throat. "I'll let you two handle this." He tipped his hat to Maisy, then gave Bowman a look. "When I couldn't find you, I gave Maisy a call." Maisy wiped at the tears now flowing down her face. "She offered to come out and help with Dulce."

One look at Maisy suggested Dulce had very little to do with her decision to hightail it out to the ranch.

"Thanks," Bowman said.

Ash disappeared down the aisle. Maisy watched him go, then walked up to the stall gate, tears rolling down her cheeks. She pushed them back with the palm of her hand. "Is Dulce okay?"

Dulce answered the question on her own, standing abruptly and licking the foal in earnest.

Bowman slipped out of the stall, closing the gate behind him. "She did great."

Maisy was still crying, still focused on the

momma and baby. The little guy untangled his legs and tried to stand but landed back on the ground.

"You okay?"

"Am *I* okay?" She turned to him, scared and furious, the way she got sometimes. "I'm not the one who went missing tonight."

Bowman let out a breath. Nothing like someone hurting your feelings, then getting mad at you for trying to deal with them. "I needed to cool off."

Maisy pressed her lips together, unable or unwilling to see his point of view. He moved away from the stall. Dulce and her foal didn't need to be in on this.

"What am I supposed to say here? I thought..." He trailed off. It didn't matter what he thought. He was wrong, and there was no use stewing about it or getting mad at Maisy for being Maisy.

"Where were you?" she asked.

Bowman ran his hands through his hair. She'd get even angrier when he told her.

And there was a part of him that wanted to make her angry.

"I was bouldering. Spent some time on Fort Rock. It was beautiful."

Her eyes raced along the ground. "On the east side, under the pine trees?"

"On the west side. Over the creek."

A flush raced up Maisy's neck. "Why? Why do you have to climb like that? Why are you constantly putting yourself in danger?"

"I wasn't in danger."

"You weren't? Fifty feet off the ground, over boulders, no rope? That's not dangerous?"

Bowman stalked over to the crossties, where one of the kids had left out a currycomb. He kept his back to Maisy as he shelved it.

"Bowman, you could have slipped and died."

He focused on the grooming equipment as he spoke. "You know what people die of in America? Heart disease. Cancer. Auto accidents. Very few people die bouldering."

"Because most people don't go bouldering, alone, in the middle of the night."

"Right. Instead, they don't take care of themselves, let stress eat away at them, drive themselves to an early grave. I don't see you out there yelling at those guys."

"I promise to start, the minute I get set up at the clinic, but right now we're talking about you. Why would you do that?"

Bowman finally turned around, letting his gaze connect with Maisy's. "Because I was hurt, and tired of thinking about it."

Maisy blinked. She took a step toward him, then stopped.

It felt like all the words he'd held back over the years were unleashed. He walked up to her, allowing himself to experience the pain of how precious she was to him. "I mean… Josh? Really? You couldn't have told me about Josh?"

"I didn't know—"

"You can do whatever you're going to do. That's your call, Maisy. But if you want to line up all the men you know and compare all their pros and cons, take me out of the picture."

He started to walk past her when her hand shot out and caught his arm. Her fingers ran down his forearm, past his wrist, then she settled her palm against his, intertwining their fingers. Bowman gazed down at her hand in his.

"There is no comparison to you, Bowman."

Her gaze met his, sweeping the breath out of him. She meant it. She felt this, too. But *how*, if she felt anything like he did, could she even consider these other guys?

Bowman took her other hand, willing her to say more. To explain away the pain threatening to crack his chest.

Maisy closed her eyes and swallowed. Feeling his request, she nodded. "I have… I have something I want to show you. I need to show you."

She tugged at his hand, leading him to a hay

bale. He sat next to her, his body turning to hers instinctively, protectively.

She swallowed hard, then pulled out her phone. She tapped the screen, her fingers navigating by rote, as though she had a system for digging back into a certain digital memory. Finally, she pulled in a deep breath and handed him the phone. Bowman was staring at a picture of a boy a few years younger than Kai, straddling a bicycle, a big grin on his face.

She blinked hard and opened her mouth to speak but wasn't able to get anything out. Bowman wrapped an arm around her, then kissed the top of her head. She snuggled closer to him.

"That's my brother."

Bowman took another look at the phone, his brow furrowed. "I thought you didn't have any siblings."

"I don't. Anymore." She pressed her lips together and glanced up at him. "Elliot died. He was five. I was eight."

Bowman pulled her to his chest, tucking his chin over her head. Silently, he urged her to release the sadness into him. She shuddered, then relaxed.

"Elliot died," she said again. "He was in a bike accident. It was… He just rode out into the street. The passing car barely bumped him, but he hit his head on the pavement, then… he died."

Bowman wrapped his arms tighter around her.

"My mom never got over it. I don't blame her. I don't know how you *could* get over it."

Bowman bent his head to look into her eyes. There were no words to say how sorry he was, to communicate how wrong it was that her family had to go through this.

She pulled in a stuttered breath. "It was horrible for my parents. I can't imagine anything worse. I don't know how they got out of bed, day after day."

He brushed his fingertips across her cheek, pushing the tears away, inviting her to say more.

"My mom didn't mean to blame me. I don't think she even remembers blaming me—" Maisy's throat seemed to close up, the painful memories shifting through her eyes. Her voice was thin, her face completely white as she said, "She thought I should have been watching him. No one told me to watch him, but I should have been. I didn't know I was supposed to."

I need to know what's expected of me, she'd said the first day Linda Sands arrived. *I don't want to be held responsible for things I didn't know I was supposed to be doing.*

He pulled her close again and whispered against her hair, "It wasn't your fault."

She nodded, eyes closed tight. Everything came into focus: the plans, the rubrics, the difficulty she had letting the time with the kids unfold naturally. He'd been annoyed with her for fears that were deeply wired in her past.

"I became a doctor. I've been working *so hard* to become a doctor, so I could… It sounds stupid now. I became a doctor to try to make up for his death. But nothing can make up for it."

"Maisy, I'm amazed by you."

She opened her eyes, questioning him.

"Here I was, whining about having to work with kids. You must have felt that pressure and fear every minute."

"It's been pretty hard. But good for me, too." She gave him the glimmer of a smile. "I'm so glad we did this."

"Me, too." He'd been trying at camp, with the kids, with her. Now he was going to try even harder.

Maisy slipped a hand along the side of his face. "I've been worried about you since I saw your poster, two days before I even met you."

Bowman melted at her words. He turned his face and kissed her palm. "You don't have to worry about me."

"But don't you see?" She exhaled. "I can't help it. I lost it when Ash called tonight. I was sure you were hurt, or worse."

"I take care of myself, Maisy," he said. It was mostly true.

Bowman leaned forward, wrapped up in her scent of spring flowers. He kissed her cheekbone. Everything around them vanished as his lips brushed across her pretty freckles. She readjusted her palm at the side of his face and looked into his eyes.

"I can't fall in love with you."

The words fell around him, out of order and confusing. He opened his mouth to contradict her. She shook her head, pulling back further.

"I can't fall in love with you. I will worry about you every minute of every day. And then you'll get hurt, and I won't recover."

"Maisy, I'm not going to get hurt."

"But aren't you?"

Frustration tangled up in his chest. "I mean, sometimes, sure. But, Maisy, you're it for me. I know—" He took her hand and placed it on his chest. His heart pulsed with the intentions he had for her. "I know this is what I'm supposed to feel like, the way I feel when I'm with you."

But she couldn't hear him—she shook her head against the truth. He struggled to find words, pressing her hand harder against his heart in an attempt to express how he felt.

"Bowman, please. I'm trying to tell you I can't let myself love you."

"I'm trying to change your mind," he said, exasperated.

"Every time you go to work, or climb on your own, I'm going to lose it like I did tonight."

He tried to speak. Words got trapped, rattling in his skull. *We can work on this. We can compromise. Why won't you let us be together?*

She gazed into his eyes, and he willed her to read every one of his thoughts. But she only said, "It's no use."

The pressure in his chest intensified. Bowman dropped her hand. This wasn't fair. "What, then? I'm supposed to fall in love with you, then quit my job?"

"It's not the job, it's the way you approach it."

He stood, paced away from her, then pushed the argument. "I get you, or rock climbing?"

She raised her chin. "There's nothing wrong with rock climbing. The issue is *you*, climbing alone, without a rope in the middle of the night. You could easily bolt the west side of Fort Rock, put in an anchor at the top and climb on a rope."

This was wrong. Unfair.

"I'm not telling *you* to change. Yeah, we have some differences, but I don't want you to be anything other than..." He gazed at her. *Smart, tough, frustrating, fun.* "I don't want you to be anything other than Maisy Martin."

She broke eye contact. "I'm *not* asking you to change, that's my point. At your core, you thrive on danger. I can't handle worrying about you for the rest of my life. I won't live in fear."

The exhaustion of the day, along with a cold streak of sadness, washed through him. He needed energy to get out the words to help Maisy understand. He swallowed hard, trying to keep the tears dammed up, the emotions locked down in his chest. "So we just say we can't do this? We're not gonna work?"

"We're *not* going to work."

The words finally settled around him. He did like the intensity of danger. He loved the focus that came with stretching the limits of what was possible. He didn't have a death wish, just a desire to live life to the fullest.

He was someone Maisy couldn't love, or didn't want to let herself love. She didn't like who he was on the deepest level, and he didn't have any words to make her feel differently.

The fault lines running through his heart sent tremors through his chest, warning of complete and catastrophic devastation. He needed to get away, out of her company, before he fell apart.

Movement caught his eye. The foal managed to get his legs under him and wobble to a stand. Dulce kept over him, protective.

"Okay." Bowman stood, waiting for Maisy to do the same, to walk away and let him deal with this. She didn't move. He gestured toward Dulce. "I need to stay in here tonight."

It wasn't technically true. Momma and baby were doing great. But it felt good to imagine somebody needed him.

Maisy stood, as shaky as the foal. "I—I didn't mean to hurt you."

He shrugged. People never meant to hurt him. They assumed because he didn't talk about how he felt, he must not be feeling anything.

People could be pretty stupid sometimes.

Maisy wiped at the tears on her cheek with her palm. He didn't know what to do here. Was he supposed to comfort her because she'd rejected him? That felt like a raw deal.

"O-okay."

Bowman allowed himself one final look at Maisy. She was beautiful. Just as pretty in the middle of the night, breaking his heart, as she was laughing with the kids at camp, or taking on a plate of sweet-potato fries at Eighty Local.

"See you Monday." He turned back to the stall. It wasn't his job to make her feel better after she'd come in here and dropped a boulder on their future. He felt her take a few steps toward the bypass door. He kept his focus on Dulce.

"See you Monday, then."

CHAPTER SIXTEEN

"KAI, GET YOUR behind back in here," Bowman called, for the fourth time that morning. The humor in his voice was strained, and it certainly wasn't reflected in his eyes.

"I think Spinach might be kinda sick." Kai's voice floated back from the stalls. Sunlight sliced through the arena, illuminating shimmering dust in the air. Maisy felt suspended in time. She was like the dust, floating with no purpose or landing in sight.

"Spinach is fine."

"His legs are wobbly."

"He's four days old." Bowman mugged an exasperated expression for the kids, but the humor didn't radiate from him like it normally did. Nothing seemed to resonate from inside Bowman over the last few days. There were no pre-grins peeking out from under his Stetson, no bad jokes, no singing. He was still great with the kids, still committed to their last week at camp, but it felt like the soul had been washed out of him.

Maisy risked a glance, because he was also still gorgeous.

"Want me to go?"

"Naw." He kept his eyes on the packed earthen floor. "I got it."

Bowman trotted out of the arena, leaving Maisy with the rest of the kids, and an abnormally heavy heart.

She'd walked out of the barn around 2:00 a.m. on Saturday morning and hadn't really spoken to Bowman since. His truck was parked at Eighty Local on Sunday, but he hadn't shown his face in the dining room. Jet and Hunter had clamored in and out of the addition as they worked, but Bowman didn't seem to need sustenance, at least not while she was in the building.

On Monday morning he'd come jogging out of the barn when she arrived. Silently, he'd handed her a card, then walked away.

A fall chill had laced the August morning as she watched him retreat into the stables. She opened the envelope to see a simple, handmade card.

I can't imagine losing one of my siblings, and I hate that you have to live with this. I'm so sorry, Maisy.

She'd read and reread the card until the familiar sound of tires against gravel pulled her focus and the kids started to arrive. She'd tucked the card, and the pain and loss, into her back pocket, and they started the day.

The newborn foal was a blessing, as the kids were too absorbed in him to pay one mite of attention to the silence between the adults on the premises.

"Maisy, we only have two and a half days left of camp!" Sami cried.

Two and a half days. Her whole mantra for the camp since she'd learned about it was "get through." Now she wanted to draw the kids, and Bowman, in close and extend it forever.

"I know. Can you believe it?"

"Can we go back to Fort Rock today?" Marc asked.

Maisy's stomach clenched at the thought of Bowman at Fort Rock.

"We should go every day." Juliet grabbed Maisy's arm and swung it.

Bowman, with a reluctant Kai in tow, returned to the arena.

"Can we take Spinach to Fort Rock?"

"He's too little to be away from his momma," Bowman told Kai.

"You know, Mr. and Mrs. Wallace are going

to rename him," Sami said, leveling a gaze on Kai. "Then they're going to sell him."

Kai turned to Bowman to confirm this heresy. Bowman hesitated a moment, then crouched so he was at eye level with Kai. He looked exhausted. "All the horses we raise here go to families who have plenty of space and can take good care of them. To help keep track of things, each year, all the newborn horses are given names that start with the same letter. This year, the letter is *F*."

Kai looked suspicious, glaring out from under his lashes. Then he crossed his arms. "So call him Fresh Spinach."

For the first time in days, Bowman threw his head back and laughed. The tension evaporated, and everyone joined in.

Except for Kai, whose lips twisted in a smile he wouldn't allow to crack. "Doesn't matter, anyway. When I grow up, and I'm a veterinarian, I'm going to buy him and Midnight. I'll call him whatever I want."

Bowman tousled his hair as he stood. "Sounds like a plan. Speaking of plans, what's up next, Doc?"

Maisy consulted her clipboard, and was about to suggest they shorten the afternoon's lesson and head to Fort Rock, when they heard a truck pull up outside the stables.

"Is Linda back?" Marc asked.

"Maybe." Maisy blinked, then tried to catch Bowman's eye again. "It doesn't matter when she comes back, we're prepared."

Bowman didn't respond. He'd done everything in his power to make this camp work for her, and she'd repaid him with a promise to do her best not to care about him.

Good work, Maisy.

Sami ran to peek over the railing. "Dad!"

Both Bowman and Maisy turned to the entrance, where Sami was skidding around the half wall to the gate and launching herself at Josh.

Josh swung her up in a hug, continuing his stride into the arena. His eyes met Maisy's briefly. She'd canceled their date for Saturday, telling him she enjoyed getting to know him, but didn't want to take things further. He'd been an absolute gentleman about it.

"Hi," she said, like a mature adult who could handle such things. "Are you here for Sami?"

Josh shook his head. Maisy noticed he was wearing his turnout gear. She followed his gaze to Bowman.

Bowman looked surprised, then curious. Maisy fought the urge to remind both of them that Bowman was still on suspension.

"You willing to suit up?"

"That legal?"

"We need everyone we can get. I just got a call from the Old Wright Mill. Something went wrong with the renovation. The rest of the crew is already on their way, along with the guys from Redmond."

Bowman didn't respond, but Maisy could feel the questions rising off him. He glanced at her, his brown-green eyes conflicted.

"There are horses," Josh said. "If you're coming, we need to move, now."

Bowman kept his gaze on her, and she answered what she thought was his question. "I can handle camp. Ash is up at the house in case anything comes up."

He nodded, taking a few steps toward Josh. Then he glanced back. "This is my job," he reminded her.

"I know." She tried to infuse her words with confidence, excitement even, at the idea of him crashing around in a fire, using his intuition as a guide. "Go get it done."

Bowman crossed the arena to Josh, speaking over his shoulder. "Kai, you help Doc Martin, and stay out of the stables. When I get back, I want a good report. You help out with camp, and I'll ask your parents if you can help me with Spinach next week."

"I always help Maisy," he said.

"Then keep at it." Bowman waved over his shoulder.

Then he was gone.

THE HEAT OF the fire and the weight of the gear felt familiar, good. Bowman ran toward the mill, next to Josh. The crew was already working on the main blaze. He'd be the most help getting the horses out of the stable and off to safety before the fire spread any farther.

The Old Wright Mill was being converted into a rustic hotel by an entrepreneur out of San Francisco. Folks in Outcrop didn't know much about her, or her plans, but no one wanted to see this place go up in flames.

Bowman took in his surroundings. The stables were significantly closer to the mill than he'd remembered.

He looked at Josh and the fire chief nodded.

Bowman scanned the property as he ran past the main blaze. The horse community was already showing up. With the increase in wildfires over the last decade, horse owners in Oregon had learned to respond to news of a fire by hitching up their horse trailers and heading to the blaze so they could transport animals to safety. Jet was already there, directing traffic, as people backed their trailers up to the pasture.

The only question was why weren't the horses *in* that pasture already? The weather was great, and it was weird the owner had her horses locked up in their stalls. Then again, she was new to the area.

Bowman pulled open the bypass door and stepped into the stables. The place felt alive with the helplessness of fear and stress. The horses kicked at their stalls, turning in the small spaces. A black glossy coat flashed and the thick flow of a mane caught his eye. The horses towered in their stalls, a good two hands higher than most of the Canadian horses his family raised.

These massive animals were purebred Friesians, a favorite for dressage competitions. The horses were worth substantially more than the entire property the rest of the team was working to save.

Bowman unlatched a stall gate. The horse reared back, eyes rolling as he tried to back into his stall, away from Bowman.

"Come on, boy." Bowman kept his shoulders relaxed. "I know I look funny in this getup, but you can trust me."

The horse cut to the right. Bowman stepped

in front of him, ushering him toward the open door. "It's gonna be okay. We'll get out of here."

The gelding's increased fear upset the rest of the horses in the stable. If Bowman could get him calmed down and moving along, it would be a lot easier to get everyone else out.

A mare behind him let out a nervous cry. The smell of the burn intensified. Bowman forced his breath to steady.

"Let's go. Just a few steps and we're out of here."

He ushered the horse through the stall gate and got him halfway to the door. Bowman felt something shift. The wind outside had turned. He glanced back at the six other horses. Without running a single calculation or receiving word on the radio, Bowman figured he had less than two minutes before flames hit the stables.

He slapped the gelding on the rump and it headed out the door. Jet was there—he'd wrangle the horse into a trailer once it got out.

Bowman sprinted back and opened the other stall gates. Most of the horses weren't sure how to react. If this group had a lead mare, she could help him commandeer the others to safety. He just needed to find her.

Bowman glanced into the final stall to see an agitated mare. He steadied his breath and considered the possibilities. Then he smiled, unzipping his jumpsuit a few inches and slipping a hand into the pocket of his shirt. A little slice of apple never hurt anyone.

"Help me out here, girl." He stepped into the stall. The mare's eyes were wild and angry, as though Bowman had set the fire himself just to vex her.

He flattened his hand, offering the apple. She snorted, annoyed he was offering a treat in the situation, but still interested in it. Bowman backed out of the stall. She followed, snapping for the apple, then trotted past him toward the door. The other horses moved with her. Bowman exhaled in relief, following close behind, ready to usher the horses into the trailers. He heard a distinctive crackle coming from above. Flames had reached the roof overhead. He placed a hand on the mare's back as she encouraged the others ahead of her out the door.

The horses flowed through the bypass door in a gorgeous mass of black, shining coats and long manes. He stepped out behind the pack as a woman rushed at them, screaming.

The words were incomprehensible, but her distress was clear. As was her inability to handle the situation. This must be the owner. She ran straight for the herd, questions spewing as Jet tried to calm her down.

The lead mare turned sharply in the face

of the onslaught. The other horses lost their purpose and shuffled in agitation. One tried to bolt back into the stables, but Bowman blocked his path. Flames and smoke created an eerie, confusing light. The mare reached her breaking point, reacting in fury to protect the others. She reared up, teetering on her back legs. Bowman stepped around her, holding a hand out to keep the owner back. Jet tried to steady the woman, but she shrugged him off and screamed. The mare responded in distress and anger, her hooves thundering toward the ground.

Bowman felt what would happen before it did. A glassy black hoof caught his shoulder, the weight of the magnificent horse falling to the earth, taking him down with her.

CHAPTER SEVENTEEN

MAISY PUSHED OPEN the door to Redmond General Hospital, cold air rushing around her, creating an icy gust in the hot August afternoon. She closed her eyes briefly, then kept walking.

Bowman was okay.

Ash had called her just after Bowman was admitted. He gave her the facts like an attending doctor, straightforward and scientific: Bowman had been knocked down when trying to calm a horse, and kicked. He had a laceration in his left shoulder that required stitches. There was significant pain, but he wasn't complaining. They planned to keep him overnight to make sure he hadn't sustained any other injuries. He had a reputation for not being completely forthcoming about his injuries. Apparently, one time Bowman had patiently sat through stitches in one arm, not bothering to mention a dull ache in the other, and walked out of the hospital with an untreated fracture. They had his number now.

"He'll be fine. He's the human bouncy ball,"

Ash had joked. Then, more seriously, he'd added, "Bowman's okay, but I bet he'd love to have your opinion on the X-rays."

Maisy didn't imagine Bowman wanted her opinion on anything these days.

Their conversation in the stables came back to her. The accusation she'd hit him with over and over in their short friendship, *The problem is you.*

Nothing like telling an incredible man that he was inherently problematic.

Bowman had struggled his whole life with not fitting in the mold. He didn't value endless chatter and rowdy collaboration. He went with his intuition when it served him well, with horses, in his work and the people he loved. When his gut couldn't lead him in the right direction, he was more than willing to let others take the lead.

And when he had to, he stepped up and did counterintuitive things, like create a plan for acing the HLI rubric.

And she'd sat on the hay bale and told him flat out she couldn't love him.

Like it was even possible to love anyone else at this point.

Her feet slowed as she made her way to Bowman's room. He wouldn't want her here.

He'd turn away, like he had in the stables that night.

Maisy watched the square tiles drift beneath her feet, one after the next, receding down the hall behind her like the years in her life. She'd spent so much of her precious time on earth chasing this one goal: being a doctor. Why did it seem like the moment she'd finally arrived, she was more lost than ever?

Early childhood memories, caught in the few images her mother snapped on her phone, showed a young Maisy wearing her dad's white button-down as a lab coat, lost in the dog-eared pages of a DK human anatomy book. Had she really wanted this, or did she just let a childhood whim shape her life? She'd been a good student, following each rubric with reverence, until she walked out of residency and wound up here.

"Hey there, Doctor!"

Maisy looked up to see Michael Williams heading toward her. He wore blue scrubs, orthopedic shoes and a lab coat, big glasses and a bigger smile. He was at ease here in the hospital, doing what he was born to do.

"Hi." Maisy waved awkwardly. She couldn't feel less like a doctor. She'd always imagined being a doctor would make her feel strong, powerful. Right now, she just felt confused.

"Are you coming in to see Bowman?"

"Yes."

"He's doing great." Michael paused, then asked, "You okay?"

Was she okay? It felt like her nerves had twisted her stomach and tied it up with her esophagus, like a balloon animal at the fair.

"Let's talk." Michael gestured to a bench, brow furrowed with concern.

Maisy knew from reputation that Michael was incredible with both his pediatric patients and their parents. He was clearly fulfilling his destiny.

She just felt like she was filling up space.

"What's going on?"

Maisy studied a bright picture of sea turtles on the wall opposite her. Keep Swimming! the poster admonished.

And that was just too much. *Keep swimming where? And why?*

"I just… I don't know what I'm doing with my life. How did I get here?"

If Michael was surprised by the turn of conversation, he was kind enough not to show it. He smiled kindly. "Starting out is hard. And you've got the extra pressure of HLI."

And the extra pressure of having to absolve herself for letting her brother slip away, down the driveway, into the street. Why had she thought being a doctor would change anything?

"Sometimes, I'm not sure why I even pursued this profession. You know? Like what do I even have to offer?"

"Kindness, intelligence..." He mugged a thoughtful expression, as though searching for the right words, "Oh, yeah, and four years of in-depth study, along with three years of practice that has resulted in a bank of knowledge to help people live longer, happier lives."

Maisy laughed softly.

"And if there were no doctors, who would wear these fabulous coats?"

She swallowed and looked up at Michael. "I don't think I went into medicine to help others. I told myself that at the time, but..."

"There are a lot of reasons people go to medical school—the money, the status. I always imagined I'd come out the other side cool, the type of guy to drive a sports car." He shook his head.

Michael seemed far more likely to drive a bumper car at the county fair than a Ferrari.

"You're not a sports-car guy?"

He brushed off his sleeves, imitating a wealthy, well-dressed man. "I'm more of a Subaru connoisseur."

Maisy cracked a smile, then pushed her hair

back out of her face. "I guess I thought I'd be different on the other side of med school, too. I wanted to be confident, an adult."

Michael laughed. "I'll never be an adult."

"You know what I mean."

"No, seriously, I rush into everything like a five-year-old. I always eat the cookie. I had a bouncy house at my own wedding. I will not be growing up anytime soon."

Maisy laughed.

"That's who I am. But I'm also a skilled medical professional." He put a hand on her shoulder. "You're a doctor now, but you're still you. When you get the coat, the residency, the first job, it doesn't magically change you. The work you did to get here, *that* changed you. The time and effort you'll put in with each patient? That will change you, too. But the day you start work is just another day."

Maisy gazed at Michael. If he could get here, maybe she could, too. She didn't feel like a doctor right now, but starting Monday she'd have her own clinic. Everyone in Outcrop and the surrounding areas would come to her. Including Bowman. She might not always feel like a doctor, but everyone else was depending on her to be one.

Michael handed her a file with flourish. "You want to do the honors?"

She opened the file to find printed copies of X-rays. She held it up to view a muscular shoulder with really great alignment.

Okay, this made her feel a little more like a doctor.

"This looks pretty good for being hit in the scapula."

"From what I understand, he's probably fine. They keep him overnight as a rule, in case something comes up. Bowman's not always forthcoming about where and how he got hurt."

The image of him grinning in the Firefighter of the Year poster came to mind. He felt good in these situations. She didn't understand it, but she could at least acknowledge it was his reality, and it wasn't wrong.

Michael's pager buzzed. He checked it, then gave her an apologetic smile. "I'm off. You'll talk Bowman through those?"

"Sure."

"Great. He's in Room 409."

Maisy headed down the brightly lit hallway. Encouraging posters engaged a riot of color, trying to make up for the stark white walls. Maisy breathed in, battling the dizziness with each step she took toward Bowman's room.

"I literally don't understand how you still have your arm at this point." Piper's voice floated into the hallway. "Seriously. I'm surprised it hasn't just given up and fallen off on its own."

Maisy pressed her lips together and stepped into the room.

Bowman was propped up in the hospital bed, one arm in a sling. His face was still dusted with soot from the fire, but he was laughing.

That laugh came to an abrupt stop when he saw her. Maisy held up the X-rays, her defense and excuse for being here. "Hi. I have…your shoulder?"

Bowman's gaze met hers, and all the pain and confusion of their night in the barn flooded between them, then his eyes flickered to the window. "Okay."

"You wanna hear about it?"

Bowman shrugged, then winced.

"Yes," Piper answered for him. "And I need an espresso. Maisy, can I get you one?"

She shook her head. Caffeine was the last thing she needed right now. "I'm good. Thanks."

Piper delivered a meaningful look to Bowman. He turned his head away.

There were a million things Maisy wanted to say. But there were also a million things she *didn't* want to say. She wasn't going to continue to pummel their friendship by putting her fears onto him, chastising him for responding to danger differently than she did. This was

Bowman. He was more comfortable with danger than others. That's who he was.

"How are the horses?" she asked.

He raised his head, surprised at the question. "They're fine. It was a rowdy group, but we got 'em all out."

"That's great." Bowman seemed confused at her interest, but pleased to not be under attack. Maisy pushed forward. "Where will the horses stay?"

"Jet and Clara are going to stable a couple of them. Ash will take a few. The community will make sure they have homes until the stable is rebuilt."

Maisy nodded. Bowman leaned back and stared at the ceiling. She stood awkwardly, holding the X-rays. Finally, he asked, "You gonna yell at me?"

Of all the things she wanted to do to Bowman right now, yelling was pretty low on the list.

"I'm glad the horses are okay. And I'm sure their people are happy about it, too."

Bowman met her gaze for the first time, probably shocked she wasn't losing it. She held eye contact, trying to apologize Bowman-style, with no words, just feelings, being truly sorry.

Piper cleared her throat.

Because apparently his sister was still in the room.

Maisy spun to find Piper already on her feet, heading for the door. "Espresso." She gestured, as though the continued beating of her heart depended on the substance. "I'm off."

Bowman gave Maisy the slightest grin. It made her feel so much better that she smiled back. She held up the X-rays. "Want to hear about your shoulder?"

BOWMAN WAITED A BEAT, not entirely willing to let go of being hurt. His body, however, had different ideas. Without exactly meaning to, Bowman scooched over so Maisy could sit next to him with the X-rays, ignoring the twinge of pain in his left arm and shoulder.

"Your real doctor will be in to go over these with you on the monitor, but Michael managed to get a set for friends and family."

"Didn't know doctors had a family special, too."

She grinned at him. "Less delicious than Hunter's family special, but still useful."

Bowman tried not to smile. His heart was far more battered than his shoulder. Still, it was kind of funny.

Maisy perched on the side of the bed and Bowman wished he'd made more room for her.

But then again, if he'd made more room, she wouldn't be as close.

She pointed to a flat bone.

"You see that?" She tapped the image. "That's your completely not-broken scapula."

"I told 'em I was fine."

"Yeah, not so fast, cowboy. Trauma to the scapula is rare, but associated with major internal injuries like a ruptured aorta or punctured lung. Yours isn't fractured, but you did get smashed by a fourteen-hundred-pound horse, so there could definitely be complications. You're going to stay right here until every single one is ruled out."

Bowman kept his eyes on the X-ray. He sensed he was fine, but logically could see where Maisy was coming from.

"Are you worried?" he asked.

A flush bloomed at her neck. "I'm always going to be a little bit worried," she admitted. "But my gut tells me you're fine." She gave him a grin. "And Ash tells me you're the human bouncy ball."

Bowman couldn't quite stop himself from readjusting his right arm so it rested above her shoulders. She scooched a fraction of an inch closer, inspiring him to point randomly at the X-ray as he asked, "What's that?"

"This beautiful blank space is your cartilage."

"And it's okay?"

"I have no idea. It doesn't show up on this X-ray." She gave him a patient expression. "But I can tell you that, overall, you have fantastic cartilage."

He leaned in closer, much more interested in the wash of freckles across her nose than his cartilage. But he had no claim to those freckles. He could admit he was happy Maisy was here—thrilled, grateful. But she'd been clear. They were friends, and only friends, because she didn't want to love a man who the X-ray techs knew by name at this point. He refocused on the picture. "How do you know it's fantastic if it's blank?"

She ran her finger along the image of his shoulder. "You see how much space there is between the bones? That represents a nice, thick cartilage."

"That's what all the ladies say. I have great cartilage."

Maisy laughed and Bowman was struck again with how much he liked her, no matter what she thought about him.

"To be clear, I suspect you've done *nothing* to earn this good cartilage."

"Are you sure? We can't grow good cartilage

by eating our vegetables and getting a good night's sleep?"

"Not unless you've been stretching regularly and doing your yoga. My guess is you were born with it. Like some people are born with good teeth."

Bowman groaned. "None of us Wallace kids were born with good teeth. We all had braces." He tapped the space between his front teeth. "I should have worn my retainer."

Her eyes flashed to meet his. A flush crept up her cheeks as she said, "I'm so glad you didn't."

Maisy leaned in closer, keeping her eyes on the X-ray as she explained it. Bowman dropped his arm onto her shoulder. She snuggled into him, the scent of her hair making him feel better than any medication they could come up with in this place. She explained the possible issues with a scapula injury, why he had to keep his arm and shoulder immobilized, the probable time frame for recovery. Bowman listened to the meaning behind her words, rather than the words themselves. She wasn't mad. She accepted he had his reasons for risking his safety, and that he was going to be okay.

The words warmed him, like morning sunshine on the front stoop of the bunkhouse.

It was all good until Piper clipped back into

the room, holding two cups. "Okay, Maisy, I didn't know what you like, so I got you an Americano. It's hard to go wrong with an Americano. And I know you said you *didn't* want an espresso, but I don't trust people who don't want coffee. I trust you, ergo, I got you coffee."

Piper finished her monologue, pulling her focus from the coffee. She gazed at Bowman, then Maisy, with mild interest. She narrowed her right eye.

"Intriguing X-rays?" she asked.

"I have good cartilage," Bowman told her.

Maisy finally seemed to realize he had his arm around her, and that her head had come to rest on his good shoulder as she talked him through the injury. She sat up abruptly. The loss of her warmth made his right shoulder feel even worse than his supposedly injured left shoulder. She blinked, looking around like she'd just landed in the room.

Piper pressed the coffee into her hand, cementing Maisy's departure from his side.

"I should, uh, probably take off." Maisy gathered up the photocopies of the X-rays. "I just wanted to stop by and check in."

Bowman reached for her hand. He might not be the man for her, but he was gratified all the same when she wound her fingers through his.

"That's sweet of you," Piper said. "You're very thorough."

Bowman glared at his sister, attempting to communicate that he was gonna let her have it if she said one more word.

Piper smiled and sipped her coffee.

Maisy turned to Bowman. "I won't see you tomorrow. You need to lay low until they're sure there are no further injuries."

"I'll be there if I can."

"No, you won't." She squeezed his hand. "I can handle it."

"I know you can."

Maisy gave him a sad smile, then turned to Piper and raised her cup. "Thank you. I've got a meeting with the two previous docs at the clinic. This will come in handy."

"See you back at the ranch," Piper said.

Maisy gave Bowman a quick smile, then slipped out the door.

Bowman pulled his pillow from behind his back with his one good arm and threw it as hard as possible at Piper.

"What was that for?"

"Take your pick."

"You and Maisy are supercute."

"There is no 'me and Maisy.'"

"Really? Do all doctors snuggle while reading X-rays? Because if they do, I'm going to try to get my allergist to take some X-rays."

Bowman started to cross his arms over his chest, but the pain in his left shoulder reminded him that wasn't a good idea.

"Bowman, she's great." Piper sat on the end of his bed. "If Clara and I could have sat down and brainstormed the perfect partner for you, we couldn't have come up with anyone better than Maisy."

Bowman snorted and looked out the window. The muddy blue emotions washed through him again. She might be perfect for him, but she'd made it abundantly clear he wasn't the man for her.

"Walk me through it, brother." Piper leaned forward, cradling her coffee in her hands. "I can't read your mind on this one."

Bowman was surprised by the pain that bloomed up in his chest, making it hard to breathe. He wanted Piper's help but didn't know what to ask.

"I can't do this," he finally admitted. "It hurts."

"What, snuggling with a cute doctor as she pores over your X-ray?"

Bowman glared at her. Then he reached out his hand. "Can I have my pillow back?"

Piper grabbed the pillow and handed it to him. He hit her with it.

"Stop it!"

"Stop acting like this is funny." He hit her with the pillow again.

"You didn't see how cute you were, actually caring about your cartilage."

Piper let out a yelp, protecting her coffee as he brought the pillow down on her head in a series of soft, puffy blows.

"Everything okay?" The deep, serious voice startled them. A nurse poked his head in, eyebrows set in a way that suggested everything *wasn't* going to be okay if they kept this up.

Piper smoothed back her hair and smiled at the man. "We're fine."

He nodded. He didn't seem to believe her, but he nodded.

The nurse moved on. Piper gave Bowman a wry smile. "You have to tell me what happened with Maisy."

He turned his gaze out the window.

"I'll get you started. A brilliant, fun, athletic woman shows up in Outcrop to help out with the camp. You two shock everyone by doing a fantastic job. You work together, you balance each other's flaws and the kids thrive."

Bowman breathed in deeply. Pain throbbed in his shoulder. Piper's description brought back all the best memories of the last few weeks.

"Then she comes to family karaoke night, where she rocks."

Bowman's heart flipped over. Maisy, in a red sundress, under the twinkling lights. Ash's big guitar in her small, capable hands.

"That was cool."

"It was amazing. You two couldn't keep your eyes off each other."

Bowman shook his head. "She had her eyes on Clara, asking her to set her up with as many guys as possible."

"Bowman, how stupid are you when it comes to women?"

"Very. Deeply." He thought about all the men he knew who were dumb when it came to women, and concluded, "Probably the stupidest."

"Did you ever wonder *why* Maisy wanted to get set up with so many different men her first few weeks in Outcrop?"

"She's running an experiment. She wants to line up all the available men and evaluate them against her rubric."

Piper shook her head. "She asked Clara to set her up because she's in love with you."

Bowman scoffed.

"She is."

Bowman shifted, then glared at Piper. "If you and Clara thought she was in love with me, why did Clara agree to this?"

"Because it wouldn't matter how many men Clara set her up with, she's in love with you, and probably has been since day one. None of the guys she went out with are right for her. You are."

Bowman grunted his acknowledgment. "I thought maybe Clara was losing her edge."

"Clara is the best sister ever. She wasn't going to let the legal counsel to the town of Madras walk off with the girl you're falling for. I mean, can you imagine how excited she is to have her accident-prone brother in love with a doctor? She wasn't going to miss the chance to make that work."

"You couldn't have told me this earlier?"

"*You* needed to put some effort into Maisy. Relationships take work and you never learned how to do that."

He wanted to believe her. But she hadn't seen the way he'd reacted when Josh spoke to Maisy. She hadn't been in the stables Friday night when Maisy walked away.

Bowman shook his head. "I messed it up, Piper. We went on this date, and we ran in to Josh..."

"Hold up. How'd that date go?"

"Not good."

"And you didn't ask for my help planning it?"

Bowman reached for the pillow but Piper

grabbed it first, then walked it across the room. She resettled with her coffee and fixed her gaze on him.

"What happened?"

"I couldn't do anything right. I thought it would be like when Clara and Jet were at Outcrop Outside. You should have seen them. They were so into each other, having so much fun. I thought Maisy and I would have fun like that."

"And you didn't?"

"I thought we were having fun, but it was so crowded, and people kept talking to me. I tried to show her the town. I even took her into the yarn shop."

"Why?"

Bowman glanced at the ceiling. *Why?* "Women like yarn, right?"

"Do we?"

"I mean, most of the time it's women in the yarn shop."

"Has Maisy given you any indication that she's at all interested in fiber arts?"

"No." Bowman ran his right hand through his hair. "But you should have seen Clara and Jet. When they came out of the yarn shop, she looked like she was ready to marry him on the spot."

Piper shook her head, closing her eyes slowly as she let out a sigh.

"It does sound kinda stupid now that I'm saying it."

"What did you think they were going to do? Tie you together?"

The problem with landing in the hospital was that a man couldn't walk away when he was called out by his bossy younger sister.

"Whatever. I'm hopeless at dating. Then I got mad, because I found out she'd been out with Josh, and I left her there."

Bowman didn't want to go into what happened next.

Unfortunately, with Piper it didn't matter what you wanted to go into, she had a way of making you talk.

"I left. I was rude and just walked off."

She narrowed her right eye.

"Then I went climbing," he admitted.

"At night?"

"Yeah, and Maisy already yelled at me about it. She got all upset and then told me flat out she couldn't love me."

"Okay, back up. She can love you. She clearly does love you."

"But she doesn't *want* to. That's what she told me. I'm too reckless and she doesn't want to fall in love with someone who takes unnecessary risks."

Piper quieted. Then she reached out and took his hand. "You're going to be okay."

Bowman wanted to contradict her but his throat closed up. He rolled his left shoulder, letting the pain distract him.

"I haven't been here for you like I should," she said. "I've been out of touch."

"I know. Way to pick a time to blow me off."

Piper pressed her pinky finger to the corners of her eyes, blocking tears that might mess up her mascara. "I, um, I got dumped." She chuckled. "Liam dumped me." She nodded, as though she still needed to say this out loud to accept that it was real.

Bowman didn't know how to respond. For her entire life, Piper was the one with the answers. Even though she was two years younger, she'd been bossing him around from day one. When the worst tragedies struck, Piper was the one to rally the family and work on a solution. But right now, she just looked lost.

Bowman didn't know what to say, besides the obvious. "He's an idiot."

Piper tilted her head, as though that was debatable.

"Come here." He gestured with his good arm. "Hug."

She shook her head. "I didn't tell you about it to get sympathy."

"You're getting it, anyway."

Piper sighed, and allowed herself a three-second, half hug. Then stood up and paced to the window.

"The point I'm trying to make is that this *is* hard. Dating isn't a walk in the park. Clara and I have built an entire business around love, because most people can't figure it out on their own." She gazed out the window. "Not even me."

"I'm not sure I'm up for it, Piper. This really hurts."

She turned back to him, a spark of mirth in her eye. "You know what's really good for a heartache? Taylor Swift."

Sadness swirled through his gut again at the thought of Maisy's favorite musician. Taylor Swift might be good for a heartache, but no amount of music was going to bring Maisy back.

CHAPTER EIGHTEEN

MAISY CLOSED THE door to the clinic and leaned against it.

What a day.

Camp had gone fine in Bowman's absence, if she didn't count her overworrying about Bowman's absence. Then she'd received the call from Ash, made it to the hospital, then back to the clinic barely in time to meet with the outgoing docs. They couldn't be more excited to have her there, and ready to take over.

She'd spent the meeting trying to replay Michael's words of encouragement, but her brain kept getting stuck on the warmth of Bowman's arm across her shoulder.

Her cheeks burned as she remembered how she'd babbled at him about the X-rays.

You have fantastic cartilage.

Seriously? Ugh.

Disgusted with herself, Maisy forced her attention onto her present surroundings. This was it. The clinic. The end goal of two decades of planning and hard work. What would her eight-year-old self think about this place? She looked to the white walls of the clinic for answers, but they only echoed back her emptiness.

A banging sound and a faint call of "Maisy!" jolted her out of her thoughts. She glanced up at the front window.

Speaking of her eight-year-old self, Sami was waving gleefully. Josh was a few paces behind her, still in his turnout gear.

Maisy opened the door and held it for them. "Hey!" She glanced at Josh. "How's the fire?"

"Under control. How's Bow—"

"This is your clinic!" Sami interrupted, pushing past the adults into the room. She scrambled from the door to the counter, then poked her head into the exam room. "This is so cool," she said. "Can I be your first patient?"

"I'd love that, but are you sick?"

"No. But I could get a checkup."

Maisy glanced at Josh, who waved a hand to indicate that if his child wanted an update on her wellness, he wasn't one to stand in the way.

Sami grabbed her hand and headed back into the exam room. Maisy took her height and weight, and checked out her eyesight, all while Sami chattered about how she was going to tell everyone at camp that she got the first checkup from Doctor Maisy.

"When did you know you wanted to be a doctor?" Sami was perched on the exam table, swinging her feet as she asked the innocent question.

Maisy swallowed, tapping a tongue depressor on the counter. There were two answers to the question: the dull litany of wanting to give back to the community and the painful secret of Elliot's death.

Maisy opened her mouth to give the first reason, when it struck her that neither answer had ever really been true. She'd *always* wanted to be a doctor. As a toddler, she'd been entranced by her pediatrician. The pictures of her in her dad's short-sleeved white shirts, her "lab coat," were taken long before the accident. She'd been studying human anatomy books since she was old enough to hold them open.

She hadn't pursued medicine because Elliot died, she'd done it because she wanted to. She'd loved her brother, and been as good a sister as anyone could expect. He'd been tragically stolen from her family. That tragedy would always be a part of her story, but it didn't have to be the whole story.

Maybe it was time to open up to a new chapter?

"I wanted to be a doctor my whole life." Maisy nodded. It felt good to recognize herself before the accident. "I like science. I think the human body is fascinating, like a beautiful miracle. And I like solving puzzles." She paused, then said, "And when I was your age, my little brother died in an accident. I worked extra hard in school to make the grades necessary to be a doctor, hoping to honor him by helping others live long happy lives."

Sami pulled her head back, surprised.

"Your brother died?"

"He did."

Sami held out her arms. Maisy leaned in and let herself take the child's hug and sympathy.

"I'm sorry he died," Sami said as Maisy hugged her small frame. "But I'm glad you're a doctor."

"Me, too."

The weight eased by some tiny fraction. The loss would never go away, but it might not always be as heavy. It wasn't the accomplishment of becoming a doctor that could blot out the pain, but rather the connections with others that would ease it over time. Her parents didn't need her to punish herself for the freak accident. They needed her to live a happy productive life.

That was the only real way she could honor her brother.

After being declared in perfect health, Sami

marched back into the waiting room and threw herself into one of the chairs. "This room is ugly."

Maisy sputtered out a laugh as Josh reprimanded his daughter. "Sami. That's impolite."

"No, she's right. This—" she gestured to the blank walls and gray carpet "—needs help."

"You need to paint it. Yellow."

"I like yellow."

"And I'll draw you some pictures."

It would make a pretty good start.

"You need new carpet, and these chairs are really uncomfortable," Sami said. "Bowman can help with everything else."

"Bowman's going to be pretty busy." She glanced up at Josh. "He'll be back with the fire department, right?"

"He's already been reinstated." Josh set his hands on Sami's shoulders. "He asked to finish up camp, then he's back in the firehouse Saturday."

Maisy nodded. He was going back to work. Wildfires would intensify over the next month. He'd be busy with a job that was inherently dangerous.

Josh looked up from his daughter and smiled kindly at her. "But I imagine he'll be able to find plenty of time to help you out, Maisy."

Would he? Was it even possible to come

back after her hurtful words? She'd done well at the hospital, caring for Bowman without chastising him about being in danger. He'd done well, too.

For this to work, she'd need to trust him, and accept that he lived closer to the edge than most. It wasn't unreasonable that he set some limits, too. Finding the line might take some work, and inspire a few more arguments.

Then again, some of Bowman's best jokes came in the middle of an argument.

Josh cleared his throat. Maisy looked up abruptly from her thoughts.

She smiled sheepishly. "How long was I out?"

"Long enough for us to get a pretty good idea of who you were thinking about."

Heat crept up her neck. Maisy didn't try to hide her smile.

"So, Bowman?" Josh asked.

The heat flooded her face, and for once she didn't try to stop it. "Yeah." She shook her head, still not quite able to believe it herself. "Bowman."

BOWMAN RESTED HIS feet on the railing of the front porch and tilted back his chair, settling the brim of his hat lower to fend off the rays of the setting sun. Most days he loved to be out as the sun settled behind the Cascade mountains.

This evening all he could think about was how much Maisy would like this.

Bowman blew out a breath and brought his boots to the plank floor of the porch, leaning forward to cradle his face in his hands. Pain shot through his shoulder and he settled with cradling his face in one hand. The noise of his family laughing and arguing swirled inside the house on the other side of the picture window. Maybe he should go down to the barn to check on Spinach. But if he headed out, Piper would send up her radar and realize he was more than thirty feet away and come looking for him. He didn't want to disrupt the family gathering. But he sure didn't want to join it, either.

He'd made his own mess of his friendship with Maisy. He could lay a certain amount of blame on the world for not letting a guy off the hook for going with his gut, and not wanting to talk all the time. But he alone was responsible for not listening to Maisy's concerns. Not telling her how he really felt.

The door creaked open behind him. Bowman felt his oldest brother, heard his boots clunk across the porch. He gazed out at the fields, not wanting to talk to Ash, but not exactly wanting him to leave, either.

"How's it going out here?" Ash asked.

Bowman shrugged his good shoulder.

"You want some company?"

"Nope."

Ash sat in the chair next to him, anyway. The sun slipped a notch lower, bathing them in warm, pink rays.

"I gotta say, you did a heck of a job with camp this year."

Bowman nodded. He had surpassed everyone's expectations. They'd been incredibly low expectations, but still.

"I knew you could do it." Ash gazed out at the stables. "I had no idea you'd do it all so well."

"That was all Maisy. I just helped."

"It wasn't all Maisy. You kept her grounded." Bowman opened his mouth to argue but Ash cut him off. "You can't see it from my perspective, but she needed you as much as you needed her. You two did great."

"Thanks. Despite everything, I'm glad you roped me into it." The sun dipped further, painting the mountain ice caps a dark red. "It was good for me."

"It was good for the kids, too."

It had been good for the kids. All of them, but especially Kai. If Bowman were worth his salt, he'd agree to extend the camp with riding lessons. Kai could use the time out here.

"I might do it again next year if I can get the time off."

"Good call. What I don't understand, though, is why you're out here moping, rather than in the house gloating while you have the chance."

Bowman chuckled. "I don't know. Everything seems so different. It's like..."

"It's like Maisy should be here, right?"

Bowman glanced up at Ash from under the brim of his hat.

"Yeah. She should be here. I just don't know how to make her want to be here."

"You can't make her do anything."

"That's for sure."

"Look, I'm not the relationship expert in this family, not by a long shot. But it seems to me you need to meet her in the middle."

"Where even is that?"

Ash laced his fingers together. "The middle is trusting your gut, but listening when other people voice their concerns. If people are worried, they're worried, and you blowing them off doesn't help anyone."

Bowman nodded.

"It's taking a calculated risk at work, but knowing you'll have to explain it to someone who loves you at the end of the day."

Bowman liked that idea, especially the part about talking with someone who loved him at the end of each day.

"And let me be honest. Climbing alone, without a rope, over the creek—that's not the middle. If Mom knew you were still free soloing she'd take out Fort Rock on her own with a mining pick and homemade explosives."

"That's an image."

"One I'd prefer not to see."

Bowman nodded in agreement, then ran his good hand through his hair. "I don't even know how to start with Maisy at this point. I've never been good at putting things into words, and this is so complicated it'd be tough for Shakespeare."

Ash nodded. He glanced over at the old red barn, then said, "She seemed to like your singing all right."

"I can't sing her back."

"Can't you? A little Taylor Swift might go a long way with Maisy."

Bowman sat back in his chair.

"You think she's got a song for this?"

Ash grunted. "Taylor Swift's got a song for everything."

"Amen."

Bowman thought it through. After camp, when everyone was gone, maybe they could walk out to Fort Rock and he could sing quietly to just Maisy?

His gaze flickered over to Ash, who was giving him the classic, big-brother, do-the-right-thing face. He knew exactly what his brother was thinking.

Bowman kicked out his boots, trying to get comfortable in his chair. Trying to get comfortable in his skin. Loving Maisy was the easy part of all this. Expressing his feelings, and finding the middle ground where those feelings could grow, was the challenge. He needed to show Maisy how serious he was about her, and that meant stepping out of his comfort zone.

He needed to show her that while he might be hard to love in some respects, there would be positives to the relationship.

Lots and lots of positives.

Bowman pulled himself up out of the chair with his good arm. "Alright. Let's get the karaoke machine."

CHAPTER NINETEEN

MAISY HOPPED OUT of her Jeep, plans and anticipation running through her as she slammed the door. The rising sun worked the chill out of the morning air, promising a glorious, late-summer day for the close of camp.

Maybe it was the good phone call she'd had with her parents the night before. No big epiphanies, just a nice conversation that Maisy let herself enjoy. Maybe it was the fantastic night of sleep she'd finally managed. Most definitely, it was the decision she'd made about Bowman. Whatever the mix, Wallace Ranch looked more beautiful than ever. And she wanted to spend as much time here as Bowman and the Wallace family would let her.

To do that, she needed to have an honest talk with Bowman, and hope he was willing to listen to her apology.

Maisy readjusted the fawn-colored Stetson Bowman had given her, and took determined steps toward the arena.

"Hey!" Bowman emerged from the farmhouse, rather than the stables or the bunkhouse, where he normally spent his time. He waved his good arm, the other still lashed to his side in a sling. He was smiling, but also running. "Last day. I'll get things set up in the arena."

"Wait. Hi."

Bowman slowed, walking backward. "Hi." His grin broke out. "Nice hat."

"Do you want to go over the schedule?"

He shrugged, then winced. "We've got the kids for a few hours to prepare for the open house, then we open the house."

"Yeah. So could we talk—"

"Looks like Kai's here! Send him to the stables." Bowman turned and ran the last few steps.

"Um, okay. Just...keep your sling on," she called to his receding back. "Your soft tissue needs to be immobilized for at least a week!"

He waved his good arm in acknowledgment. Then he glanced back at her, his lips twisted in a pre-grin, and slipped through the bypass door.

What was that?

Kai, true to form, gave Maisy a quick high five, then tore off into the stables with Bowman. That wasn't strange at all. What was weird was how Kai came sprinting out of the barn every time a new car arrived, whispered something to the camper and then ushered them back to the stables.

By the time she went in to have everyone circle up, everyone was already there. In a circle.

Highly suspicious.

"What's going on?" she asked.

Glances shot back and forth around the circle like an invisible, high-speed game of cat's cradle. The kids alternately shook their heads, or shrugged way too casually.

"Nothing! What's the circle question today?" Sami asked.

Maisy looked each camper in the eye. No one was close to breaking.

"Oka-a-ay. Question of the day—which of the healthy habits we've learned about during camp will be the easiest for you to implement, and which will be the most difficult?"

"What's *implement*?" Juliet asked.

"It's something you farm with," Marc said. "Farming implements. Like a tractor."

"Well, yes, but in this case I mean—" A familiar tune came floating across the circle.

"What are you whistling?" she asked Bowman.

He flushed. "Was I whistling?"

"You're always whistling," Juliet said.

Bowman shook his head. "I don't think I was."

"I didn't hear any whistling." Kai raised his hands, as though he, too, was innocent.

But Bowman had definitely been whistling, and it sounded like midcareer Taylor Swift.

He winked at Kai, then said, "By *implement* Maisy means which of the habits are you going to keep. Which will be easy, and which will be harder?"

After check-in, they walked through the plan for the day. In the morning they'd take one last ride, then visit the ant colony and Fort Rock. Parents would arrive after lunch. They'd gather in the arena, where each camper was in charge of presenting information about a different aspect of healthy living and horse care.

"Let's hit the trail," Bowman said, backing out of the circle to bring in the horses. "Ash and Clara are coming in to set up chairs for your parents, so we should get out of here."

He started jogging toward the stalls. Maisy caught his arm. The touch stilled him. He looked down into her eyes and the whole barn seemed to shift sideways.

"I want to talk to you," she said.

His eyes traveled from her hand, up to her eyes, a slow smile spreading across his face. "I want to listen."

She opened her mouth to speak but Bowman cut her off. “We have a really big day, though. We need to keep on schedule.”

Maisy rolled her eyes. “Since when are you the one who wants to stick with the plan?”

“Bo-o-owman!” Juliet called.

“Let’s get through this.”

“What’s going on here?” Maisy gestured, indicating him, her, the kids and the entire world.

He stepped closer to her, his warm scent wrapping around her. “Trust me?”

She drew back, letting the words swirl through her. That was his request. Trust.

“Okay.”

The morning sped by. The trail ride was fun. Each camper was confident on their horse, with Liya leading the way on Jorge. They visited the ant colony, and the kids gathered up sticks and pine needles and brought them close in case the worker ants wanted to enlarge the mound. Finally, they enjoyed a picnic lunch at Fort Rock. It was a perfect morning.

“This is the best camp ever,” Sami proclaimed as they walked back to the stables to meet their families. “When I grow up, I’m going to help out.”

“Me, too,” Liya said. “I’m going to help kids learn how to ride a horse.”

Maisy turned and walked backward so she

could see the rest of the group. "Anyone else gonna help out in the future?"

"Me!" Bowman said. Juliet clung to his back, and he was flanked by Marc and Kai.

"I'll let Spinach come help out if he wants to," Kai said.

Bowman laughed as they emerged from the pine trees and turned toward the stables. Then his face fell and the laugh, along with his feet, stopped abruptly.

"You gotta be kidding me," he muttered.

Maisy spun around, searching for whatever had offended Bowman.

Next to the red barn were at least fifty cars, parked every which way. Was he upset about how they'd parked?

"How many parents do you all have?" she joked.

"Those aren't all parents," Bowman grumbled.

"Who is it, then?" Maisy asked.

"My family."

"You don't have *that* many siblings."

"No, but they all have huge mouths." He shook his head, then glanced at her. "Whatever happens over the next hour, I want you to know it's only partially my fault."

"That's ominous."

He let out a breath. "Not ominous so much as humiliating."

The door to an old International Harvester Scout slammed and Coach Kessler and Christy Jones emerged, waving broadly.

"All these people are here to see us," Juliet said, leaning over Bowman's shoulder.

"They're here to see something," he muttered.

"Is this…normal?"

"Nothing in Outcrop is normal." Bowman straightened his shoulders and readjusted Juliet on his back. "Let's go get it done."

The arena was buzzing with people, and all the people seemed particularly interested in Bowman. But these weren't groupies. They were community members. Maisy recognized Mr. Fareas, and the women from the chocolate shop. As expected, Linda Sands was here, grading rubric at the ready.

"Are all of these people here to learn about healthy living?" she asked.

Sami grinned up at her. "Probably."

The kids assembled in front of the guests. They were excited and having way more fun with this than she would have expected.

Everything started out fine. The campers each gave a short presentation. Kai compared the horse named Spinach to the leafy green vegetable. All the while Bowman seemed to be growing more and more nervous.

The presentation finally finished with all the kids singing "The Veggie Song," to thunderous applause from the community. Maisy stepped forward.

"Thank you all for coming," she said. "I didn't expect such a huge turnout but we're glad you're here."

"Show's not over!" Coach Kessler called from the back.

Maisy felt the strong urge to explain that the show *was* over. She turned to Bowman, knowing he wouldn't want to speak in front of the crowd, but hoping he could shed some light on the situation.

That's when she noticed the karaoke machine.

"Bowman, what's the—"

"Maisy, sit here!" Sami grabbed her hand and pulled her to a lawn chair Hunter had set up. Juliet pushed her from behind as Sami pulled.

Maisy glanced at Bowman. A sheepish grin crossed his face. "You're gonna want to sit down for this."

THE QUESTION WAS whether to disown his family now, or after the performance. When Bowman told his family about his decision to step out of his comfort zone by singing to Maisy in public, he'd imagined the kids, their parents and possibly his horse.

He hadn't expected the whole town.

Bowman glanced out into the audience. Maisy looked curious, and completely beautiful. If he was going to ask her to overcome her fears, he could do the same.

"It's, uh, good to have you here, Outcrop."

The crowd erupted into cheers. Coach whistled from the back.

"As you know, there's a new doctor in town. Maisy Martin." Bowman gestured to where she sat and the crowd cheered again. "We got real lucky with Doc Martin. I'm glad she's here." Bowman gazed at Maisy, who was flushed red, but hopefully happy.

He took a deep breath. If he did this right, it was likely he'd get to kiss her when all of these people were gone.

Let's get it done.

"We got real lucky, and the kids and I all hope she'll…stay."

That was Hunter's cue. He turned on the machine and the base beat of the Taylor Swift song "Stay Stay Stay" filled the air.

Maisy's eyes lit up, and that somehow made the entire arena full of people disappear.

Bowman grinned at her and started singing. He'd rewritten the words for her, and while the intention—*please stay!*—remained the same, the song was now an apology, and an offer of love. The kids sang backup, and danced with a few simple moves he'd taught them, each bringing their own flair to the performance.

And singing for Maisy, in front of all these people, wasn't horrible. In fact, as she rolled her eyes when he made a pun about sweet-potato fries, it was kind of fun.

When her laugh rang out, it became really fun.

As he sang, his intuition took over, and the dance moves broke out, at least the ones he could do without hurting his arm.

The crowd went wild.

The song finished to a standing ovation, with the kids bouncing around, cheering for their own performance.

Bowman set down the mic, because no matter how good the performance, a microphone was still an expensive piece of equipment and Hunter would have his hide if he dropped it.

Maisy stood and walked straight up to him, placing her hands along the side of his face. Her blue eyes shone, and if the crowd had any reaction, he was completely unaware.

"You are too much, Bowman Wallace."

Bowman wrapped his one good arm around her waist, tethering her close. "I was going for just enough."

She grinned, her freckles shifting as she pulled his face to hers. The soft touch of her lips, the scent of her hair and all the good that was Maisy wrapped around him. They could have been completely alone as he melted into the pull of her kiss.

But they weren't alone.

"Bow-man!" a voice hollered. He looked down and saw that he and Maisy were being swarmed by the kids. A quick glance around showed the audience on their feet, cheering and clapping. Maisy pressed her deep red face against his chest, and Bowman ran his hand along the back of her head.

"Okay," he called out. "Thanks for coming, everyone. Show's over!"

She shook her head, stepping back. "Actually, it's not over." She cleared her throat and addressed the crowd in her confident, doctor voice. "Linda Sands, a representative from the Healthy Lives Institute, has offered to fund an extension of camp." She glanced around at the kids. "We have a few spots for horseback-riding lessons, and if anyone is interested, I'd like to start a club, too, so we can all meet once a week."

"I'm in," Bowman said.

"Are you willing to put up with a few more of my plans?" she asked.

He wrapped his arms around her and pressed his forehead to hers. "Guess I'm hoping I get to put up with all your plans."

EPILOGUE

A Thank You, Firefighters! sign in Outcrop Eagles red flashed by as Bowman approached the ranch. Underneath the print was a hand-scrawled message that read, And Thank You for Being Cognizant of Your Own Safety!

He grinned, despite the exhaustion. It was good to be home.

Wildfire season had been intense this year, but now that they had the Fallen Ridge blaze under control, and rain had returned to much of the state, they were in the clear. Bowman never liked being away from his family for weeks at a time. Being away from Maisy was torture. But several weeks on the far eastern side of Oregon had provided plenty of time to think. With time to think came clarity about his future.

And right now, he was ready to get started on that future.

Less than an hour before, his crew had returned to the firehouse after an all-night drive from Joseph. He'd barely taken a moment to shower and change his clothes before hopping in his truck and heading home. *Home.* It was where he wanted to spend his time, and he knew who he wanted to spend that time with.

Bowman pulled onto the property, heart lifting as he crested the rise. The leaves in the massive oak trees surrounding the house would turn soon, and the aspen covering the hillside shimmered as a morning haze drifted across the pastures. Cars and trucks were parked in front of the house, along with a dusty Jeep. Bowman grinned, remembering Maisy's first trip to Wallace Ranch.

Would she be up for a chin-up competition this morning? Naw, maybe tomorrow. Today he had other plans.

The front door banged open and a gorgeous doctor flew onto the porch and into the yard. Bowman had never gotten his truck in Park so quickly.

And suddenly his arms were full of Maisy. He pulled her close, closer. She nestled her face into his neck, and he felt her welcoming words, rather than heard them. A warm, joyful feeling flooded through him, like a pool of warm sunlight. He lifted her off the ground and spun her around, the smell of her hair, the sound of her laugh, all he needed.

Unfortunately, his family wasn't so easily satisfied.

"Okay. You've hugged her. She still exists, come in the house."

"Piper," Mom admonished, "give them a minute."

"It's literally been ten minutes."

Bowman tucked one arm around Maisy and headed up to the front porch toward his family. He knew there'd be a welcoming committee, and he could be patient. Scents of cinnamon, freshly baked bread and bacon wafted from the house.

"Is that breakfast?" he asked Hunter.

"It's not just breakfast, man. It's cinnamon-toast casserole, eggs, bacon and cranberry jumbles."

"Thank you." Bowman put a free hand on his twin's back. He was so deeply grateful for his brother, and knew Hunter could feel his intention, even if all he managed to say was "I'm starving."

"Cookies for breakfast?" Maisy asked, a glint of humor in her eye.

"Oatmeal," he reminded her with a wink.

The family ushered him into the house. It felt so good to have everyone here, and together. He didn't need to talk, and just enjoyed listening to them as they caught him up on what had been going on in his absence.

From their phone conversations, he knew Maisy's work at the clinic was going well, but seeing her assured him that she was thriving as a small-town doctor. Outcrop couldn't have gotten luckier.

Hunter was closing in on the addition to Eighty Local, but there was still a lot to be done. Knowing his brother, it all had to be done perfectly. Piper was better, a lot better. But Bowman continued to worry about the breakup. So few things had the power to throw Piper off-kilter like this had. That said, he knew his sister well enough not to bring it up at the table.

The big topic of conversation was Clara and Jet, with their wedding just around the corner. It was awesome to see his sister so happy, and he looked forward to having Jet officially in the family.

He glanced at Maisy, his heart picking up pace as he thought about adding new people to the family.

"I'm so glad you're back in time," Clara said, her dimples flashing as she grinned at him, then her fiancé.

"I wouldn't miss it." Bowman took a deep breath, then said, "And, yes, I'm going to sing."

The family burst into cheers. Maisy bit her lip as she smiled up at him. "I can't wait."

He nodded, then looked down at his mostly empty plate.

He couldn't wait any longer, either.

Bowman stood abruptly and reached out a hand to Maisy. "Wanna go for a quick walk? We could check out Fort Rock." It was technically a question, but since he had a hold of her hand and was pulling her out of her chair, she didn't really have much of a choice.

"Sure." She snagged one more cranberry jumble as she stood. "That sounds great."

Piper cleared her throat. Bowman gave his sister a look to stop any comment that might give away his intentions, then nodded at his family and took long strides toward the door. "We'll be back in a bit."

Piper's voice stopped him. "Did you remember to grab some yarn?"

"Not funny," Bowman warned, trying to repress a smile at the memory of Piper grilling him about taking Maisy into a yarn shop on their first, ill-fated date.

"I just want to make sure you get everything all tied up," she quipped.

"Leave him alone." Ash dropped a hand on Piper's shoulder.

"I thought the whole point was for him *not* to be alone," Hunter countered.

Maisy raised her brow in question at Bowman. He shook his head, unsure if he should apologize for his family, or encourage her to get used to it.

Then she smiled at him, her freckles shifting and rearranging across her nose, and nothing else seemed to matter anymore. He grinned back and tugged her hand. "Let's get out of here."

MAISY AND BOWMAN made a break for the door, not slowing until they hit the back steps.

"Your family is something else," she said.

"Yeah." He gripped her hand tighter, weaving his fingers through hers. "But you like them?"

"I love them." She swung his arm as they walked along. "I couldn't love them more. But sometimes they're a little—"

"Yeah. I know." He shook his head, but his affection for his family was evident. "And that's never going to change."

"I wouldn't want it to."

He smiled at her, then looked away, still grinning.

The cool of the morning had burned off by the time they made it to Fort Rock.

Maisy's feet slowed, then stilled under the pine trees, wanting to remain on the safe side of Fort Rock. Bowman tugged at her hand. "I have something I want to show you."

She nodded. Bowman loved this rock. He talked about building a home near this outcropping.

And she loved Bowman. Knowing him had encouraged her to grow and open up to life. If he had something to show her on the west side of Fort Rock, she was going to approach it with an open mind.

They emerged from the trees, rounding the end of the rock. The creek came into view. She glanced up at the steepest part of the crag. Something was different. Shining, new bolts stood out at regular intervals. She followed the bolt line up to the top of the rock and saw anchors that would hold a rope to keep Bowman safe as he climbed.

"Did you—"

"Yeah. I bolted the whole thing before I left for the Fallen Ridge fire. Now I can be responsible for my own safety on both sides of the rock." He gave her a little grin.

Maisy threw her arms around him. She knew this was hard for him, making a change to help her feel more comfortable. There had been growing pains over the last few months, but he was enthusiastic about working on this issue. "Thank you," she whispered in his ear.

He reached up a hand to the side of her face, drawing her into a kiss. Bowman, she'd learned, communicated in a number of different ways. This kiss said, "You're welcome," and "you were right about climbing without a rope here," and "I'm happy to do this for you."

The kiss also suggested he'd like to keep kissing her for the rest of the morning. His other hand coming to rest on her jaw corroborated the sentiment. But after a moment he drew back and said, "It's part of something I need to do."

"Okay?"

Bowman took both her hands in his. He studied her fingers as he spoke. "I want to meet you in the middle, with everything. I'm not always going to know where that is, but it's where I want to be."

Maisy laced her fingers through his, breathing in his scent. She wanted this, too. Bowman urged her to grow past her fears and open up to a life beyond chasing a future.

It was life in the present moment, here and now.

She leaned her forehead against his chest. "There's no one I'd rather meet in the middle."

"Or get stuck in the middle with."

She grinned at him, then flexed onto her toes and turned her face toward his, hoping that by *middle* he was speaking literally. Like their lips meeting right between the two of them.

Bowman gazed down into her eyes, then in a swift movement dropped to one knee.

Her heart beat fast, and a flush prickled at the back of her neck. A good, excited, happy flush spread its way straight up into her face.

"Maisy." He pulled in a breath, and held out a ring. "Maisy, you are *it* for me. You're music and sunshine and home. All I know is that you make me better. I want you to be a part of my family. Maisy Martin, please let me be your husband."

Maisy wasn't even tempted to use a question mark.

"Yes!"

Bowman gazed up at her, his beautiful, heart-stopping smile shining out more brilliantly than the ring he slipped on her finger.

Although the ring really was quite brilliant. Still, there was plenty of time for looking at gold and diamonds. Right now, she wanted Bowman.

"Yes. Always and every time, yes."

He gazed into her eyes, and she could feel everything good unfolding in their future, together.

"Okay then, Doc Martin." He stood, tugging at her hand, then bent to lift her onto his back for a piggyback ride. She wrapped her arms around his neck and kissed his cheek.

"Let's go make some plans!"

* * * * *

Don't miss the next book in Anna Grace's Love, Oregon miniseries, coming October 2023 from Harlequin Heartwarming

COMING NEXT MONTH FROM

HARLEQUIN

HEARTWARMING

#471 HER ISLAND HOMECOMING

Hawaiian Reunions • by Anna J. Stewart

When by-the-numbers accountant Theo Fairfax arrives in Nalani, Hawai'i, to evaluate free-spirited pilot Sydney Calvert's inherited tour business, he just wants this assignment behind him. Until he begins to see Hawai'i's true beauty. And Sydney's, too...

#472 THE LAWMAN'S PROMISE

Heroes of Dunbar Mountain • by Alexis Morgan

Shelby Michaels wears several hats in her professional life, including museum curator in Dunbar, Washington, and acting as protector of the town's most prized possession. But after clashing with police chief Cade Peters, she'll have to guard her heart, too!

#473 HER KIND OF COWBOY

Destiny Springs, Wyoming • by Susan Breeden

Hailey Goodwin needs a cowboy to help her run trail rides at Sunrise Stables, not the big-city businessman who volunteers for the role. Opposites may attract—and Parker Donnelly is *certainly* attractive!—but can they find a happily-ever-after?

#474 HIS MONTANA STAR

by Shirley Hailstock

Cal Masters can't stand to see his temporary neighbor and former Hollywood stuntwoman Piper Logan feeling sorry for herself after a stunt gone wrong. He hopes re-creating it with her will help—but now he's falling for her...